PRAISE FOR ...

In Plain Sight

"Startling . . . well-plotted . . . an explosive conclusion . . . full of tense suspense and believable, emotional, well-crafted characters." —*Lansing State Journal*

"Edge-of-the-chair suspense . . . Heart-stopping action . . . [An] unforgettable mystery." —*Library Journal* (starred review)

"More violence than C. J. Box's other novels and shows the ethical changes in his detective from a bumbling but happy professional to a man with a lot on his conscience." —*The Dallas Morning News*

"The sixth in the series, and the best." —*The Toronto Globe and Mail*

"Thrilling and frightening . . . Will satisfy C. J. Box fans well into the night." —*The Jackson (MS) Clarion-Ledger*

"Any mystery fan . . . can get drawn in just by reading the opening page of *In Plain Sight*. Just be warned, you'll want to keep the lights burning." —*Billings (MT) Gazette*

"Box continues to write the sharpest suspenses west of the Pecos." —*Kirkus Reviews* (starred review)

continued . . .

"C. J. Box vividly evokes life in the West." —*People*

Winterkill

"Well-crafted." —*USA Today*

"Exquisite descriptions . . . Moves smoothly and suspensefully to the showdown." —*The Washington Post*

"*Winterkill* proves that Box . . . is one of the best new voices in the mystery game. [It's] a full-fledged thriller, Wyoming-style." —*Rocky Mountain News*

"Fast moving, intelligent." —*Fort Worth Star-Telegram*

"Box proves he knows how to make every storm into a story." —*Houston Chronicle*

Savage Run

"The suspense tears forward like a brush fire." —*People*

"Hunker down and hang on tight for an intense, twisting ride that lasts to the final page." —*The Denver Post*

"Impressive . . . tense." —*The Washington Post*

"Riveting . . . Box weaves in a history that gives the action a rich context . . . Harrowing." —*USA Today*

"Brilliantly crafted . . . bears comparison to the best work of mystery giants such as Tony Hillerman and James Lee Burke." —*Minneapolis Star Tribune*

continued . . .

Open Season

"Buy two copies of *Open Season*, and save one in mint condition to sell to first-edition collectors. C. J. Box is a great storyteller."
—Tony Hillerman

"Intriguing, with a forest setting so treacherous it makes Nevada Barr's locales look positively comfy, with a motive for murder that is as unique as any in modern fiction. Pickett is a refreshingly human and befuddled hero . . . But it's Box's offbeat way of telling the story that puts it on the best of the year track."
—*Los Angeles Times*

"A muscular first novel . . . Box writes as straight as his characters shoot, and he has a stand-up hero to shoulder his passionate concerns about endangered lives and liberties."
—*The New York Times Book Review*

"A fascinating, well-scripted debut novel. It's a classic tale of Wild West justice."
—*USA Today*

Also by C. J. Box

In Plain Sight

C. J. BOX

BERKLEY PRIME CRIME, NEW YORK

THE BERKLEY PUBLISHING GROUP
Published by the Penguin Group
Penguin Group (USA) Inc.
375 Hudson Street, New York, New York 10014, USA

Penguin Group (Canada), 90 Eglinton Avenue East, Suite 700, Toronto, Ontario M4P 2Y3,
Canada (a division of Pearson Penguin Canada Inc.)
Penguin Books Ltd., 80 Strand, London WC2R 0RL, England
Penguin Group Ireland, 25 St. Stephen's Green, Dublin 2, Ireland
(a division of Penguin Books Ltd.)
Penguin Group (Australia), 250 Camberwell Road, Camberwell, Victoria 3124, Australia
(a division of Pearson Australia Group Pty. Ltd.)
Penguin Books India Pvt. Ltd., 11 Community Centre, Panchsheel Park, New Delhi—110
017, India
Penguin Books (NZ), 67 Apollo Drive, Mairangi Bay, Auckland 1311, New Zealand
(a division of Pearson New Zealand Ltd.)
Penguin Books (South Africa) (Pty.) Ltd., 24 Sturdee Avenue, Rosebank, Johannesburg
2196, South Africa

Penguin Books Ltd., Registered Offices: 80 Strand, London WC2R 0RL, England

This is a work of fiction. Names, characters, places, and incidents either are the product of
the author's imagination or are used fictitiously, and any resemblance to actual persons,
living or dead, business establishments, events, or locales is entirely coincidental. The
publisher does not have any control over and does not assume any responsibility for author
or third-party websites or their content.

IN PLAIN SIGHT

A Berkley Prime Crime Book / published by arrangement with the author

PRINTING HISTORY
G. P. Putnam's Sons hardcover edition / May 2006
Berkley Prime Crime mass-market edition / May 2007

ISBN: 978-0-425-21579-1

For Molly Jo
. . . and Laurie, always

April

Family quarrels are bitter things. They don't go by any rules. They're not like aches or wounds; they're more like splits in the skin that won't heal because there's not enough material.

—F. SCOTT FITZGERALD

The great plain drinks the blood of Christian men and is satisfied.

—O. E. RÖLVAAG, *GIANTS IN THE EARTH*

1   *Twelve Sleep County, Wyoming*

WHEN RANCH OWNER OPAL SCARLETT VANISHED, NO one mourned except her three grown sons, Arlen, Hank, and Wyatt, who expressed their loss by getting into a fight with shovels.

Wyoming game warden Joe Pickett almost didn't hear the call over his radio when it came over the mutual-aid channel. He was driving west on Bighorn Road, having picked up his fourteen-year-old daughter, Sheridan, and her best friend, Julie, after track practice to take them home. Sheridan and Julie were talking a mile a minute, gesticulating, making his dog, Maxine, flinch with their flying arms as they talked. Julie lived on the Thunderhead Ranch, which was much farther out of town than the Pick-etts' home.

Joe caught snippets of their conversation while he drove, his attention on his radio and the wounded hum of the engine and the dancing gauges on the dash. Joe didn't yet trust the truck, a vehicle recently assigned to him. The check-engine light would flash on and off, and occasionally there was a knocking sound under the hood that sounded like popcorn popping. The truck had been issued to him as revenge by his cost-conscious superiors, after his last vehicle had burned up in a fire in Jackson Hole. Even though the suspension was shot, the truck did have a CD player, a rarity in state vehicles, and the sound track for the ride home had been a CD Sheridan had made for him. It was titled "Get with it, Dad" in a black felt marker. She'd given it to him two days before after breakfast, saying, "You need to listen to this new music so you don't seem so clueless. It may help." Things were changing in his family. His girls were getting older. Joe was not only under the thumb of his superiors but was apparently becoming clueless too. His red uniform shirt with the pronghorn antelope Game and Fish patch on the shoulder and his green Filson vest were caked with mud from changing a tire on the mountain earlier in the day.

"I think Jarrod Haynes likes you," Julie said to Sheridan.

"Get out! Why do you say that? You're crazy."

"Didn't you see him watching us practice?" Julie asked. "He stayed after the boys were done and watched us run."

"I saw him," Sheridan said. "But why do you think he likes *me*?"

" 'Cause he didn't take his eyes off of you the whole time, that's why. Even when he got a call on his cell, he stood there and watched you while he talked. He's hot for you, Sherry."

"I wish *I* had a cell phone," Sheridan said.

Joe tuned out. He didn't want to hear about a boy targeting his daughter. It made him uncomfortable. And the cellphone conversation made him tired. He and Marybeth had said Sheridan wouldn't get one until she was sixteen, but that didn't stop his daughter from coming up with reasons why she needed one now.

In the particularly intense way of teenage girls, Sheridan and Julie were inseparable. Julie was tall, lithe, tanned, blond, blue-eyed, and budding. Sheridan was a shorter version of Julie, but with her mother's startling green eyes. The two had ridden the school bus together for years and Sheridan had hated Julie, said she was bossy and arrogant and acted like royalty. Then something happened, and the two girls could barely be apart from each other. Three-hour phone calls between them weren't unusual at night.

"I just don't know what to think about that," Sheridan said.

"You'll be the envy of everyone if you go with him," Julie said.

"He doesn't seem very smart."

Julie laughed and rolled her eyes. "Who cares?" she said. "He's fricking awesome."

Joe cringed, wishing he had missed that.

He had spent the morning patrolling the brushy foothills where the spring wild turkey season was still open, although there appeared to be no turkey hunters about. It was his first foray into the timbered southwestern saddle slopes since winter. The snow was receding up the mountain, leaving hard-packed grainy drifts in arroyos and cuts. The retreating snow also revealed the aftermath of small battles and tragedies no one had witnessed that had taken place over the winter—six mule deer that had died of starvation in a wooded hollow; a cow and calf elk that had broken through the ice on a pond and frozen in place; pronghorn antelope caught in the barbed wire of a fence, their emaciated bodies draping over the wire like rugs hanging to dry. But there were signs of renewal as well, as thick light-green shoots bristled through dead matted grass near stream sides, and fat, pregnant does stared at his passing pickup from shadowed groves.

April was the slowest month of the year in the field for a game warden, especially in a place with a fleeting spring.

It was the fifth year of a drought. The hottest issue he had to contend with was what to do with the four elk that had shown up in the town of Saddlestring and seemed to have no plans to leave. While mule deer were common in the parks and gardens, elk were not. Joe had chased the four animals—two bulls, a cow, and a calf—from the city park several times by firing .22 blanks into the air several times. But they kept coming back. The animals had become such a fixture in the park they were now referred to as the "Town Elk," and locals were feeding them, which kept them hanging around while providing empty nourishment that would eventually make them sick and kill them. Joe was loath to destroy the elk, but thought he may not have a choice if they stuck around.

The changes in his agency had begun with the election of a new governor. On the day after the election, Joe had received a four-word message from his supervisor, Trey Crump, that read: "Hell has frozen over," meaning a Democrat had been elected. His name was Spencer Rulon. Within a week, the agency director resigned before being fired, and a bitter campaign was waged for a replacement. Joe, and most of the game wardens, actively supported an "Anybody but Randy Pope" ticket, since Pope had risen to prominence within the agency from the administrative side (rather than the law-enforcement or biology side) and made no bones about wanting to rid the state of personnel he felt were too independent, who had "gone native," or were considered uncontrollable cowboys—men like Joe Pickett. Joe's clash with Pope the year before in Jackson had resulted in a simmering feud that was heating up, as Joe's report of Pope's betrayal made the rounds within the agency, despite Pope's efforts to stop it.

Governor Rulon was a big man with a big face and a big gut, an unruly shock of silver-flecked brown hair, a quick sloppy smile, and endlessly darting eyes. In the previous year's election, Rulon had beaten the Republican challenger by twenty points, despite the fact that his opponent had been handpicked by term-limited Governor Budd. This in a state that was 70 percent Republican. Rulon grew up on a ranch near Casper, the grandson of a U.S. senator. He played linebacker for the Wyoming Cowboys, got a law degree, made a fortune in private practice suing federal agencies, then was elected county prosecutor. Loud and profane, Rulon campaigned for governor by crisscrossing the state endlessly in his own pickup and buying rounds for the house in every bar from Yoder to Wright, and challenging anyone who didn't plan to vote for him to an arm-wrestling, sports-trivia, or shooting contest. The word most used to describe the new governor seemed to be "energetic." He could turn from a good old boy pounding beers and slapping backs into an orator capable of delivering the twelve-minute closing argument by Spencer Tracy in *Inherit the Wind* from memory. His favorite breakfast was reportedly biscuits and sausage gravy and a glass of Pinot Noir. Like Wyoming itself, Joe thought, Rulon didn't mind leading with his rough exterior and later surprising—and mildly troubling—the onlooker with a kind of eccentric depth.

He was also, according to more and more state employees who had to deal with their new boss, crazy as a tick.

But he was profoundly popular with the voters. Unlike his predecessor, Rulon reassigned his bodyguards to the Highway Patrol, fired his driver, and insisted that his name and phone number be listed in the telephone book. He eliminated the gatekeepers who had been employed to restrict access to his office and put up a sign that said GOV RULON'S OFFICE—BARGE RIGHT IN, which was heeded by an endless stream of visitors.

One of Rulon's first decisions was to choose a new Game and Fish director. The Board of Commissioners lined up a slate of three candidates—Pope included. The governor's first choice was a longtime game warden from

Medicine Bow, who died of a heart attack within a week of the announcement. The second candidate withdrew his name from consideration when news of an old sexual harassment suit hit the press. Which left Randy Pope, who gladly assumed the role, even declaring to a reporter that "fate and destiny both stepped forward" to enable his promotion. That had been two months ago.

Trey Crump, Joe's district supervisor, said he saw the writing on the wall and took early retirement rather than submit to Pope's new directives for supervisors. Without Trey, who had also been Joe's champion within the state bureaucracy, Joe now had been ordered to report directly to Pope. Instead of weekly reports, Pope wanted *daily* dispatches. It was Pope who had nixed Joe's request for a new pickup and instead had sent one with 150,000 miles on it, bald tires, and a motor that was unreliable.

Joe had been around long enough to know exactly what was happening. Pope could not appear to have a public vendetta against Joe, especially because Joe's star had risen over the past few years in certain quarters.

But Pope was a master of the bureaucratic Death of a Thousand Cuts, the slow, steady, petty, and maddening procedure—misplaced requests, unreturned phone calls, lost insurance and reimbursement claims, blizzards of busywork—designed to drive an employee out of a state or federal agency. And with Pope, Joe knew it was personal.

"*DAD!*"

Joe realized Sheridan was talking to him. "What?"

"How can he tune out like that?" Julie asked Sheridan, as if Joe weren't in the cab.

"I don't know. It's amazing, isn't it?" Then: "Dad, are we going to stop and feed Nate's birds? I want to show Julie the falcons."

"I already fed them today," he said.

"Darn."

Joe slowed and turned onto a dirt road from the highway beneath a massive elk-antler arch with a sign hanging from chains that read:

THUNDERHEAD RANCHES, EST. 1883.

THE SCARLETTS

OPAL

ARLEN

HANK

WYATT

Julie said, "My grandma says someday my name is going to be on that sign."

"Cool," Sheridan replied.

Joe had heard Julie say that before.

EVEN THOUGH JOE had seen the Thunderhead Ranch in bits and pieces over the years, he was still amazed by its magnificence. There were those, he knew, who would drive the scores of old two-tracks on the ranch and look around and see miles and miles of short grass, sagebrush, and rolling hills and compare the place poorly with much more spectacular alpine country. Sure, the river bottom was lush and the foothills rose in a steady march toward the Bighorns and were dotted with trees, but the place wouldn't pop visually for some because it was just so open, so big, so sprawling. But that was the thing. Because of the river, because of the confluence of at least five significant creeks that coursed through the property and poured into the Twelve Sleep River, because of the optimum diversification of landscape within a thousand square miles, and the vast meadows of thick, nutrient-enriched grass, the Thunderhead was the perfect cattle ranch. Joe had once heard a longtime rancher and resident of the county, Herbert Klein, say that if aliens landed and demanded to see a dog he would show them a Labrador, and if they demanded to see a ranch, he would skip his own and show them the Thunderhead.

It was also an ideal ranch for wildlife, which posed an opportunity for Hank, who ran an exclusive hunting business, and a problem for Joe Pickett.

"Look," Sheridan said, sitting up.

A herd of pronghorn antelope, a liquid flow of brown and white, streamed over a knoll ahead of them and to the right, raising dust and heading for a collision with the pickup.

"They don't see us yet," Joe said, marveling, as always, at the graceful but raw speed of the antelope, the second-fastest mammal on earth.

When the lead animals noticed the green Wyoming Game and Fish pickup, they didn't stop or panic but simply turned ninety degrees, not breaking stride, their stream bending away from the road. Joe noted how Sheridan sucked in her breath in absolute awe as the herd drew parallel with the pickup—the bucks, does, and fawns glancing over at her—and then the entire herd accelerated and veered back toward the knoll they had appeared from.

"Wow," she said.

"'Wow' is right," Joe agreed.

"Antelope bore me," Julie said. "There are so many of them."

For a moment he had been concerned that the lead antelope was going to barrel into the passenger door, something that occasionally happened when a pronghorn wasn't paying attention to where he was going. That was all he needed, Joe thought sourly, another damaged pickup Pope could carp about.

That's when the call came over the mutual-aid channel.

Joe said, "Would you two please be quiet for a minute?"

While the entire county was sheriff's department jurisdiction, game wardens and highway patrolmen were called on for backup for rural emergencies.

Sheridan hushed. Julie did too, but with attitude, crossing her arms in front of her chest and clamping her mouth tight. Joe turned up the volume on the radio. Wendy, the dispatcher, had not turned off her microphone. In the background, there was an anxious voice.

"Excuse me, where are you calling from?" Wendy asked the caller.

"I'm on a cell phone. I'm sitting in my car on the side of the highway. You won't believe it."

"Can you describe the situation, sir?"

The cell-phone signal ebbed with static, but Joe could clearly hear the caller say, "There are three men in cowboy hats swinging at each other with shovels in the middle of the prairie. I can see them hitting each other out there. It's a bloody mess."

Wendy said, "Can you give me your location, sir?"

The caller read off a mile marker on State Highway 130. Joe frowned. The Bighorn Road they had just driven on was also Highway 130. The mile marker was just two miles from where they had turned onto the ranch.

"That would be Thunderhead Ranch then, sir?" Wendy asked the caller.

"I guess."

Joe shot a look toward Julie. She had heard and her face was frozen, her eyes wide.

"That's just over the hill," she said.

Joe had a decision to make. He could drive the remaining five miles to the ranch headquarters, where Julie lived, or take a fork in the road that would deliver him, as well as Sheridan and Julie, to the likely location of an assault in progress.

"I'm taking you home," Joe said, accelerating.

"No!" Julie cried. "What if it's someone I know? We've got to stop them."

Joe slowed, his mind racing. He felt it necessary to respond, but did not want to put the girls in danger. "You sure?"

"Yes! What if it's my dad? Or one of my uncles?"

He nodded, did a three-point turn, and took the fork. He snatched the mic from its cradle. "This is GF forty-three. I'm about five to ten minutes from the scene."

Wendy said, "You're literally there on the ranch?"

"Affirmative."

There was a beat of silence. "I don't know whether Sheriff McLanahan is going to like that."

Joe and the sheriff did not get along.

Joe snorted. "Ask him if he wants me to stand down."

"You ask him," Wendy said, completely breaking protocol.

AS THEY POWERED up the two-track, Joe could see that Sheridan and Julie had huddled together.

"Can you keep a secret?" Julie whispered, loud enough for Joe to hear.

"Of course I can," Sheridan said. "You know that. We're best friends."

Julie nodded seriously, as if making up her mind.

"You can't tell your parents," Julie said, nodding at Joe.

Sheridan hesitated before answering. "I swear."

"Swear to God?" Julie asked.

"Come on, Julie. I said I promise."

"Tighten your seat belts, girls," Joe cautioned. "This is going to be bumpy."

The scene before them, as they topped the hill, silenced Julie and whatever she was going to tell Sheridan. Below them, on the flat, there were three pickups, each parked haphazardly in the sagebrush, doors wide open. Inside the ring of trucks, three men circled each other warily, raising puffs of dust, an occasional wide swing with a shovel flashing the late afternoon sun.

Out on the highway, two sheriff's department SUVs and a highway patrolman turned from the highway onto an access road, their lights flashing. One of the SUVs burped on his siren.

"Jesus Christ," McLanahan said over the radio, as the vehicles converged on the fight. "It's a rodeo out here. There's blood pourin' outta 'em . . ."

"Yee-haw," the highway patrolman said sardonically.

Joe thought the scene in front of him was epic in implication, and ridiculous at the same time. Three adults, two of them practically legends in their own right, so blinded by their fight that they didn't seem to know that a short string of law-enforcement vehicles was approaching.

And not just any adults, but Arlen, Hank, and Wyatt Scarlett, the scions of the most prominent ranch family in the Twelve Sleep Valley. It was as if the figures on Mount Rushmore were head-butting one another.

It was darkly fascinating seeing the three of them out there, Joe thought. He was reminded that, in a situation like this, he would always be an outsider looking in. Despite his time in Twelve Sleep County, he would never feel quite a part of this scenario, which was rooted so deeply in the valley. The tendrils of the Scarlett family ranch and of the Scarletts themselves reached too deeply, intertwined with too many other people and families, to ever completely sort out. Their interaction with the people and history of the area was multilayered, nuanced, too complicated to ever fully understand. The Scarletts were colorful, ruthless, independent, and eccentric. If newcomers to the area displayed even half of the strange behavior of the Scarletts, Joe was sure they'd have been run out of the state—or shunned to the point of cruelty. But the Scarletts were local, they were founders, they were benefactors and philanthropists—despite their eccentricities. It was almost as if longtime residents of the area had declared, in unison, "Yes, they're crazy. But they're *our* lunatics, and we won't have anyone insulting them or judging them harshly who hasn't lived here long enough to understand."

Arlen was the oldest brother, and the best liked. He was tall with broad shoulders and a mane of silver-white wavy hair that made him look like the state senate majority floor leader he was. He had a heavy, thrusting jaw and the bulbous, spiderwebbed nose of a drinker. His clear blue eyes looked out from under bushy eyebrows that were black as smears of grease, and he had a soothing, sonorous voice that turned the reading of a diner menu into a performance. Arlen had the gift of remembering names and offspring, and could instantly continue a conversation with a constituent that had been cut off months before.

Hank, the middle brother, was smaller than Arlen. He was thin and wiry with a sharp-featured bladelike face, and wore a sweat-stained gray Stetson clamped tight on his head. Joe had never seen Hank without the hat, and had no idea if he had hair underneath it. He remembered Vern Dunnegan, the former game warden in the district, warning Joe to stay away from Hank unless he absolutely had the goods on him. "Hank Scarlett is the toughest man I've ever met," Vern had said, "the scariest too."

Hank had a way of looking coiled up when he stood still, the way a Brahma bull was calm just before the chute gate opened. Hank was an extremely successful big-game guide and outfitter, with operations in Wyoming, Alaska, and Kenya. His clients were millionaires, and he was suspected of using less-than-ethical means to assure kills of trophy animals. Hank had been on Joe's radar screen even before Joe was assigned the Saddlestring District, and Hank knew it. All the game wardens knew of Hank. But Joe had never found hard evidence of any wrongdoing. Hank's legend was burnished by rumors and stories, such as when Hank single-handedly packed a two-hundred-pound mountain sheep twelve miles across the Wind River Mountains in a blinding snowstorm. Or Hank crash-landing a bush plane with mechanical problems into the middle of a frozen Alaskan lake, rescuing two clients, amputating the leg of one of them while they waited for rescue. And Hank dropping from a tree onto the back of a record bull moose and riding it a quarter of a mile before reaching forward and slitting its throat.

Wyatt was the biggest but the youngest. His face was cherubic, without the sharp angles his brothers' had. Everything about Wyatt was soft and round, his cheeks, his nose, the extra flesh around his soft brown eyes. He was in his early thirties. When people within the community talked about the historic Scarlett Ranch, or the battling Scarlett brothers, it was understood they were referring to Arlen and Hank. It was as if Wyatt didn't exist, as if he was as much an embarrassment to the community as he was, no doubt, to the family itself. Joe knew very little about Wyatt, and what he had heard wasn't good. When Wyatt Scarlett was brought up, it was often in hushed tones.

Joe was close enough now that he could see Arlen clearly. Arlen was bleeding from a cut on the side of his head, and he shot a glance over his shoulder at the approaching vehicles. Which gave an opening to Hank, the middle brother, to swing and hit the back of Arlen's head with the flat of his shovel like a pumpkin on a post.

Julie screamed and covered her face with her hands.

Joe realized what he was thrusting her into and slammed on his brakes. "Julie, I'm going to take you home . . ."

"No!" she sobbed. "Just make them stop! Make them stop before my dad and my uncles kill each other."

Joe and Sheridan exchanged glances. Sheridan had turned white. She shook her head, not knowing what to say.

Joe blew out a breath and continued on.

. . .

ARLEN WENT DOWN from the blow as the convoy fanned
out in the sagebrush and surrounded the brothers. Joe hit
his brakes and opened his door, keeping it between him and
the Scarletts. As he dug his shotgun out and racked the
pump, he heard McLanahan whoop a blast from his siren
and say, in his new cowboy-slang cadence, "DROP THE
SHOVELS, MEN, AND STEP BACK FROM EACH
OTHER WITH YOUR HANDS ON YOUR HEAD. EX-
CEPT YOU, ARLEN. YOU STAY DOWN."

The officers spilled out of their vehicles, brandishing
weapons. The warning seemed to have no effect on Hank,
who was standing over Arlen and raising his shovel above
his head with two hands as if about to strike it down on his
brother the way a gardener beheads a snake.

Joe thought Arlen was a dead man, but Wyatt suddenly
drove his shoulder into Hank and sent him sprawling, the
shovel flying end-over-end through the air.

"Go!" McLanahan shouted at his men. "Go round 'em
up now!"

"Stay here," Joe said to Julie and Sheridan. His daughter
cradled Julie in her arms. Julie sobbed, her head down.

Joe, holding his shotgun pointed above the fray, stepped
around his truck and saw three deputies including Deputy
Mike Reed rush the three prone Scarlett Brothers. Reed
was the only deputy Joe considered sane and professional.
The others were recent hires by McLanahan and were, to a
man, large, mulish, quick with their fists, and just as quick
to look away if an altercation involved someone who was a
friend of the Sheriff's Department—or, more specifically,
McLanahan himself.

Arlen simply rolled to his stomach and put his hands behind his back to be cuffed, saying, "Take it easy, boys, take
it easy, I'm cooperating . . ."

Wyatt, after watching Arlen, did the same, although he looked confused.

It took all three deputies to subdue Hank, who continued to curse and kick and swing at them, one blow connecting solidly with Deputy Reed's mouth, which instantly bloomed with bright-red blood. Finally, after a pepper spray blast to his eyes, Hank curled up in the dirt and the deputies managed to cuff his hands behind him and bind his cowboy boots together with Flex-Cuffs.

AFTER TWO YEARS as county sheriff, McLanahan still seemed to be somewhat unfinished, which is why he had apparently decided in recent months to assume a new role, that of "local character." After trying on and discarding several personas—squinty-eyed gunfighter, law-enforcement technocrat, glad-handing politician—McLanahan had decided to aspire to the mantle of "good old boy," a stereotype that had served his predecessor Bud Barnum well for twenty-four years. In the past six months, McLanahan had begun to slow his speech pattern and pepper his pronouncements and observations with arcane westernisms. He'd even managed to make his face go slack. His sheriff's crisp gray Stetson had been replaced by a floppy black cowboy hat and his khaki department jacket for a bulky Carhartt ranch coat. Rather than drive the newest sheriff's department vehicle, McLanahan opted for an old county pickup with rust spots on the panels. He bought a Blue Heeler puppy to occupy the passenger seat, and had begun to refer to his seven-acre parcel of land outside the city limits as his "ranch."

McLanahan squatted down in the middle of the triangle of handcuffed brothers and asked, "Can one of you tell me just what in the hell this is all about?"

Joe listened.

"Mama's gone," Hank said, his voice hard. "And that son-of-a-bitch there"—he nodded toward Arlen—"thinks he's going to get the ranch."

McLanahan said, "What do you mean she's gone? Like she's on a vacation or something?"

Hank didn't take his eyes off of Arlen. "Like that son-of-a-bitch killed her and hid the body," he said.

"What?" McLanahan said.

There was a high, unearthly wail, an airy squeal that seemed to come down from the mountains. The sound made the hairs on Joe's neck stand up. It was Wyatt. The big man was crying.

Joe looked over his shoulder at his pickup truck, to see if Julie had heard. Luckily, the windows were up and she was still being held by Sheridan.

"Mind if I stand up now?" Arlen asked the sheriff.

McLanahan thought it over, nodded his assent, and told Deputy Reed to help Arlen up but to keep him away from Hank.

Joe squatted down a few feet from Wyatt.

"Are you okay?" Joe asked. "Are you hurt?"

Wyatt just continued to sob, his head between his knees, his back heaving, tears spattering the ground between his boots. Joe asked again. Wyatt reached up with his cuffed hands and smeared his tears across his dirty face.

"Where's my mom?" Wyatt asked, his words mushy. Joe noticed Wyatt had missing teeth. "Where did she go?"

"I don't know," Joe said. "She can't be far."

"But Hank says she's gone."

Joe said, "I'm sure we'll find her."

Wyatt's eyes flared, and for a second Joe thought the man would strike out at him.

"Where's my mom?" Wyatt howled.

"Pickett!" McLanahan yelled, "What are you doing over there?"

Joe stood uneasily, searching Wyatt's upturned, tragic

face for a clue to his behavior. "Making sure Wyatt's okay," Joe said.

"He's not," McLanahan said, and one of the deputies laughed. "Trust me on that one."

Joe looked at Arlen, and Hank. Both brothers were turned toward Wyatt, but neither said anything. They simply stared at their younger brother as if they were observing an embarrassing stranger.

Joe walked over to Deputy Reed, who was holding a bandanna to his split lip.

"What do you think the deal is with Opal?" Joe asked, out of earshot of the Scarlett brothers.

"Don't know," Reed said. "But I do know that old woman's just too goddamned mean to die."

WHILE SHERIFF MCLANAHAN interviewed each of the brothers quietly and individually, Joe concluded that he was no longer needed and, by inadvertently bringing Julie, he had done more harm than good.

"I've got Julie Scarlett, Arlen's daughter, in my truck," Joe told Reed. "I don't want her to see any more. I think I need to get her home to her mother." Joe gestured toward Arlen.

"You mean Hank?" Reed asked.

"No," Joe said. "I mean her dad, Arlen."

Reed squinted. "Arlen isn't her dad."

Joe wasn't sure what to say. He had dropped Julie off before at the big ranch house where she lived with Arlen, her mother, and Opal. As far as Joe knew, Hank lived alone in a hunting lodge on the other side of the ranch.

"What do you mean?" Joe asked.

Reed shrugged. "When it comes to the Scarletts, nothing is as it seems. Julie and her mother moved out of Hank's place years ago, but from what I understand, Hank is her dad."

Joe wondered if Sheridan knew this, if Julie had told her. Or if Reed was mistaken.

"Either way," Joe said, "I think I should get her home."

Reed nodded. "If you see Opal, give us a call."

"I will. Do you really think she's missing?"

Reed scoffed. "Do you really think those men would be out here beating each other with shovels if she was back home baking cookies? The whole damned county has been scared of the day when Opal passed on and those three would start fighting for the ranch. Now it looks like that day has come."

As Joe turned toward his truck, he heard McLanahan shout at him. "Where do you think you're going?"

"To the ranch," Joe said over his shoulder. "It looks like you've got things handled here."

"It's okay," Reed told his boss. "He's got Hank's little girl with him."

"I'll need your statement," McLanahan said. "It sounds like you were one of the last people to see Opal alive."

Joe turned, surprised. He had talked to Opal the day before about charging fishermen access fees. One of the brothers must have told McLanahan that.

"When do you need the statement?"

"Tonight."

Joe thought of Marybeth's last words to him that morning. She asked him to be home on time because she was cooking dinner and wanted to have the whole family there for a change. With her business thriving, that was a rarity. He had promised he would be home.

"Can it be tomorrow morning?" Joe asked.

The sheriff's face darkened. "No, it can't. We've got to jump all over this one, and what you've got to tell us may help."

Joe looked up. He saw that Julie's head was up, her eyes on her uncles and father. He wanted to get her away from there, and quickly.

"Tonight," McLanahan called after him.

"Tonight," Joe said, walking away.

He opened the door to his truck and said, "I'm so sorry you saw this, Julie."

She cried, "Please, just take me home."

2

ON THE MORNING OPAL SCARLETT VANISHED, A MUD-streaked green late-model SUV with Georgia plates pulled off I-80 at exit 214 and into the parking lot of Rip Griffin's Truck Stop outside Rawlins, Wyoming. The driver left the car running while he climbed out, stretched, and dug through his army duffel in the back seat for a clean shirt. He had been driving all night and all morning, stopping only to fill the tank and buy pork rinds, bottled water, and cashews. The floor of the car was littered with the wrappers.

As he walked across the parking lot toward the store, he breathed in deeply and looked around him. It was high and desolate, this country, as if the prairie had been pushed from below the earth way up in the air. He thought of seeing the sign just an hour ago that read CONTINENTAL DIVIDE, thinking, *That's it?* Not a single damned tree. The smell in the air was of diesel fumes from the trucks lined up on the far side of the lot and something sweet that he guessed was sagebrush. Even with the interstate highway humming behind him, there was an immense blanket of quiet off the road. The air was light and thin, and the terrain wide open as far as he could see. He felt exposed, like everybody who could see him would know why he was there, what he was up to. He thought of the herds of pronghorn antelope he had seen in the distance as the sun came up. Hundreds of them out there, red-brown and white, glowing when the sun hit them and lit them up. Unlike the animals he was used to at home who survived by hiding in the dark timber and the swamp, and moved only at night, these antelope stood out there in the wide-open plains, bold as you please, using the openness and long-range visibility as a defense measure. If you could see them, he thought, they could see you. Hide in plain sight, that was the way out here. He would learn something from that.

In the bathroom, he stripped off his greasy sweatshirt, balled it up, and tossed it in a garbage can. He filled the sink with water, splashed his face and rubbed it under his arms, across his chest, and dried off with paper towels. He stared at his reflection in the mirror, liking what he saw. Liking it a lot.

His blue eyes burned back from shadowed sockets. There were hollows under his sharp cheekbones, and his three-day growth of beard added an edge to his gaunt features that had once been described by the wife of his last hunting client as "haunted." He didn't know if that was good or bad, but he didn't forget the word. He tilted his chin up and surveyed his pectorals, and liked the clean definition of them, and the blue, green, and red tattoo of a striking water moccasin that stretched from one nipple to the other. The way the head of the snake turned out with an open mouth and dead black eyes always gave him a little thrill. It scared some women, another thing that was all right with him.

He pulled the rubber band out of his long brown hair, combed it back with his fingers, and then snapped it back on. With his hair pulled back so tight, it looked as though he wore a skull cap, and his eyes appeared even more piercing. He liked that too.

Teeth bared into a half grin, he made his eyes go dead. This was his most fearsome look. He had showed it to the lady who said he seemed haunted, and it had the desired effect. She was terrified, her eyes so wide they looked about to pop out, her mouth forming a perfect little hole. That felt good, to have that kind of power over a rich, stupid lady who shouldn't have been in his hunting camp in the first place.

The bathroom door wheezed open and a trucker came in. He was big through the shoulders but had a fleshy face and a big belly. When the trucker saw him standing there at the sink he started to say something smart-ass, something like "Doing a little primping, eh?" or "Did you forget your hair spray?" but when their eyes met in the mirror it was as if the fat man suddenly choked on a piece of meat. All the man did was nod, turn away, and pass behind him for the shelter of a stall.

He winked at himself in the mirror, pleased with the effect he had on a man outweighing him by at least ninety pounds, then pulled his new shirt on and walked out of the bathroom.

As he passed the counter, which was stacked with displays for all-natural amphetamines and cigarette lighters in the shape of cell phones and hand grenades, he asked the bored, washed-out clerk, "Is this the right road to get to the Wyoming State Pen?"

"The *pay-un*?" the clerk said, mocking his accent. He was so surprised by her insolence that he didn't know what to say. His first instinct was to reach over the box of beef jerky and pull her tongue out by the roots.

"Yeah," she continued, either too empty-headed or jaded to care about how he felt, "this is the exit. Just get back on the road and go over the hill and you'll see it." She gestured vaguely over her head, to the south. "You visiting or checking in?"

Again, she insulted him! He could feel the rush of blood to his face, feel his fists involuntarily clench. If only she knew what he was capable of, he thought. If only that clerk knew about what had happened to that hunter and his wife back in Mississippi, she wouldn't be doing this. That couple should never have left Atlanta to go hunting in their green SUV.

THE SIGHT OF the prison complex, a bunch of low-slung gray buildings sprawled across a sagebrush-choked valley, cooled him down a little. As he passed the sign that read NO TRESPASSING: ALL VEHICLES AND INDIVIDUALS ARE SUBJECT TO SEARCH BEYOND THIS POINT, his mind focused again, his anger venting out like the *kack-kack-kack* of a pressure cooker releasing steam, the reason for his arrival coming back into prominence.

Not that he didn't think about that woman behind the counter, how he could come back later and wait for her in the employee parking lot so that he could break her face— and that mouth!—open with an iron bar. But he had work to do, information to get, and it had been long in planning. He couldn't let her insolence set him back, add an unnecessary complication. That clerk would never know how close she had come to . . . what? He wasn't sure. He would have just let his rage take over, seen where it took him. One thing he was sure of: she was the luckiest woman in Rawlins, Wyoming. Too bad she didn't know it.

The prison was close to the interstate, but a high rocky ridge separated the two. Every day, thousands of travelers took that interstate going either east or west, and few if any of them knew how close they were to a maximum-security prison just over the hill, a place filled with murderers, rapists, kidnappers, and other scum of the earth. He had known plenty of ex-cons. Some he'd grown up with, some he'd hired, some he'd gone drink for drink with at a bar. In fact, technically, he was an ex-con, although he didn't feel like one. Five years in his state pen down South for aggravated assault. He'd spent most of his time observing the makeup of the general population. To a man, they were stupid. Even the ones with some intelligence had a stupid blind spot that later tripped them up. They *deserved* to go to prison. They didn't think, they just did. They were nature's mistakes, human bowel movements. Prison was too good for most of them. And he'd told a couple of them that right to their faces, because he didn't care what they thought of him.

He cruised through the parking lot, looking at the cars. Half of the plates were from Wyoming, the rest from all over. He saw a flash of brake lights from a yellow ten-year-old Ford pickup with a camper shell and Wyoming plates. The truck had just pulled in. He parked the SUV two rows behind it. While he waited, he emptied all the metal from his pockets into a dirty sock and put it in the glove compartment. The occupants of the truck, an older man wearing red suspenders and a pear-shaped woman with tight gray curls, finally got out to go inside. They were no doubt the parents or grandparents of some stupid convict, and in a way it was kind of a sweet, sad thing to see. Were they wondering what they could have done differently? Did they ask themselves where they had gone wrong, to turn out a son like this, a human bowel movement? *But,* he said to himself, *at least they have family.*

He took a quick look in the mirror, smiled at his reflection, and followed. The old couple walked so slowly he overtook them at the entrance to the building. The man flinched a bit when he darted in front of them and grabbed the handle to the door.

The old man snorted, said, "What in the . . . ?"

But instead of rushing inside, the man who had driven

all night opened the door for them, stepped aside, and said, "Let me get this here heavy door for you."

The woman looked from her husband to the man, and smiled. "Thank you," she said.

"My pleasure."

WHILE HE WAITED for the old couple to check in at a desk inside the waiting room, he read the notices on the bulletin board. The room was clean and light, built of cinder block painted pale lime green. The check-in desk was on one side of the room and a row of lockers was on the other.

The couple gave their names while the woman in uniform behind the desk found their names in her notebook.

The guard handed them a key and told them to remove all metal objects and to put everything in one of the lockers before going through the metal detector.

In order to visit, a sign posted on the bulletin board said, *visitors shall be MODESTLY DRESSED to be permitted inside. The following will not be allowed: bare midriffs, see-through blouses or shirts, sleeveless shirts, shorts, tube tops, halter tops, extremely tight or revealing clothing, dresses or skirts above the knee, sexually revealing attire . . .*

He glanced over at the old couple while they emptied their pockets. The woman seemed flustered. She clucked at her husband, asking him whether he thought her thick old nurse's shoes would be okay. The old man shrugged. She wore a billowy print dress that did little to disguise her bulk. Thick, mottled ankles stuck out below the hem of the dress and looked stuffed into the shoes. *Nothing sexually revealing there,* he thought, and smiled.

. . . Visitors must wear undergarments; children under the age of ten may wear shorts and sleeveless shirts. No rubber slippers or flip-flops will be allowed.

It took the couple three tries to get through the metal detector. First, the old man had to remove his suspenders because of the metal clips. The second time, the woman had to confess that the bra she wore to hold up her massive breasts contained wire. Then, the man had to remove his work boots because of the hobnails in the heels. Finally, the guards allowed the old couple through provided the suspenders be put away in the locker.

He watched the old man close his locker door and noted the number: 16.

He approached the check-in desk, smiling.

"You are . . . ?" the guard asked.

He said his name.

"Give me your ID so I can hold on to it here."

He handed his driver's license to her. She looked at it and matched up the photo.

"That's quite a name," she said, and the corners of her mouth curled up a fraction. Was she amused? Contemptuous? Flirty? He couldn't decide.

He said, "It never bothered me none."

"All the way from Mississippi. And you're here to see . . ." She paused, following her finger across the page, then said it.

"That's right."

She handed him a key to locker number 31, and gave him a speech about metal objects she had memorized. He'd heard it before down South.

"All I got with me is this," he said, digging in his pocket for a can of Copenhagen chewing tobacco. "I want to give it to him."

She took the Copenhagen from him and screwed the top off. The strong smell of powdered black tobacco filled the room. He felt his stomach muscles clench, but he tried to keep his face expressionless. He could not smell anything other than tobacco, and he doubted she could either. So far, so good.

"I guess that will be okay," she said, handing it back.

"Oh," he said, smiling his warmest smile and letting his eyes drip on her a little, "and I ain't wearin' any underwear."

This produced an amused shake of her head. "That's just for women visitors," she said.

"I shoulda figured that out," he said. "You live around here?" He'd be willing to take her home, even though she was a little too heavy and plain in the face. Or at least he'd take her out to his car. She had a nice full mouth.

"Of course I do," she said, sitting back in her chair, looking at him closely, making a decision. She voted no, he could see it happen. Maybe it was his beard. "Where do you think I'd live if I work for the Department of Corrections in Rawlins? Hawaii? Now please proceed through the metal detector."

HE PLACED THE locker key in a plastic basket and showed the two guards at the metal detector the can of Copenhagen.

"She said it was okay," he said, gesturing to the waiting room.

"She did, huh?" a guard wearing horn-rimmed glasses said, taking the can and opening it. Unlike the woman, the guard stuck his bare finger into it and swirled it around.

"What are you looking for?" he asked. "You're getting your germs in it."

The guard looked up, not sympathetic. "People try to smuggle things in here all the time," he said. "How do we know you didn't mix something in here?"

He felt his neck get hot. "But she said it was okay. It's a gift."

"Nope," the guard said. "Leave it here. You can get it on your way out." The guard replaced the top, and wiped his finger on his uniform pants.

Go wash your hands . . . Don't put your finger in your

mouth, he wanted to warn. But all he said was, "Oh, come on . . ."

The guard shook his head no. It was final.

"For Christ sake," he said. His plan was already going a little awry. But he had a backup.

"Keep Him out of it," the guard said. "Do you want to go inside or not?"

"Yes, sir."

"Then leave it here and go get in the van."

He nodded, figured he'd better shut up. As he went down the hallway where another guard was waiting at an open door, he heard a metal clunk as the tobacco was tossed inside a metal waste can. He let out a breath and walked ahead. A van was outside.

He settled into the first seat behind the driver. He was the only visitor in the van. The driver climbed in after him, turned on the motor, shut the door, and did a slow U-turn. He looked outside the window at the bare, rocky hills. There were wisps of clouds in a high blue sky and nothing, absolutely nothing, else. Except some antelope, up there on the hillside. Hiding in plain sight.

IT WAS A mile from the Administration Building to the prison. The driver said, "First time?"

"Yep."

"You want to know what you're looking at?"

He really didn't care, but to be friendly, he said, "Sure."

"That's the ITU," the driver said, nodding in the direction of a boxy gray building behind a fence topped with razor wire. "Intensive Treatment Unit. Ultra-rehab. That's where the drug addicts get sent when they arrive. Or if an inmate needs extensive psychological treatment."

"That's probably a lot of them, I'd guess," he said.

"You're right about that.

"This is a state-of-the-art prison," the driver continued,

saying it in a way that suggested he had repeated it a hundred times, like a tour guide at a theme park. "It's a city unto itself. Everything is on premises, cooking, laundry, hospital, everything. It would continue to function if the rest of the world didn't, at least for a while. We have six hundred and eighty inmates in A, B, C, and E buildings, or pods. The inmates are segregated based on their crimes and their behavior, and you can tell their status by the shirts they wear. Yellow means newbie, or rookie. Blue shirts and red shirts are general population. Orange means watch out, that man is in trouble or he's dangerous. White means death row.

"The whole place is watched twenty-four/seven by two hundred cameras that are everywhere. I mean it, everywhere. There are also motion sensors everywhere, and I mean everywhere. No one moves in this place that somebody isn't watching him.

"That includes visitors," the driver said, looking at him in his mirror to make sure he had heard him.

"It's slow today for visitors. Summer weekends, we get more than a hundred people. The average day is fifty. Are you meeting your inmate in the contact or noncontact area?"

He wasn't sure. "Noncontact, I think."

"Who is it?"

He told him.

The driver nodded. "Yeah. Noncontact. He's in for murder, right?"

He said yes. Multiple homicide. Death row. He'd be wearing white.

"He doesn't get many visitors," the driver said, leaving it at that.

HE STOOD IN another waiting area. He wished the driver hadn't told him about the cameras, even though he should have known. If he'd felt exposed standing in a parking lot, he really felt exposed here. He'd been told the conversation he was about to have wouldn't be recorded. But how could he be sure of that? He'd have to keep his comments obscure, the way he had in his letters to the inmate. Get things across without actually saying them.

Beyond the waiting room, through three-quarter-inch glass, was the big visiting room with tables and chairs in it. A guard, a woman, sat at a desk in the corner, doing paper-work. On the desk was the biggest box of sanitizing wipes he had ever seen. He grimaced, thinking about what it was she had to wipe up out there, what kinds of fluids oozed out of these people, this scum. There was a table with an urn of coffee and columns of white Styrofoam cups. Bright plas-tic toys were stacked in a corner. A television was on with a game show on it. *Jesus, the place is almost cheery,* he thought. It reminded him of a modern high school without windows.

A guard came into the room with a clipboard.

"You're John Wayne Keeley?"

"Yessir."

"You're here to see Wacey Hedeman?"

"Yessir."

"Follow me."

SIX YEARS BEFORE, Wacey Hedeman had gone crazy. Un-til it happened, he had been a game warden working for the Wyoming Game and Fish Department in northern Wyoming, near the Bighorn Mountains. He had a good reputation and was well liked; a former champion rodeo bull rider in the PRCA, star of the university rodeo team, state champion wrestler before that. He was gregarious, ambitious, and cut a wide swath. He was, in practically everyone's opinion, paid the highest compliment a Wyomingite paid another: He was thought "a good guy."

But that was before he got the urge to run for Twelve Sleep County sheriff. He had needed money and influence to win, and he hooked up with former supervisor and mentor Vern Dunnegan, who had reappeared in the area as an advance landman for a natural-gas pipeline. Dunnegan could deliver the office to Wacey because he had the goods on the current sheriff, if Wacey would clear the way and anyone in it for the pipeline project. The situation spiraled downward into places no one anticipated and in the end, Wacey murdered four men and shot a pregnant woman before he was stopped.

Keeley had been told some of the story, and had looked up the rest. Wacey Hedeman had been sentenced to die by lethal injection, but he was still waiting for it to happen. His partner in crime, Vern Dunnegan, was serving out his sentence in the same prison, but in the general population, not maximum security.

KEELEY WAS TAKEN through a door labeled NONCONTACT VISITS and down a narrow hallway. The guard opened another door and Keeley went into a narrow cubicle with a desk, a stool bolted to the floor, a foot-wide counter, and a thick piece of glass that revealed a setup on the other side that was similar. A half-inch slot was cut in the glass near the counter, enough room to pass papers through. A black phone was mounted on the wall.

He sat down, straddling the stool, his palms flat on the counter, his nose just a few inches from the glass.

The door in the other room opened, and Wacey Hedeman stepped in and looked at him.

Hedeman was smaller than he thought he would be, Keeley thought. The old newspaper photos he had seen of Hedeman made him look taller, and more than a little dashing. His drooping gunfighter mustache was still there, though, but streaked with some gray. He had a bantam rooster kind of cockiness to his step, and the way he looked at Keeley from beneath his eyebrows . . . he looked like someone you wouldn't want to mess with. One of Wacey's sleeves flopped around as he moved. *That's right,* Keeley thought, *his arm got shot off. Idiot.*

The guard behind Wacey Hedeman said, "I'll be right outside"—Keeley could read his soundless words through the glass by watching his mouth—and Hedeman nodded but didn't look back at him. The guard withdrew and the door closed. Wacey sat down. Their faces were no more than eighteen inches apart, through the glass. They reached for the handsets simultaneously.

"Thanks for agreeing to meet me," Keeley said.

"Did you bring me what you said you would?"

Keeley raised his eyebrows. "They wouldn't let me bring it through security. I tried, though. The first lady let me but the guy at the metal detector took it."

Wacey's face started to turn red. He glared at Keeley through the glass, and lowered the handset from his face. Keeley thought for a second that Wacey might just stand up, turn around, and demand to be let out.

"I'm sorry," Keeley said.

Wacey just stared at him.

"Don't fuck with me," Wacey said, after bringing the phone back to his face. "Do you know how much I crave that stuff in here? Do you have any fucking idea?"

"No."

"Some of these guys have it," Wacey said, nodding toward the inmates with visiting families in the open room. "How is it they get it and I don't? Why is it okay to smoke but not okay to chew? It pisses me off. This is Wyoming. A man ought to be allowed to chew here."

Maybe because you're on death row? Keeley thought but didn't say. "I don't know. It don't seem too fair. I'm sorry."

"Quit saying that," Wacey said, his eyes on Keeley. "You sound like one sorry son-of-a-bitch."

Keeley felt his always-present anger flare up, and fought to stanch it. He would let this man humiliate him if it would get him the information he needed. Who cared if a stupid con treated him badly? It wasn't as if he'd ever see the guy again.

"Let's start over," Keeley said. "Thanks for seeing me, putting me on your visit list."

Wacey rolled his eyes and his mouth tightened. "Yeah. I had to bump twenty visitors to the bottom of the list just to get you in. And you didn't even bring me what I wanted."

"I said I was sorry. I tried. Maybe I can send you a roll of it."

Wacey scoffed. "Everything gets searched. The guards would take it and use it themselves."

While he talked, Keeley dropped one hand under the counter and unzipped his fly. He found what he was looking for, and raised it up so Wacey could see it. It was a can of Copenhagen, all right, but much thinner than a normal plastic can, with a plastic lid that wasn't picked up by the metal detector.

"This is how they give out samples as you probably know," Keeley said. "At rodeos and county fairs and such. It's about a quarter the size of a real can. I picked it up last summer, and used it as my backup in case they took the real one, even though you said it'd get through. It's better than nothing, I guess."

Wacey's eyes were focused on the can of tobacco. "Give it to me."

Now Keeley felt in control. "I will. But I got a couple of questions for you first. That's why I'm here."

Keeley could see Wacey lick his lips, then raise his eyes back up, then back to the can. He was like a drug addict, Keeley thought. He *needed* the Copenhagen. But how could he need it so much if he'd gone six years without it? Then he remembered: Convicts are stupid. Even Wacey Hedeman.

Wacey looked up, eager to talk. Keeley thought, *Pathetic*.

Keeley said, "I think you know why I'm here. I got a big interest in you. See, my brother moved out here to Wyoming eight years ago. He was an outfitter up in Twelve Sleep County. Name of Ote. You remember him?"

Wacey seemed interested now. "I remember."

Keeley watched Wacey's eyes for a hint of guilt or remorse. Nothing.

"He got killed," Keeley said.

Wacey just nodded.

"He used to send me letters. That's when I first heard your name. And the name of the other game warden. You remember him, don't you?"

Again, the nod. Keeley knew Wacey was wondering where this was going, since it had been Wacey who shot his brother in an elk-hunting camp. Keeley proceeded as if he weren't aware of that fact.

"What I'm interested in is this other game warden."

Wacey swallowed, said, "What about him?"

"You don't like him much, do you?"

"He was the one put me in here," Wacey said. "So no, I'm not real *fond* of him." He spat out the word *fond*.

"You hear about what happened a couple of years ago up in that same country?" Keeley said. "A big confrontation where some good people got burned up in the snow? A woman and her little girl?"

"I heard."

"She was my sister-in-law, and her child, God bless them. They was also Keeleys," he said. "They was the last Keeleys, 'cept for me. And you know what?"

Wacey hesitated. Then, finally, "What?"

"That same damned game warden was involved in that too. Can you imagine? The same guy involved with the end of our family name."

Wacey stared at him through the glass. "That wouldn't be the end of it," he said. "You got the same last name. Whyn't you just go out there and make a bunch more? Isn't that what you people do in the South?"

Now the anger did flare up. Keeley lashed out and thumped the glass with the heel of his hand. Wacey sat back in reaction, even though there was no way Keeley could have broken through.

The door behind Wacey Hedeman opened and the guard leaned his head in. "Knock off the noise," the guard said, and Keeley could hear him through the handset.

"You don't understand," Keeley said, after the guard had left. Wacey looked back, wary. It was obvious he hadn't expected that blow to the glass.

"Don't understand what?"

"Just shut up, and answer a couple of questions. I drove all the way here for this, and I don't need your mouth. I drove through Arkansas, Oklahoma, Kansas, and Nebraska to meet you, Mr. Wacey. I don't need to hear your shit-for-brains views of my people, or my name."

Wacey swallowed again, shot a glance at the miniature can of Copenhagen.

"Tell me about him," Keeley said. "Tell me what makes him tick. Tell me how to get under his skin."

Wacey seemed to weigh the question, his head nodding almost imperceptibly. Then: "He's not going to look or act the way you might expect. In fact, when you meet him, I predict that you'll feel . . . underwhelmed. That's his trick, and I don't even know if he realizes it." Wacey paused for a moment. "I take that back—I think he does. But that doesn't mean he acts any different."

"What are you talking about?"

"He likes being underestimated. He doesn't have any problem with playing the fool. But just because he isn't saying anything doesn't mean he's stupid. It means he's listening."

Keeley nodded, go on.

"The worst thing about him, or the best, depending on how you look at it, is that when he thinks he's right, there isn't anybody that can change his mind. The son-of-a-bitch might even act like he's going along with you, but deep down, he's already set his course. And nothing, I mean fucking *nothing,* will get him out of it. He's a man who thinks he's looking at everything for the very first time, like no one else has ever looked at it before so he's got to figure it out for himself. You know what I mean? There's some real arrogance there, but he'd never admit that.

"Once you set the hook in him," Wacey said, "he won't shake it out. Even if he knows you set it. He'll see it through to the bitter end, no matter what happens. Just realize that. Once you start with him, you better be prepared to hang on."

AFTER ANOTHER TWENTY minutes of talking, Keeley slipped the can of tobacco through the slot, and Wacey grabbed it before it was all the way through. Keeley watched Wacey twist off the top and plunge his nose almost into the black tobacco and breathe in deeply, his eyes closed. Without another word, he put the lid back on and stuffed the can in his pocket, then reached up and hung up his phone. His part of the conversation was over.

Keeley couldn't detect the chew in his side of the room, but he tried to imagine it. He also tried to imagine the other odor, the one that was overpowered by the tobacco. The smell of almonds.

"I'm going to enjoy this," Wacey said soundlessly.

Keeley smiled through the glass. Wacey didn't smile back, but stood and knocked on the door so the guard would let him out.

AS HE RODE in the van back to the Administration Building, John Wayne Keeley thought over what Wacey had told him.

"Good visit?" the driver asked.

"Good enough," Keeley said.

WHEN HE PASSED back through the security area, he fished the large can of Copenhagen he had brought out of the garbage can, and slid it back in his pocket. The guard saw him, and winked. *They didn't care a whit what you took out of the place,* Keeley thought, *only what you brought* in.

At the desk he retrieved his driver's license from a guard who had replaced the woman. He quickly cleaned his wallet and keys out of the locker, while noting that number 16 was locked. The old couple were still inside, visiting.

IN THE PARKING lot, he wiped down all the surfaces in the SUV with a soft cloth, then removed his duffel bag from the back seat and the sock of valuables from the glove compartment of the SUV. He carried them across the pavement to the old yellow Ford pickup and tossed the duffel into the back beneath the camper shell.

As he guessed, the cab of the truck was unlocked. He opened the door and tripped the hood latch. After a glance toward the Administration Building to make sure no one was coming, he leaned under the hood. It took less than a minute to locate the red coil wire, strip it, run half of it to the positive side of the battery coil and tie it off, and trigger the starter solenoid. The engine roared to life. These old Fords were easy to hot-wire, and he'd had plenty of practice on his own when some dumb-shit camp cook lost the keys. That's why he'd targeted the truck right off, rather than any of the other vehicles in the lot that were nicer. He slammed the hood shut and slid behind the wheel. The steering wheel unlocked as he jimmied the locking pin on the column with the flat screwdriver blade on his knife. Easy.

He peered over the dashboard to make sure no one had watched him. No one had.

John Wayne Keeley backed up and drove out of the parking lot, up the service road, beneath the NO TRESPASS-ING sign. He steered with his left hand while he threw the old couple's belongings out the passenger window: a thermos, some women's magazines, sunglasses, cassette tapes of polka hits. Before he took the entrance ramp to the interstate, he pulled the can of Copenhagen out of his pocket, the one of two he had laced generously with potassium cyanide stolen from a jewelry store in Kansas, and tossed it out the window.

That was the difference, once again, between those stupid convicts in there and John Wayne Keeley out here. If one of those jokers had broken into a jewelry-restoration shop he would have walked right past the chemicals used to refurbish diamonds and gold—cyanide—and straight to the jewelry itself. And then he'd have had a bunch of worn trinkets to try and fence. Not John Wayne Keeley. Not J.W., as he liked to be called. Keeley stopped when he found the cyanide in a locked drawer of the little workroom. And he only took as much of the white powder as he needed, before reshelving the bottle. The proprietors would know they'd been broken into, of course, but would be flummoxed by their good fortune that the thieves had stolen nothing of value. They probably wouldn't even notice the small amount of missing chemical.

He tried to imagine what was happening back there at the prison right now. Had Wacey filled his mouth with the Copenhagen right outside the door? Or had he tried to sneak it back to his cell, where he could smell and savor the tobacco, out of view of the two hundred cameras? Either way, it would kill within minutes of ingestion. Keeley remembered a hunting client, a forensic pathologist from Texas, telling him how it worked. The victim looks flushed, then has a seizure, like he's had a heart attack. He collapses, fighting for breath. His skin turns pink, and his blood inside his veins has turned cherry red. Bright pink foam might burble out of his nose, looking like something . . . festive. Then, *Sayonara*!

"Have a good chew, Wacey!" he hollered. "That was for Ote!"

And he was thinking that he really hadn't learned all that much from Wacey, because he already knew what he wanted to do to Joe Pickett—hit him where he lived. Make him hurt. Take him down. Make that son-of-a-bitch game warden find out what it's like to feel lonely, worthless, unable to protect his own.

3

AT THE TWELVE SLEEP COUNTY SHERIFF'S OFFICE, THE Scarlett brothers sat in molded-plastic chairs, with an empty chair between each of them, across from the sheriff who was at his desk. Arlen was on one end of the line, Hank on the other, Wyatt in the middle. All three were still cuffed. Wyatt's and Hank's hands were bound behind their backs but Arlen had his cuffed in front, so he could dab his head wound with a cloth. Deputies stood close to the brothers. Joe had found them like this when he arrived, and was surprised emotions had cooled down enough that McLanahan had chosen to put them all into the same room. Joe sat on the edge of McLanahan's desk, a gesture sure to annoy the sheriff. *Fine,* Joe thought. Arlen had apparently persuaded the sheriff to forgo the hospital for the time being, and he held a bloody cloth to the side of his swollen head. His eyes were alert, Joe thought, and his expression was mildly amused.

Robey Hersig, the county attorney, had been called

away from dinner with his family to come to the sheriff's office and interview the brothers.

"You asked what happened," Arlen said to Robey. "I'll tell you. As you know, the legislature broke for the session Tuesday morning. I stayed in Cheyenne that night to pack, and drove back to the ranch. Two nights ago, I had a nice supper with my mother and Wyatt at the Holiday Inn here in town, and we went back to the ranch."

"They got good prime rib," Wyatt interjected, then looked back at his big hands in his lap.

"Yes, well," Arlen said, looking at Wyatt with an expression that wasn't quite sympathy, wasn't quite annoyance, but a kind of uncomfortable acceptance. "Anyway, we were home that night around ten, which is late for Mother. She's an early riser. The game warden can attest to that," he said, nodding at Joe.

Robey looked to Joe for an explanation of why he had been brought into the conversation.

"I saw her early yesterday morning when I floated the river," Joe said. "I guess it was about seven." But he wasn't sure why Arlen had thrown it to him, other than to make the point, yet again, that Joe might have been the last person to see her.

"And why were you there, Mr. Game Warden?" McLanahan asked from behind his desk.

Joe bristled at the way McLanahan asked, knowing there was sarcasm in the question.

"Fishing access," Joe said, and left it at that.

"How did she appear when you had your conversation with her about . . . fishing access?" McLanahan asked.

"She was fine," Joe said, "her normal self."

"Did you two have a dustup?" the sheriff asked.

"No more than usual."

Joe was grateful when Arlen jumped back in. "As I said, she's an early riser. Yesterday, we had a nice breakfast in the house, Mother, Wyatt, my niece Julie, and me."

At the mention of Julie's name, Hank suddenly sat up. His mouth was now pulled back into an ugly grimace. Joe noted that Arlen had confirmed what Reed had told him about Julie being Hank's daughter.

"Yes, Julie," Arlen said, aware of his brother's reaction but pretending, Joe thought, not to notice it. "Such a sweet, sweet girl. She's developed a real interest in political science and history, and she's a good student. We talked about the legislature, how laws are made, how the system works. Things she never would have learned at home if she'd stayed with her father . . ."

At that, Hank twitched, and his neck and face got darker. His eyes were boring into Arlen now, as Arlen continued in a pleasant voice that was somehow grating.

"This morning, Mother wasn't around, which was highly unusual. Nevertheless I assumed she'd gone to town so I made breakfast for Julie and myself and then took her out to the main road in my pickup so she could catch the bus to school. Then I went back to the main house, to my office on the third floor, and remained there all day catching up on correspondence and paperwork. You'd be amazed how many things pile up while I'm away at the session.

"I remember hearing a bit of a discussion outside near the bank of the river. I heard raised voices, one of them being Mother's."

Joe leaned forward, asked, "Who was the other?"

McLanahan cleared his throat, a signal to Joe that he'd intruded on the interview.

Arlen shrugged. "A local fishing guide. I'm not sure I know his name. They were having an argument about trespass fees. This wasn't that unusual, really. It happened all the time. In the end, Mother always got them to pay up."

"Then"—Arlen furrowed his brow, trying to recall something—"I believe it was about three when Wyatt pounded on the door. It was three, wasn't it?" Arlen asked Wyatt.

Wyatt shrugged.

"It was three," Arlen said. As he spoke, his voice lapsed into a bit of a singsong. Joe thought the cadence of Arlen's speech was another way to get at his brother Hank. It was probably a way of speaking that had been established long ago *specifically* because it enraged Hank, who hardly talked at all. "Wyatt said our brother Hank called in a rage. Apparently Hank had been to the house and couldn't find Mother, or her car. And, Hank being Hank—who isn't really supposed to be on our side of the ranch in the first place—immediately came to the conclusion that Mother met with foul play . . ." Joe watched, amazed, as Hank's face turned almost purple and a vein in his throat swelled to look like a writhing baby snake. ". . . and of course if there was foul play involved, then in my brother's twisted mind, that meant I must somehow be involved with it. My brother needs professional help in the most serious way, which is obvious to all who meet him, and especially to those of us forced to, um, *coexist* with him. So, Hank being Hank, he assumed the worst and was ready to act out his own western movie. That's pretty much what Hank told you, isn't it, Wyatt?"

Wyatt didn't look up, but said reluctantly, "Pretty much. Not all the movie stuff, though."

Arlen chuckled in a condescending way Joe found irritating. "In an effort to stave off another violent confrontation, of which there have been many over the years, I decided to drive over to Hank's side of the ranch and try to calm down the situation. Wyatt decided to follow me in his truck. I spotted Hank just across his side of the line . . ."

"Hold it," Robey said, raising his hand. "You've made a couple of references to 'his side of the ranch' and 'our side of the ranch.' And now you say there's a line. What's that about?"

Arlen smiled paternalistically at Robey, as if graciously offering an explanation that should have been well known by all. "In order to keep the peace, Mother decided a few years ago that we should live on opposite sides of the ranch. Hank built a fine hunting lodge on the east side, and the rest of the family remains on the original homestead on the west side. There's an old fence line that more or less cuts the ranch in two, and we'd all come to understand that it wasn't to be crossed. Nothing legal, just an understanding until Hank decided to lock all of the gates. Julie and her mother moved down to live with us. I have adopted Julie as my own. Unofficially, of course, and much to Hank's dismay. He would rather they both stay up there on his side, pining for him while he takes clients to Kenya to hunt for months on end. But Julie needs some stability."

"Thanks," Robey said. "Go on."

"I saw Hank's truck tearing across the ranch toward our side at the same time we were trying to find him. I pulled over and waved him down, so we could talk. After all, Wyatt and I are just as concerned about where Mother might be as Hank is. I thought, for once, we could put the animosity aside and try to work together and figure out where she was."

Joe was struck by how Hank and Arlen used the word "Mother" when they spoke. Men their age should say, "My mom," "my mother" or "our mother," or "our mom," it seemed.

"So I got out of the truck and went to talk to Hank. Wyatt came up behind us. But alas"—Arlen paused, and again took the rag away from his head—"instead of talking, Hank grabbed his irrigation shovel and started swinging. I grabbed mine in self-defense. I guess that's when you were called."

Arlen stopped speaking, and winced, as if a sudden jolt of pain had coursed through his head. Either that, or a conspicuous play for sympathy, Joe thought.

"Is that how it happened, Wyatt?" Robey asked.

Wyatt slowly nodded his head, but refused to look up.

"Hank, you agree?" Robey asked warily.

Instead of answering, Hank sighed and stood up, a movement so swift and unexpected given his previous stillness that the deputy beside him didn't reach out. Joe slid off the desk, ready to step between Hank and Arlen if necessary.

"It's pretty accurate," Hank said, his voice tight. "I ain't gonna dispute what he said about the fight. I think he left out the part about what he did to Mother, and where he hid her."

Hank turned to Arlen, who was still seated. Arlen looked back calmly, knowing, Joe thought, he had already done as much damage as he could do. Wyatt took that moment to look up, see what was happening, and drop his head again, as if figuring that if he didn't watch it nothing could happen.

Hank couldn't raise his hand to point since it was cuffed behind him, so he set his shoulders in a way that seemed to point at Arlen's face. Hank said, "And I don't want to hear another fucking word about Julie coming out of your mouth."

Arlen arched his eyebrows. "Why? Because she's come over to my side? Just like her mother?"

That did it. Hank emitted a guttural, anguished sound and hurled himself at Arlen, head down, closing the space between them so quickly that neither the deputy nor Joe could stop it.

Hank head-butted Arlen square in the face, and the force of his body took them both backward, smashing into the filing cabinets. Framed photos fell from the wall and broke on the floor. Both deputies pulled at Hank's bound arms and shirt collar, but his thrashing legs tripped Reed and the officer fell heavily on the pile. Joe and the other deputy grabbed Hank's ankles and pulled him away, facedown along the floor, leaving a smear of blood on the linoleum.

"You got no idea what he's capable of!" Hank shouted.

Arlen's face was covered with blood from his broken nose, and he shouted: "THROW THAT ANIMAL IN A CAGE!"

Joe breathed deeply after the scuffle and watched the

deputies carrying Hank through the door to a cell. While Robey helped Arlen to his feet, he looked at Wyatt, who had not moved. Wyatt sat still, his head hung low, his huge body settled into the cupped seat of the molded-plastic chair. As Joe watched, Wyatt reached up and covered his head with his huge hands, lacing his thick fingers through his hair.

Joe saw where the Flex-Cuffs had bitten into Wyatt's fleshy wrists, and what remained of the cuffs on the floor under the chair where Wyatt had snapped them off during the fight. Joe had never encountered a man strong enough to snap cuffs before. Next to the shredded cuffs, Joe saw a splat of moisture. Then another. He realized Wyatt was shaking, his big shoulders heaving up and down as he sobbed.

TWO HOURS LATER, after Joe had finished giving his deposition to Robey concerning his recent encounter with Opal Scarlett, Deputy Reed stuck his head into the office.

"I thought you guys would want to know we've sent a couple of cars out to pick up a fishing guide named Tommy Wayman," Reed said, glancing at his notepad. "His wife, Nancy, called it in. They had a fight and Nancy said Tommy told her he would do the same thing to her that he did to Opal Scarlett if she didn't shut up."

After a beat, Joe said, "Which was . . . ?"

"'Throw her in the river like fish guts,'" Reed said, looking at his pad to emphasize that he was quoting.

SO IT WAS Tommy Wayman, Joe thought. Tommy was a longtime local, a throwback, given to white snap-button shirts and stretch Wranglers. He ran three boats and two rafts on the Twelve Sleep River, his business doing well despite the fact that Tommy would much rather fish himself than tend to detail. The guided operation was flourishing now, though, due to MBP Management, Marybeth's company.

Wayman had the oldest fishing service in the valley, and was the first to change from live bait to flies, flat-bottomed jon boats to beautiful McKenzie-syle drift boats, the first to preach catch-and-release instead of killing and taking caught fish. It had been a nod to progress and a realization that the resource was unique but limited. Joe encouraged Tommy and urged other guides to change their methods while he managed the river for quantity and quality of trout instead of meat in the water.

Tommy had contended with Opal Scarlett for years. Maybe he had finally snapped.

4

IT WAS AFTER TEN WHEN JOE DROVE TOWARD HIS
home on Bighorn Road. Maxine was asleep on the passenger seat, tucked in on herself, her deep breathing punctu-
ated by occasional yips as she dreamed of what? Chasing
rabbits? Watching men beat each other with irrigation
shovels?

The night was remarkably dark, the moon a thin white
razor slash in the sky, the stars hard and cold. There were
no pole lamps this far out of town, and it was one of those
nights that seemed to suck the illumination out of the stars,
rather than transmit the light, leaving pinpricks.

He had called Marybeth to tell her he'd be late.

"Sheridan told me what happened," Marybeth said.
"Julie, that poor girl. I wish she hadn't seen her father and
uncle fighting like that."

Joe said, "My fault."

Marybeth was silent, which meant she agreed with him

that he'd screwed up. But at least she didn't say it. For the past six months, since Joe returned from his assignment in Jackson, Marybeth had been unerringly patient with him, as if she were overcompensating for something that had happened while he was gone. While he wasn't sure what that was, he knew it involved Nate Romanowski. He didn't ask because he trusted her judgment more than his own and, frankly, he liked how things were going between them. Plus, he had a secret of his own—his surprising attraction to a married woman in Jackson. Nothing had happened, but it could have, which was nearly as bad. So things had been rocky for a while, like all marriages, he supposed, but the storm had passed over them without fatal damage. Now they were on smooth water again, which he preferred. He saw no good reason to dredge up past feelings with probing questions. She didn't either. Life was good in general, as it should be, he thought. Except for his job, his boss, and now Opal Scarlett's disappearance.

IN SPRING THE animals came out, so he was cautious as he drove. The deer, rabbits, badgers, elk, and occasional mountain lions were on the move, reestablishing their hierarchy and territory, having babies, kicking up their heels after a long winter. Joe imagined them puzzling over new human and natural developments on the land, processing the changes, and moving forward with slight instinctive variations. He slowed when two bright blue lights winked just beyond the arc of his headlights, and he stopped the truck while a badger, her belly fat quivering while she scuttled, crossed the two-lane blacktop. Her young one, which was sleek and shiny, froze in the roadway for a moment and displayed its attitude with a teeth-rattling display of juvenile aggression as it rocked from side to side, then followed her. Both vanished into the darkness of the barrow pit beside the road.

He was always grateful for the drive home, because it allowed him to wind down, to sort out the events of the day, to try to put them in a mental drawer for later.

Joe was still buzzing from what had happened at the sheriff's office with the Scarlett brothers. Although the rift between them—especially Arlen and Hank—was the stuff of local fable, he had not seen it for himself in its fury.

TOMMY WAYMAN HAD been brought to the county building as Joe left. Before starting his truck, Joe watched as Wayman was pulled out of the car and steered toward the door by two sheriff's deputies. Curiosity got the best of him, and Joe went back inside to hear what Tommy had to say.

Someone had tipped off the Saddlestring *Roundup,* and a reporter (who, to Joe, looked all of seventeen years old) had arrived with a digital camera. The flash popped and lit Tommy's face in stark relief, freezing an image of tiny eyes set in a face of deep tan from spending so many hours on the river, and a bulbous red nose from drinking so many beers *while* spending so many hours on the river.

Tommy looked scared, Joe thought, as if he were ready to flinch from blows that could come from anywhere. Joe could see a bandage on Tommy's neck. The adhesive strip holding on the gauze had pulled loose to reveal a wound that looked, at first, as if someone had tried to slit Tommy's throat from ear to ear.

"What happened to your neck?" Joe asked.

"Opal Scarlett," Tommy said. "Joe, she should have been stopped a long time ago." His voice slurred with alcohol. Since his hands were cuffed behind him and he couldn't point, Tommy raised his chin to indicate the wound across his throat. "This time, she just about cut my head off."

Before he could say more, the deputies took him into the building to be processed.

Joe had watched Tommy's thin back until the guide was taken into the building. Joe followed, pieces falling into place.

JOE HAD FIRST met Opal Scarlett three years before as a result of a complaint by the very same Tommy Wayman. Wayman had come to Joe's office at his house and claimed Opal was blocking access to the river and charging fees for his boats to float through her ranch.

"She's been doing it for years," Wayman said, sitting down in the single chair across from Joe's desk.

Joe said, "You're kidding me, right?"

Wyoming law was long established and well known: it was perfectly legal for anyone to float in a boat through private land as long as the boaters didn't stop and get out or pull the boat up to shore and trespass. The land belonged to the landowner but the water belonged to the public. While it was perfectly fine for a landowner to charge a fee for access to the river over private ground, it was illegal to charge for simply floating through private land.

"The rumor is that she collects enough money from float fees—as she calls 'em—to buy a new Cadillac at the end of every summer," Tommy Wayman had said while cracking the top off a bottle of beer he had pulled from his fishing vest. "She's been collecting money for years, but nobody turns her in because, well, she's Opal Scarlett."

Wayman told Joe that Opal collected her fee by standing on the bank near her house and calling to passing boats. Since Opal was white haired and tiny, most boatmen assumed there was something wrong when they heard her cries and beelined to help the old woman. When the boats pulled to shore, she pointed out to the passengers of the boat that they were now technically on her land and subject to fines or arrest. She would let it go, however, if the passengers paid a fee of $5 per person. Later, the fee was raised to $10, then $15, then $20. Word got around among fishermen to ignore Opal Scarlett when she hollered, no matter what she said.

Which led to more escalated measures on Opal's part, and for a few years she got the attention of passing boats by firing a shotgun blast into the air and making it clear they were next if they didn't pay up. That worked, Wayman said, for a while.

In order to avoid the embarrassment of paying fees in front of their customers, the outfitters and guides had learned to pay Opal up front and therefore pass through her ranch without trouble. Wayman told Joe he had done that for years, but Opal was getting forgetful and half the time couldn't recall that he'd prepaid, so she would stand on the bank, shooting her shotgun in the air, demanding her tribute.

Joe noted at the time that Wayman had not brought the situation to his attention until it was literally out of control, only when Wayman was forced to double-pay Opal.

That was when Wayman first told Joe that Opal had threatened to string razor-sharp piano wire across the river, neck-high.

"If she does that she's likely to kill somebody," Wayman said. "She thinks everybody on the river is trying to shaft her by not paying the fee, even though most of us already coughed up. If she strings that wire, somebody's going to get seriously hurt."

After his meeting with Wayman, Joe drove out to the Thunderhead Ranch, feeling that his case against Opal Scarlett was remarkably cut and dried. It was his initial experience with the Scarlett mystique, his first real look into how deep the family roots were in the county and how something as straightforward and simple as river access turned out not to be that at all.

He found Opal working alone in her magnificent vegetable garden on the southern side of the massive stone ranch house where she lived. As he parked his pickup in the ranch yard and walked toward her, she leaned on her hoe and sized him up with a kind of interested, professional detachment that resided somewhere between a friendly greeting and a trespass warning. The set of her face seemed to say, "I've been dealing with *your* kind for sixty-odd years and have yet to be surprised."

She had opened with, "So you're the game warden who arrested the governor for fishing without a license?"

Joe nodded, already on the defensive.

She was small, trim, and wiry, dressed in a kind of casual western outdoor elegance that seemed reserved for people like her—faded jeans, Ariat boots, silver ranger set buckle, an open canvas barn jacket over a plaid shirt, silk scarf. Opal was a remarkably self-assured woman who had no qualms about charging a fee to boaters who passed through her ranch, and who seemed to make it clear without saying that she had thus far tolerated him being there in the county but there was a limit to her time and patience. She explained to Joe how her father-in-law and grandfather had established the ranch. Over the years, they had graciously maintained the flow of the river even though it was their right to divert as much of it as they pleased to irrigate their land, since they had the very first water right. By maintaining the flow over the years, she told Joe, the family had not only assured a supply of drinking water to the town of Saddlestring, but had preserved the natural ecology of the valley and also allowed for an extensive guided trout-fishing economy that would have otherwise not existed.

"In a way," she said through a tight smile, "if it weren't for us, you wouldn't be here, and neither would Mr. Tommy Wayman."

Without a hint of remorse, she led Joe down to the bank of the river and described the "tollgate" she wished to build in the future. She started by pointing across the river at an immense cottonwood.

"I want to tie a wire off over there on the trunk of that tree, and stretch it all the way over to my side. I'll attach my end of the wire to a big lever I can work by myself, so I can raise and lower the wire as necessary," she said, demonstrating how she would pull on the imaginary handle.

"What if you kill somebody?" Joe asked, incredulously.

She dismissed his concerns with a wave of her hand. "Don't worry, I'll tie orange flagging to the wire so all the floaters can see it plain as day. My objective is to collect my fee, not to decapitate my customers."

"But you can't do that, Mrs. Scarlett. It's a public waterway."

She turned from her imaginary tollgate, her eyes freezing him to his spot. "It's a public waterway, Mr. Pickett," she said, "because my family has allowed it to be so. The water in that river could just as easily be diverted, by me, to irrigate my ranch and turn this place into a Louisiana bayou and my home into Venice with all the beautiful canals. But I have chosen not to do that, but to instead collect a small fee in exchange for providing free drinking water and recreation to you and several thousand other residents of our sleepy little valley.

"This arrangement," she continued, her unblinking eyes still on him, "has worked very well for three generations. Water in exchange for proper respect. I understand from others that you have a tendency to want to go your own way to some degree. I admire that in a man, generally. But I'd suggest this isn't the best battle to choose to fight when there are other more worthy ones out there."

Joe felt he'd been flayed by a rawhide whip. All he could think of to say in response was, "Nice to meet you, Mrs. Scarlett."

So when Joe saw the wound on Tommy Wayman's neck that evening, he was pretty sure he knew what had happened out on the river.

. . .

TOMMY WAYMAN CONFESSED that he had, in fact, tossed Opal in the river that morning. He said it happened like this:

He was scouting the Twelve Sleep River in his flat-bottomed Hyde drift boat, his first trip on the water since winter. After winter, there were always new hazards, new bends, new currents on the wild river to scout out. And it was a great time to fish for himself, before the spring runoff began and raised and muddied the river, before clients started to book, before he had to mess with the hassle of hiring guides and office help.

It was an unseasonably warm day and there was a mayfly hatch on. Tommy said he was alone on the river, and never saw another boat. The trout were hitting his flies so hard they were mutilating them, and he was hauling the fish in and releasing them in a steadied fury. It was an angler's wet dream, he said, the kind of day that reminded him of why he loved to fish, why he loved the river.

He was putting on a dry fly and a dropper, concentrating on tying the tippet knots, as he floated through the Thunderhead Ranch. He never saw the silvery band of wire stretched across the river until it sliced through his leader and caught him under his chin, lifting him briefly off his boat seat. He felt the wire bite into his flesh and saw blood fleck down the front of his shirt, but was able to reach up and grab the wire with his hands before the momentum of the boat carried him forward even farther and cut his throat wide open. After plucking the wire out and ducking under it, Tommy grabbed the oars and took the boat to shore. Just as Opal Scarlett came out of her house, drying her hands on a towel.

"Damn you, Opal!" he shouted, hurtling out of the boat once he reached the shore. "You just about cut my head off with your damned wire!"

Opal just stood there regarding him with what he called the look of ownership. "Like she was disappointed in the behavior of a hired hand—or a slave." Finally, she told Tommy if he had paid his river fee up front this year, as he knew he should have, he could have avoided the problem.

"There is no such thing as a river fee!" Tommy yelled.

"There is on my ranch," Opal said, arching her eyebrows.

And with that, he rushed her, grabbed her by the collar with one hand and by the belt with the other, and swung her through the air and into the river.

"Damn, she was light," Tommy said. "Like there wasn't really anything to her, just clothes and a scowl. It was like tossing my nieces and nephews around the pool or something. She didn't even struggle. I think that was the last thing she expected, to be thrown into the river like that."

Tommy said he watched her floating away in the river. She was treading water, and howling at him saying, "Next time, Tommy Wayman, you'll have to pay me a hundred dollars a trip!"

"Nuts to you, Opal," he called after her. He said he watched her bob in the river, heard her curse at him, until she was carried around a bend two hundred yards from where he stood. He never once thought she didn't simply swim to shore, he said later. He never even considered that she had drowned. That part of the river was too shallow and slow. And she was too mean to die, he said, which was something Joe had also heard from Reed.

No, Tommy said, he never saw her climb out on shore after he got back in his boat and floated downriver.

No, he never saw her body wedged in debris or trapped under the surface by an undertow. Besides, he said, in April the river was barely moving. The dangerous currents would come later, when the snow started to melt and the speed and volume of the river would increase two to three times.

No, he didn't feel any need to turn himself in at the time because, well, Opal deserved to be thrown in the river.

"I'm surprised that river didn't spit her right out," Tommy said to Joe and Robey.

Proud of his feat, he'd immediately bragged about it to his wife, Nancy, not knowing that she had spent the entire day at home fuming over photos she had found: Tommy with his arms around attractive female clients and one shot in particular—a group of flight attendants in the boat who bared their breasts to the camera with Tommy at the oars— grinning like an idiot. She was angry enough that after he fell asleep in his lounge chair with a beer, she called the sheriff's office and reported what Tommy had said. Nancy felt horrible about it now, though, since at the time she had no idea that Opal was missing.

So what had happened to Opal Scarlett's body? Or had Opal simply climbed out, had an epiphany of some kind, gotten in her Caddy, and driven away?

JOE PARKED IN front of the garage, stirred Maxine awake, and entered the house through the mudroom.

The Picketts lived in a small state-owned two-story house eight miles out of Saddlestring. Joe was thankful for darkness, so he wouldn't have to see how tired the place was looking, how it appeared to sag at the roofline, how the window frames and doors were out of plumb. It sat back from the road behind a white fence that once again needed painting. There was a detached garage filled with Joe's snowmobile, gear, and supposedly the van, but the vehicle space was now occupied by his upturned drift boat needing repair. Behind the house was a loafing shed and corral for their two horses, Toby and Doc.

The house was quiet and everyone was in bed. He left his battered briefcase on the desk in his home office off the mudroom. He left his blinking message light and unopened mail for later.

Joe thought of how things had changed for them in the past year. Marybeth's business, MBP Management, had taken off. She now managed eight Saddlestring companies, doing their accounting, inventory management, employee scheduling, federal and state compliance. The owners had gratefully ceded control to her, and told their colleagues at morning coffee at the Burg-O-Pardner how much easier their lives had become since hiring her. She had filled a void none of them knew existed when she showed up with her laptop, spreadsheets, and no-nonsense practicality. She even had affiliate offices in Sheridan and Cody, manned by women much like herself who were mothers who knew what time management and prioritization really meant and could walk into a small business, dissect it, and make it run like, well, a *business*. Her income to the family now exceeded what Joe brought in as a state employee for the Game and Fish Department. The money helped.

College funds for Sheridan and Lucy had been opened. All four burners worked on the stove. They had a new minivan, and a television that revealed, for the first time, that most actors' faces were not actually shades of green.

They had discussed the fact that MBP Management had quickly reached the point in business where Marybeth would need to make the choice to maintain what she had or expand. Maintenance, Marybeth explained, was the first step to stagnation, something she saw all the time with the businesses she managed. But expansion—hiring employees, finding bigger office space, changing her role from hands-on consultant to full-time executive of the business itself—was not what she thought she wanted to do. She enjoyed working with her clients, and expanding would mean more time away from the family and additional strain on the marriage. It was a difficult decision that faced them, she said, and one they needed to make together. Joe just wanted her to be happy, and said he'd support her in whatever she chose to do.

Before going upstairs to bed with his wife, Joe tiptoed into Lucy's room and kissed her good night (she rolled over and said "um"), then rapped lightly on Sheridan's door because he saw a band of light underneath it.

"Come in," she said.

Joe stuck his head inside. Sheridan was reading in bed, wearing her glasses instead of her contacts. She smiled at her father, but then arched her eyebrows in a "do you need something?" way.

"How are you doing?" he asked.

"Fine. I feel sorry for Julie, though."

Joe said, "Me too. I feel terrible about taking her out there. I hope she'll be okay."

Sheridan nodded.

"Has she ever told you about the situation out there?" Joe asked. "What the deal is with her father and her uncles?"

Sheridan shook her head. "I don't think she really knows what is going on. I thought she'd call tonight, but she didn't."

Joe told Sheridan how the fight continued in the sheriff's office, and that Tommy Wayman confessed to throwing Opal in the river.

"That's just crazy," she said.

"I'm curious about the Scarlett brothers," Joe said. "How well do you know them? Does Julie talk about them much?"

Sheridan looked suspicious. "Some," she said. "And I've met them all. Her dad, Hank. Uncle Arlen and Uncle Wyatt."

"What do you think of them?"

"Dad, I don't feel comfortable being your spy. Julie is my best friend."

Joe held up his hand. "Okay, not now. I understand. But I'll probably want to talk with you about them later, okay?"

Sheridan said, "Good night, Dad."

· · ·

MARYBETH WAS ASLEEP in bed with her table lamp on and a book opened on her chest. She was breathing deeply, so Joe tried not to wake her as he padded across the room. He changed out of his red uniform shirt and Wranglers and pulled on old University of Wyoming Cowboys sweats. Before he went back downstairs, he marked the page and closed Marybeth's book, putting it aside. He hesitated as he reached to shut off her lamp, and took a moment to look at her. In sleep, her face was soft and relaxed, and there was the hint of a smile on her mouth. She was a beautiful woman, better than he deserved. She'd been so busy lately that she was dead tired at night. It had been over two weeks since they'd made love, and Joe scratched tonight off his list as well.

He missed the time they used to have together, before her company took off and before the girls required nonstop shuttling among school, home, and activities. And with his schedule and the problems at work, he knew he wasn't helping the situation much.

Joe brushed her cheek lightly with the tips of his fingers, shut off the light, and went back down to his office.

He had never enjoyed the paperwork associated with his job, but considered it necessary—unlike some of Wyoming's other fifty-four game wardens, who complained about it constantly. He viewed the memos, reports, requests for opinion, and general correspondence as the price he paid to spend the majority of his working day out in the field in his pickup, astride one of his horses, in his boat, or on his snowmobile. Joe Pickett still loved his job with a "pinch me" kind of passion that had yet to go away. He reveled in his fifteen-hundred-square-mile district that included haunting and savage breaklands, river lowlands, timbered ridges and treeless vistas, and landscape so big and wide that there were places where he parked his truck and perched where he could see the curvature of the earth.

He even used to get pleasure from writing his weekly reports, coming up with a well-turned phrase or making an argument that could persuade higher-ups. But things had changed, and he now dreaded entering his own office.

Joe listened to his telephone messages. There was a complaint from a local rancher about a vehicle driving around on his land at night, possibly a poacher. The next message was from Special Agent Tony Portenson of the FBI, asking Joe to call him. Portenson was heading up the investigation into the murder of ex-sheriff O. R. "Bud" Barnum and another still-unknown male the year before. Both of their badly deteriorated bodies had been found in a natural spring the year before. Joe had reported the crime. The prime suspect in the murders was Nate Romanowski, the falconer whom Joe and the rest of his family had befriended years before. Nate had vanished before the bodies had been discovered, and Portenson was trying to track him down. The agent called Joe every month or so to find out if Joe had heard from Nate, which he hadn't. Joe felt no need to tell Portenson that he and Sheridan still went to Nate's place to feed his falcons, and that they would continue to do so until Nate returned or the birds flew away for good.

JOE YAWNED WITH exhaustion as he tapped out a terse recounting of his long day to send to Randy Pope at headquarters in Cheyenne. Pope read his reports very carefully for errors that he enjoyed pointing out.

When he completed the report, he used his slow dial-up modem to send the e-mail. As the connection was made, his in-box flooded with departmental e-mails. The volume of mail had increased fivefold since Pope took over.

Joe perused the subject lines, deciding most could wait

until tomorrow morning. The only one he opened was a press release from headquarters entitled GOVERNOR RULON NAMES NEW GAME AND FISH COMMISSIONERS.

Joe read the short list. One name punched the breath out of him. The new governor had made his second mistake.

The new commissioner for Joe's district was Arlen Scarlett.

5

JULIE SCARLETT WASN'T ON THE BUS OR AT SCHOOL
for the next two days, and when Sheridan dialed her number at the ranch the call went straight to voice mail. The
news of the shovel fight as well as the disappearance of
Opal Scarlett swept through both the school and the community so fast that it was almost unnecessary to include it
in the Saddlestring *Roundup,* but it appeared there nevertheless, with the photo of a startled Tommy Wayman exiting the sheriff's department car.

On Friday afternoon, after Sheridan finished track practice and waited inside the entryway for her dad or mom to
pick her up, a muddy three-quarter-ton pickup swung into
the alcove. THUNDERHEAD RANCH was painted on the door
of the truck, and when it opened, Julie jumped out. Sheridan
could see that it was Julie's Uncle Arlen who was driving.

Julie looked pale and tired, Sheridan thought. Her friend
wore old jeans, cowboy boots, and a too-large sweatshirt. It

was unusual to see her dressed down that way, and Sheridan felt sorry for her.

Sheridan was relieved when Julie's expression changed from distraction to joy when she saw her in the doorway. Julie broke into a quick run, opened the door, and threw her arms around her friend.

"I missed you!" Julie said, beaming. "I know it's only been, like, a couple of days, but it seems like a friggin' *month*."

Sheridan said, "I know. I've tried to call you because I was getting worried . . ."

Julie dismissed Sheridan's concern with a wave. "Sorry about that. My uncles forget to tell me I've got messages since my grandma always did that. Hey, walk with me, Sherry. I've got to go pick up my missed assignments so I can get caught up this weekend."

Sheridan turned and strode down the empty hallway with Julie.

"I'm glad school is out for the day," Julie said, speaking softly. "This way I don't have to face anyone and answer all of the questions right now. That'll have to wait until Monday. So, is everybody wondering where I've been?"

"Sure," Sheridan answered, knowing Julie wanted to find out she was the topic of all conversation, even though some of the kids had said cruel things about her and her family. "Me, mainly."

"Oh, you're sweet," Julie said.

Sheridan stood near the door of Julie's math classroom while Julie got her assignments from her teacher. She listened as Julie told her teacher how rough it had been the last few days with her grandmother missing, and with her uncles fighting. The teacher eagerly drank it in. If Julie was going to repeat the story to every teacher, Sheridan thought, they'd never get out of there. While she liked Julie and was relieved she seemed okay, her friend reveled in being the center of attention.

Finally, Julie finished and left, Sheridan beside her.

"I may not be able to stay," Sheridan said. "My ride should be outside."

Julie stopped. "Are you sure? We've got some catching up to do."

"I know," Sheridan said, thinking she would much rather do that instead of listen to Julie explain what had happened at the ranch seven more times to seven more teachers. While she had the opportunity, Sheridan asked Julie something that had been on her mind since the other day. "Remember, you were just about to tell me something in the truck before we saw the fight? Remember that?"

"Yes."

"Do you want to tell me now?" Sheridan asked.

Julie laughed bitterly, and suddenly seemed much older than her fourteen years, Sheridan thought.

"It's not really news so much anymore," Julie said. "I was going to tell you how *weird* my family is. I was thinking about your mom coming to pick you up, and your sister, and your dad. It's so friggin', like, *normal* compared to what I'm used to."

"That's what you were going to tell me?" Sheridan asked, a little let down.

"Yeah. It's just that I didn't know how strange it was until pretty recently. I guess I thought everybody lived like I do—I didn't realize how screwed up it is."

Sheridan shook her head, not understanding.

"You need to come out and see it for yourself," Julie said, grasping Sheridan's arms. "You won't believe it until I show it to you. Wait until you see the Legacy Wall."

"What do you mean?" Sheridan asked, genuinely rattled by what Julie was saying.

"Well, you know that term 'nuclear family'? Meaning, you know, a dad, a mom, some kids, a dog? Like your family? Well, mine's like, a *blown-up* nuclear family. Like somebody dropped a bomb on us." Julie giggled when she said "blown-up nuclear family," which made Sheridan smile.

"I mean," Julie continued, "I don't even live with my dad. He lives on the other side of the ranch, on the east side, all by himself. My mom lives in a cabin on a creek, and she never talks to my dad. I mean *never.* I grew up in the big house thinking my grandma was my mother because she took care of me. My mom drinks, I guess. Anyway, so it's like my grandma is my mother and my uncle Arlen is my father. Uncle Wyatt—he sometimes seems like he's more my age or my little brother than anything. I'm very fond of my uncle Arlen and my uncle Wyatt, and they're on our side of the ranch . . ."

Sheridan shook her head. "Julie, this is getting complicated."

"I know," Julie said. "That's what I wanted to tell you, how complicated it is. But I don't want anybody else around here to know, because it's embarrassing, you know? At least I hope Grandmother is back soon. Then it will feel more normal."

"What do you mean?"

"Her car is gone," Julie said. "We think maybe she took a trip somewhere. We hope she comes back soon. It's a weird situation, but it would at least be more normal if she came back. She's a good cook."

Sheridan felt even more sorry for Julie, how naked she seemed to be, how pathetic she sounded. But Julie's situation also gave her an odd, cold feeling about her friend that made her feel guilty.

"Oh-oh," Julie said, pointing over Sheridan's shoulder. "I see your dad's truck outside."

Sheridan turned and looked down the hall. The green Game and Fish truck was out there, and she could see her father's silhouette, his hat brim bouncing up and down. He was probably talking to someone. Then she could see Julie's uncle Arlen leaning out of his window, talking back.

"I gotta go," Sheridan said, relieved that she had an excuse to depart.

"I know, but thanks for hanging with me," Julie said.

"Always, Julie."

"That's why I love you the most," Julie said, smiling. There was mist in her eyes. "Come out for a sleepover. I'll show you just how . . . *fucked up* my family is."

Sheridan had never heard Julie say "fuck" before, and it startled her. It seemed to startle Julie as well, who covered her mouth with her hand.

6

IT WAS A SECTION OF FENCE OUT IN THE MIDDLE OF nowhere that made J. W. Keeley think, *This is not only another world, it's another goddamned planet.*

The fence was there when he woke up. He was parked alongside Wyoming Highway 487 headed north. The Shirley Mountains loomed over the horizon like sleeping reptiles, miles across a moonscape still covered with snow, feeling as if he were absolutely alone on the top of the world. The fence was unique in that it was only a *section* of a fence, parallel to the highway, but not connected on either end with anything else. It was a tall fence, made of fresh lumber. The morning sun fire-bronzed the planks, made it look as if it was lit up by electricity.

Because it *was* another planet, and there was no electricity. Or trees. Or power lines. Or anything resembling human presence or activity, except for that section of fence, which was obviously placed there to drive men like Keeley out of his mind, this Wyoming version of Stonehenge, as if to make him think he was hallucinating or seriously hungover.

Right on both counts, he thought. But this fence, he had to go look at it up close, prove to himself that it was real, and try to figure out why it was there.

ON THE BENCH seat of the old Ford pickup next to J. W. Keeley was a scoped rifle with a banana clip. It was a Ruger Mini-14, a carbine that shot .223 rounds. The night before, the coyote hunter at the bar in Medicine Bow told Keeley the rifle was used mainly for killing coyotes and other vermin because the cartridges shot nice and flat. The thirty-round clip was a vestige of the pre–assault rifle law days, back when some federal lawmakers still had spines, the coyote hunter said, back before they all started wearing frilly little skirts and drinking lattes and passing laws against gun owners. In fact, the hunter said he'd spent the day out in the sagebrush between Medicine Bow and Rock River, working a wounded-rabbit call and popping four coyotes, missing a few others. The dead ones were in the back of his truck as he spoke, the hunter said. Their fur was worth $90 for a good pelt, he told Keeley, plus there was a $15 bounty on account of the coyote was considered a predator.

The coyote hunter told Keeley his name was Hoot.

Keeley told Hoot his name was Bill Monroe, hoping Hoot had never heard of the bluegrass picker.

Keeley had said "coyotes" in the way he'd always heard, emphasizing the middle syllable, "kye-*oh*-tees," but Hoot had made fun of him, asked him good-naturedly where in the hell he was from, because in the Northern Rockies the creature was pronounced "kye-oat" without that fruity Hollywood flare on the end. Keeley repeated "*kye*-oat, *kye*-oat, *kye*-oat" as he followed the man outside to see the dead animals.

Hoot the Coyote Hunter was a local with a bloodstained

Carhartt and a trim goatee. He liked to talk, and told Keeley in the time it took to leave the Virginian Hotel bar and arrive at his pickup that he'd grown up on a ranch near Elmo, graduated from UW with a degree in social work, come back to the area he grew up in to work in the coal mines, which paid a hell of a lot better than social work, bought a small place and got married to a wench named Lisa, lost his job in the coal mine and got divorced, now he drove a school bus and trapped and popped a few coyotes in his spare time.

When Hoot asked, Keeley said he was headed north to Casper to look for work because he'd heard there was plenty there, with the coal-bed methane boom and all.

"Pinedale," Hoot had said once they were back inside from seeing the dead coyotes while he graciously accepted another double bourbon from Keeley "that's the place to go for jobs and gas. I hear a man can pull down sixty K just for showing up, seventy K if he can fart and walk at the same time."

Keeley bought Hoot drinks until the coyote hunter finally lowered his head on the bar and went to sleep. Then Keeley went back outside and stole Hoot's Mini-14 and an army cartridge box filled with over five hundred rounds.

He had driven north in the dark until he began to imagine he was on the surface of the moon, and realized it had been over an hour since he had seen even a single set of oncoming headlights. So he pulled over to the side of the road, covered himself and the rifle with a blanket he found behind the bench seat, and went to sleep.

IT WAS WHEN he awoke that he looked out over the sparse, open, endless vista and saw the fence.

Now, as he drove toward it off the highway, on a rough two-track still choked with dirty snowdrifts that meandered across the top of two hills, he saw a real cowboy astride a real horse, and J.W. Keeley thought he had awakened in the middle reel of a western movie.

The cowboy wore a long heavy coat and a wide-brimmed hat, and a dog tailed him. In the distance, toward the Shirley Mountains, Keeley could see a pickup and horse trailer parked on the side of a hill, glittering in the early-morning sun.

There were cows on the bottom of the basin, and the cowboy was probably headed down the slope to gather them up or count them or something. Whatever real cowboys did. Keeley wasn't sure. In movies, cowboys were always in town, having just come from somewhere else.

The real cowboy stopped his horse and turned when he heard the sound of a motor coming.

Keeley drove up and got out of the truck, but the dog started yapping at him, barking so hard it skittered stiff-legged across the ground. Keeley jumped back in the cab and closed the door, opened the window, and heard the cowboy say, "Sorry about that, mister. Pay no attention to him. He don't bite."

Keeley looked at the cowboy. Except for the heavy coat, scarf, and hat, the man looked normal, like anybody, like a shoe clerk or something. The cowboy wore round wire-rimmed glasses and had a brushy mustache. His cheeks were flushed red from the early-morning cold.

Keeley rolled down his window but didn't get out.

"What can I help you with?" the man asked.

Keeley gestured toward the hill. "I was wondering about that fence up there. Ain't they ever going to finish it?"

The cowboy looked at him for a moment, then burst out laughing. Keeley felt his rage shoot to the surface. The fucking cowboy kept laughing, and even raised a gloved hand to his stupid shoe-clerk face to wipe away a tear.

"You're kidding me, right?" the cowboy said.

"I guess I'm not," Keeley said, much more calmly than he thought himself capable of.

". . . *'Ain't they ever going to finish it?'"* the cowboy said. "Pardon me, but that's one of the funniest things I ever heard. That there's a snow fence. This must be the first time you seen one."

"A snow fence?" Keeley said. "But it's made of wood."

Which got the cowboy laughing again, and the rage boiling up in Keeley, as much at himself as at the shoe-clerk cowboy for saying that, as if the fence would be made of snow, which was stupid.

"Yer killin' me, mister," the cowboy wheezed, between belly laughs.

Keeley looked off into the distance at a single cloud that was hardly a cloud at all, just a wispy white stringer across the light blue, like egg whites dropped in hot water. He asked, "Hey, you got family around here?"

"What?" That stopped the guy.

"You work for some rancher, or is this yours?"

The cowboy's eyes narrowed. The question had obviously thrown him off stride. "Talk about apropos of nothing," he said, then: "It's a corporate operation. They hire me and a half dozen other men to manage the place."

"But you have family, right?"

"Yeah, my wife and a couple of kids, but what does that have to do . . . ?"

Keeley said, "Glad I made your day," and turned the wheel sharply and floored the accelerator. He could see the cowboy watching him—still shaking his head with profound amusement—in his rearview mirror as he drove up the hillside toward the snow fence.

At the top, he parked and got out near the fence—it was practically ten feet high—and survyed the hillside he had driven up. The cowboy had finally turned his horse and was continuing back down the hill, toward the cattle on the bottom of the basin.

Keeley got out and took a moment to look around. He had never seen country so desolate, and so mean. It reminded him of one of those old western movies, but worse. The movies always showed desert as being hot and dry. This was high and rough, with dirty snow. He preferred desert, he thought; at least it was warm. And except for that laughing cowboy down there, Keeley was the only man on earth for as far as he could see. There were no cars on the highway.

Keeley snapped back the bolt of the rifle, saw a flash of bright brass as the cartridge seated, and aimed the rifle across the hood of his pickup. He leaned into the scope, putting the crosshairs just below the nape of the cowboy's neck, on a band of pink skin between the scarf and the collar, and pulled the trigger.

The shot snapped out, an angry, sharp sound, and the cowboy slumped to the side and rolled off his horse. Keeley watched as the dog trotted over and started licking the cowboy's face, which almost made Keeley feel bad until he realized the damned dog was tasting blood, so he shot it too.

Keeley got back into the stolen pickup with his stolen gun, said, "Fuckin' cowboy, anyway," and turned the vehicle toward the highway, to drive north, to find that game warden.

7

TWO DAYS LATER, MARYBETH PICKETT THREW OPEN the front door after her morning walk and shook their copy of the Saddlestring *Roundup*. Joe and the girls were having breakfast.

"Wacey Hedeman is dead, that bastard," she said, showing Joe the front page.

Sheridan said, "Good!"

Lucy said, "You probably shouldn't say 'good,' Sherry."

"But I mean it," Sheridan said fiercely. "I hate—*hated*—that man."

Joe glanced at his wife and saw that Marybeth had the same reaction as Sheridan. Because Wacey had been the man who had shot her, causing the loss of their baby.

"You know how you wish things, bad things, on people?" Marybeth said. "I have wished harm to Wacey ever since he shot me. But to read now that he's really dead . . . it's strange. I feel sort of cheated. I wanted him to know how much I hated him."

Joe was not surprised at Sheridan's and Marybeth's reaction, but it was disconcerting to see such mutual anger on display.

Joe looked at Lucy, trying to gauge what she was thinking of all this. Lucy shot her eyes back and forth between her mother and her sister. She had been three at the time, while Sheridan had been seven. Lucy seemed to take the comments in stride, probably since she'd grown up with the whole Wacey Hedeman thing—it was part of the family history.

"It says he had some kind of seizure," Marybeth said, reading the story. "They're still investigating. He might have been poisoned."

"Poisoned? By another inmate?" Joe asked.

"It doesn't say," she said. "But I guess I really don't care, considering what he did to us."

"But we're tough!" Lucy said, repeating something she'd heard over the years. It made Marybeth smile, and wipe a tear from her cheek.

"We're tough, all right," Marybeth said.

May

We have enslaved the rest of the animal creation, and have treated our distant cousins in fur and feathers so badly that beyond doubt, if they were able to formulate a religion, they would depict the Devil in human form.

—WILLIAM RALPH INGE, *OUTSPOKEN ESSAYS*, 1922

If you walk around with a hammer, everything starts to look like a nail.

—UNKNOWN

8

IN THE MONTH SINCE SHE'D BEEN REPORTED MISSING, Opal Scarlett—or her body—had not turned up. Not only that, but her car was missing. It wasn't that she was missed for sentimental reasons. She was missed because she held the keys to so many projects, so many relationships, so much history. Not until she was gone did most people within the community realize how integral Opal Scarlett was to so many things. Opal was on the board of directors for the bank, the museum, the utility company, the Friends of the Library. She was one of three Twelve Sleep County commissioners. Her annual check to fund the entirety of the local Republican Party had not arrived. The GM dealer had already taken the order for her new Cadillac, and it sat in the lot with a SOLD sign on it.

Joe kept expecting something to happen. A call from a ranch downriver saying a body had just washed up on the bank. A postcard from some faraway island, or a phone call to one of her sons to bark an order—something.

None of those things had happened. Opal's status was in a dread state of limbo and rumors that were starting to fly had practically destabilized the entire valley.

Joe had carefully read the report issued by Sheriff McLanahan's office, and he had spoken at length to Robey Hersig. It didn't make sense that her body had not turned up. The river was, as Tommy had pointed out, surprisingly low and slow. Spring runoff hadn't started yet. There were places near town where a person could walk across the river, hopping from stone to stone. The likelihood of Opal's body washing downriver without being seen was remote.

Joe had heard some of the theories being bandied about town. Three garnered prominence:

Tommy Wayman threw her in the river, all right, but that was *after* he strangled her and weighted the body down with stones;

Hank was driving by and happened to see Opal crawling out of the river around the bend from where Tommy threw her in. Hank saw his opportunity and bashed her over the head with a shovel and took the body back to his side of the ranch and buried her, thinking he would eventually get the ranch from Arlen; and

Opal was fine. The brief swim scared her, though, and when she reached shore she got in her car, drove to Vegas, and found a young lover named Mario. She'd be back, eventually. There was even a reported sighting of her from a county resident who swore he saw her with a tall, dark young man in a casino on the strip. The report was credible enough that McLanahan dispatched Deputy Reed to Las Vegas, where he ran up an expense account that created a minor scandal at the city council meeting.

Joe stood on the sidelines with growing frustration. This wasn't his case in any way and his involvement was peripheral. But it drove him crazy that no progress had been made. He suggested to Robey that maybe he could be involved in the official investigation, and Robey shook his head no, saying the sheriff wanted no outside interference. "Since when would we call in the game warden for a missing-person's investigation?" Robey asked. And Joe knew better than to bring it up with Director Pope. Joe wasn't sure he could help the investigation along. But he knew he'd feel better if he was a part of it.

SINCE THAT MORNING in April, details started to leak out about how the Thunderhead Ranch had been run and the difficulties and complications that were resulting from the matriarch's disappearance. Joe had an appointment with Robey Hersig the next evening to discuss what was going on. Robey had been cryptic in his request for a meeting, and Joe had been intrigued.

"We may have something brewing here that none of us anticipated," Robey had said to Joe on his cell phone. "The more I dig into it, the worse it gets."

"So tell me about it," Joe said.

"Not over the phone, no way."

"Are you serious? Do you think someone may be listening?"

"You never know," Robey said, hanging up.

AFTER FEEDING NATE Romanowski's falcons after school, Joe took Julie and Sheridan to the Thunderhead Ranch so Julie could go home. As they drove down the road they were met by a yellow Ford coming the other way. There was something familiar about the driver, Joe thought, something about the pinched, hard look to his face that triggered a sour familiarity, but Joe couldn't place it. Unlike most people on a back road, the driver didn't wave or stop. In his rearview mirror Joe watched the yellow Ford drive off.

"Who was that?" he asked Julie.

She shrugged. "It wasn't one of our trucks."

As they neared the ranch house, Julie said to Sheridan, "Did you ask yet?"

"Not yet."

"Ask what?" Joe said, turning his attention to the girls but still suspicious about the Ford.

Sheridan turned to Joe. "Is it okay to do a sleepover at Julie's in a couple of weeks?"

Sleepovers were all the rage among the eighth-graders, Joe knew. Scarcely a weekend went by without an invitation to Sheridan to sleep over at someone's house, along with five or six other girls. It was a group thing, a pack thing, and Joe was helpless before it. He gratefully turned over all planning and coordination to Marybeth. Marybeth rued the change in her oldest daughter from preferring the company of her family to the company of her friends.

Joe said, "Why are you asking me?"

"Because Mom may not let me," Sheridan admitted.

This was not a place Joe wanted to go. "We'll have to discuss it later."

"Come on, Dad . . ."

He hated when she did that, since his inclination, always, was to give in. Sheridan had the ability to rope him in with such ease that even he was shamed by it.

"Later," he said.

"I'll call you," Sheridan sighed to her friend, patting Julie on the arm. Julie gave Joe a pleading look, and he shrugged as if to say, *It's out of my hands.*

9

THE NEXT WEEK, JOE WAS ON A MUDDY TWO-TRACK IN the breaklands doing a preliminary trend count on the mule-deer population when he got the distinct feeling he was being watched. It was a crisp, dry morning. A late-spring snowfall was melting into the inch-high grass as the morning warmed, and the moisture was being sucked into the parched earth. By late afternoon, he was afraid, the ground would be as bone-dry as it had been all year. It would take much more rain and snow to turn back the relentless slow death of the soil caused by the fifth straight year of drought.

He had been counting pregnant does all morning. Most of the fawns wouldn't be born until June, but from what he could tell so far it would be another bad year for the deer population. A good year could be predicted if there were eighty fawns per one hundred does, or 80 percent. So far, the ratio had been 40 percent pregnant does. The drought—not hunting or development—was severely affecting the population. He would need to recommend fewer deer licenses for the area, which would not make him very popular among the local hunters.

Joe surveyed the horizon to see if he could spot who was watching him. He saw no one, and shrugged it off.

His cell phone rang.

"Guess who this is?" said Special Agent Tony Portenson of the FBI.

Portenson was originally from Brooklyn, and his accent, if anything, had become more pronounced the longer he was stationed in the Wyoming field office.

"Hello, Tony. Where are you?"

"I'm in your town."

"I'm sorry to hear that," Joe said, knowing Portenson had been trying for three years to get a transfer out of the West to someplace more exciting, someplace where there were gangsters and organized crime, maybe even terrorists. Over the years, Portenson had bored Joe for hours with his complaints regarding the poor quality of crime he had to deal with out of his office in Cheyenne: cattle rustling, methamphetamine labs, murders of passion on the Wind River Indian Reservation.

"Can I buy you a cup of coffee?" Portenson asked.

"I'm out in the field counting deer."

"Jesus, I wouldn't want to interrupt *that*."

Joe could hear Portenson turn to someone, probably his partner, partially cover his phone, and say, "The guy is counting deer. No shit. *Counting deer.*"

"I'm counting antelope too," Joe said.

"They can wait. They aren't going anywhere, I'm sure."

"The pronghorn antelope is the second-fastest mammal on the face of the earth," Joe said. "So that wouldn't be correct."

"I'm at that place with the corny name," Portenson said. "The Burg-O-Pardner. Meet me in ten minutes."

"It'll take me twenty."

"I'll order breakfast in the meantime."

. . .

TONY PORTENSON WAS sitting in a booth in the back of the restaurant when Joe entered. He looked up from his plate of biscuits, gravy, and bacon and waved Joe back. Portenson was dark, intense, and had close-set eyes and a scar that hitched up his upper lip so that it looked as if he was always sneering. When he smiled, the effect was worse. Sitting across from him was an earnest, fresh-faced, wide-shouldered younger man with buzz-cut hair. His partner, Joe assumed.

"Have a seat, Joe," Portenson said, standing and offering his hand. "This is Special Agent Gary Child."

Rather than sit with Portenson or Child, Joe retrieved a chair from a nearby table and pulled it over.

Portenson wore standard FBI clothing—tie, jacket, and slacks, which made him stand out in Saddlestring as if he were wearing a space suit.

"This is the guy I was telling you about," Portenson said to Child.

Child nodded and looked at Joe with a mix of admiration and disdain. The FBI had a low opinion of local law enforcement that was so ingrained it was institutionalized. Although Joe operated on the margin of the sheriff's department and was rarely involved with the town cops, he was considered local and therefore less than proficient. Portenson had obviously briefed Child on both cases they'd been involved in before, probably between complaints about the wind and the snow he had to put up with during his long assignment in Wyoming, Joe thought.

"So," Portenson said as they all sat back down. "What is the fastest mammal?"

"The cheetah," Joe said.

"Does that mean a cheetah can chase down a pronghorn antelope?"

"Conceivably," Joe said, "if they lived on the same continent. But they don't."

"Hmmpf."

"What brings you up here, Tony?" Joe asked, assuming it would be either about the Scarletts or . . .

"Have you seen your buddy Nate Romanowski lately?" Portenson asked, getting right to it.

Joe felt a tingle on the back of his neck. "No."

"You're telling me he just vanished from the face of the earth?"

"I didn't say that. I said I hadn't seen him. And before you ask, no, I also haven't heard from him."

Portenson exchanged glances with Child.

Child said, "Let me set the scene. Two men are murdered. Although the condition of their bodies is deteriorated almost beyond recognition, the theory of our medical examiner is that they were each killed by a single gunshot wound to the head from an extremely large-caliber handgun. The bodies were obviously moved from where they were killed. Meanwhile, your friend Nate Romanowski was known to pack a .454 Casull revolver and was at odds with at least one of the murdered men. And according to you, he just vanished?"

Joe stifled a smile. "I have a tough time envisioning Tony here as the good cop in the good cop/bad cop scenario," he said. "This is more like bad cop/worse cop. Is this a new FBI strategy, or what?"

Child didn't waver. "We could bring you back for questioning."

"Go ahead," Joe said. "I'm telling you the truth. I don't know where Nate is, and I haven't been in contact with him."

Portenson wiped gravy from his lips with a paper napkin and studied Joe closely.

"What?" Portenson said.

"I can't believe you came all the way here to ask me about Nate," Joe said. "It seems like a waste of your time."

"Look," Child said, leaning toward Joe, his eyes sharp, "we don't need to explain to you why we do anything. We're asking the questions here, not you."

"Then I've got deer to count," Joe said, and started to push his chair back.

"Okay, okay," Portenson said, holding his hand out palm-up to Child. "Sit back down, Joe. That's not why we're here."

Joe sat.

"Actually, I just figured since we were up here I'd yank your chain a little. See if you had any new information on Mr. Romanowski."

"I told you I don't."

"I believe you," Portenson said, sighing. "Although I am going to get that guy."

Joe nodded that he understood, although he didn't think Portenson would succeed.

Child sat back in the booth. By the look he gave Portenson, it was clear he didn't like the way his boss had changed tracks.

"Are you up here on the Scarlett case?" Joe asked.

Portenson looked back blankly. Joe outlined Opal's disappearance, and the battle between the brothers.

"That's sick," Portenson said, "but that's not why we're here."

"We're here on a fucking wild-goose chase," Child said sullenly.

"Get used to it," Portenson said to him like a weary father. Then he signaled the waitress for his check.

"Double murder down in Mississippi," Portenson said. "Some hunting guide killed his clients, stole the couple's car, and took off. The car was found in Rawlins last month in the parking lot of the state pen, meaning it crossed state lines, which is where we come in. A couple of days later we got a report that an old truck was stolen from the same place."

The waitress brought the check and Portenson gave her a U.S. government credit card and asked her to charge three packs of Marlboros to it as well.

"My tax dollars at work," Joe said.

Portenson ignored him and continued. "After the old truck was stolen, it was seen south of Casper in the middle of fucking nowhere. Same day, somebody shot a cowboy off his horse in the vicinity. Left a wife and two kids. We don't know whether there's a connection or not. But since the guy was headed north, we thought we'd ask around. Does any of this ring any bells? The stolen truck is a light yellow 'ninety-four Ford with rust spots on the doors. Wyoming plates."

Joe shook his head. There was something familiar about the description but he couldn't place it. "What's the guy's name?"

"Ex-con named John Kelly," Child said from memory. "John Wayne Kelly."

"I've not heard of him," Joe said.

Portenson leveled his gaze at Joe. "My brethren are breaking up al-Qaeda cells and saving humanity. Me? I'm trying to figure out who shot a lonely cowpoke off his horsey. Does anyone but me see the *disparity* in that?"

Child snorted a laugh.

Joe shook his head at Portenson's attitude. "I bet that cowboy's widow and kids would like you to find out who did it."

"Aw fuck, Joe," Portenson said. "You're ruining the mood."

"Have you talked to the sheriff?"

Portenson snorted while he signed the charge slip. "We sent him the file but I'm delaying actually talking to him as long as I can."

"He's changed yet again," Joe said.

"I heard he's a cowpoke now," Portenson said, curling his lip in disdain.

"Something like that," Joe said.

"How could he get worse?"

"I can't explain it," Joe said, pushing back. "Good to see you, Tony."

"Good to see you, Joe. And don't forget to give me a shout if Mr. Romanowski shows up."

Joe nodded again, shook Child's hand, and got a cup of coffee to go on the way out.

10

JOE AND MARYBETH DID THE DISHES AFTER DINNER while Sheridan and Lucy watched television in the family room. Joe had made chili and the kitchen smelled of tomato sauce, garlic, spices, and ground beef.

"It was too salty, wasn't it?" he asked, scrubbing the cast-iron pot he liked to use for chili, since it was huge.

"A little," she said. "Did you rinse the beans? Sometimes they pack them in so much salt that if you don't wash them thoroughly . . ."

"Ah," he said, "that was the problem."

"It was good, though," she said. "I do wish you could learn to make a smaller pot, maybe."

Since he didn't know how to make a pot of chili for less than a dozen people, and every time he tried to make less it was a disaster, Marybeth had filled two Tupperware containers of it for the freezer. Actually, Joe didn't really want to learn how to make less chili at a time, since he liked having leftovers available, especially these days, when he was never sure when Marybeth would be home from her office or if dinner would be planned. But he didn't want to tell her that. And, like most men, he wanted her to think he was largely incompetent in the kitchen.

"What do you think of Sheridan going to the Scarlett's for a sleepover?" Marybeth asked. Sheridan had brought it up during dinner.

Joe scrubbed harder. "Julie seems like a nice girl," he said. "It's the rest of her family who're nuts."

"I know what you mean. I got calls today from both Arlen and Hank. Each wants me to meet with him and see what I can do to streamline their business operations."

"Both of them, eh?"

"Both of them."

"Uh-oh."

Since Opal's disappearance, sides had been forming in Saddlestring and the county. People were either pro-Arlen and anti-Hank, or vice versa. Both brothers kept close track of who was with them, and who was against them. Arlen preferred the Saddlestring Burg-O-Pardner for his mid-morning coffee, where he could chat with the town fathers. Hank never set foot in the place. Likewise, Hank liked his shot and a beer at the Stockman, often accompanied by several of his ranch hands. Arlen never darkened the door of that bar.

The town was just big enough that there were two of most things—two feed stores, grocery stores, banks, hardware stores, auto-parts stores, lumber stores—so the brothers could choose. In the instance that there was only one business, such as the movie theater and medical clinic, one or the other brother claimed it outright and the other traveled north to the next larger city—Billings, Montana.

Since the Scarletts spent a lot of money in town, the choice between pro-Arlen or pro-Hank was an important business decision, and one not made on a whim. Marybeth had told Joe about it, how her clients agonized over which brother to court. It was just as important, she said, that when a brother was chosen, not a single kind word be spoken about the other. That was considered disloyalty, and reason to pull their business. The loyalty to one brother or the other extended to their ranch hands as well, and merchants had to keep track of who worked for whom.

Now, with calls from both brothers on the same day, Marybeth would have to make the same decision so many of her clients had made.

THERE WERE RUMORS of war on the Thunderhead Ranch. The stories filtered through the community every day. The word was that Hank and Arlen had each hired more men than they needed for normal ranch operations. No one doubted the new men could serve as soldiers in an all-out range battle for ownership and dominance of the family ranch. Locks were put on gates, and harsh words exchanged over the fences. Sugar was poured into the gas tanks of ranch vehicles. Irrigation valves were turned off, or turned on when they shouldn't be, or the water was diverted from one side of the ranch to the other.

Robey told Joe that Arlen's new foreman claimed that someone from Hank's side had taken a shot at him, the bullet entering his open driver's-side window, barely missing his nose, and exiting the open passenger's-side window. Since there was no proof that a shot had been fired other than the foreman's account and only soiled Wranglers to confirm he'd been scared, McLanahan filed away the complaint.

Then two of Hank's men charged they'd been run off the highway by a pickup clearly belonging to Arlen Scarlett. But no pickup matching the description could be found.

An editorial in the Saddlestring *Roundup* ran a long list of bulleted items that had reportedly occurred between the two brothers on the ranch. The editorial ended with the sentence, "Will it be necessary to call in the Wyoming National Guard to prevent a full-fledged bloodletting?"

"SO, WHO YOU gonna choose?" Joe asked.

Marybeth frowned and shook her head. "I wish I didn't have to choose either."

"That's an option, isn't it?"

"Not really. They'd both see it for what it was—a snub. Arlen and Hank insist on a choice."

Left unsaid was the fact that whichever choice she made would generate a good deal of revenue for her business, and therefore benefit the family. Marybeth was routing as much as she could into college funds for Sheridan and Lucy, and having either Hank or Arlen on her client list would boost her earnings. Since Joe's salary was frozen at $32,000 by the state, there was little he could do to contribute to the college funds, which made him feel guilty and ashamed.

"My mother and Arlen both serve on the library board," Marybeth said. "They're pretty good friends. I think Arlen expects me to go with him, and I *know* my mother does." She sighed. "I'll probably go with Arlen."

Joe cringed. Last fall, Marybeth's mother, the former Missy Vankueren, had married Bud Longbrake, one of the most prominent ranchers in the valley. It was her fourth marriage, and she had traded up each time. Missy had taken to her new role—that of landed matriarch—with an enthusiasm and panache that Joe found both truly impressive and frightening. She seemed to be on every board and volunteer effort, the cochair of every fund-raiser. She was even involved, somehow, in the new addition to the Twelve

Sleep County Museum, which was to be called the Scarlett Wing. Missy had never liked Joe much, and the feeling was mutual, although a kind of grudging respect had formed on both sides. She thought her daughter could have done better for herself. Joe tended to agree with that, but didn't necessarily want to hear it said. Again.

"Arlen is pretty persuasive, and we could certainly use the business. But I really don't want to get involved with either one of them. It's a classic no-win situation," she said, folding her washrag over the edge of the sink.

"Speaking of which," Joe said, "I got two messages from headquarters today. I meant to tell you about them before dinner."

She looked at him and arched her eyebrows.

"The first one was from Randy Pope. He wants me to resubmit all of my expense logs for the past four years. *Four years!* He says I still hold the record for the most wrecked vehicles in the department." In Joe's career, he had totaled three pickups and a snowmobile.

"Yes," she said, prompting him for the second.

"And an anonymous tipster called the 800-POACHER line claiming that he knew of a guy who had dozens of game-animal mounts in his home that were taken illegally in Wyoming and all over the world. The RP—that's 'reporting party' to you civilians—said the violator is prominent, a real criminal. The RP said this guy has done enough bad things to justify confiscating all of his property and equipment and fining him out the wazoo."

"Yes . . ."

"The alleged poacher is Hank Scarlett," Joe said. "The anonymous caller knows enough about game and fish regulations to cite wanton-destruction statutes. He also said many of the animal mounts at Hank's hunting lodge are clearly illegal."

"Anonymous caller?" Marybeth said, smiling. "Or Arlen?"

"I'd guess one and the same," Joe said.

"And there was an e-mail sitting in my in-box from Randy Pope referencing the tip on Hank. It says, Wait for my authorization before proceeding on this." The message infuriated Joe. Never in his career had a supervisor injected himself so deeply into his day-to-day job, much less the director of the department. In six years of working under Trey Crump, Trey had never once told Joe to hold up on doing his job. And just what in the hell was Randy Pope waiting for before providing authorization? Or was it, as Joe suspected, simply a maneuver to once again remind Joe Pickett who was running the show, like the request for back expense logs?

She stepped up to Joe and put her hands on the tops of his shoulders. "We're going to be tangled up with these people whether we want to be or not, aren't we?" She meant the Scarletts.

"Yup," Joe said, wrapping his arms around her waist.

"And you wouldn't have it any other way, would you?"

He hesitated for a moment. That one came out of left field, but she knew him so well.

"I do want to find out what happened to Opal," he said. "There's something not right about it."

"There's something not right about the whole Scarlett clan," she said. "They've got a hold on this valley that scares me. It doesn't matter if you're with Arlen or Hank, the fact is everyone feels obligated to be with one or the other. There's no middle ground, no compromise."

As she spoke, Sheridan came into the kitchen.

"You guys decide about Friday night?"

Joe and Marybeth looked at each other.

"What we've decided," Marybeth said, "is that this valley is much too small."

"What is that supposed to mean?" Sheridan asked, looking from her mother to her father, obviously embarrassed to see them holding one another next to the sink.

The night suddenly split wide open as Maxine awoke

from her customary sleeping place in the doorway of Joe's office and barked furiously at the front door, the fur on her neck and back bristled up like a feral hog's. Joe, Marybeth, and Sheridan all turned to the door, and Lucy scrambled from the couch to join them.

"Maxine!" Joe commanded. "Maxine, stop it!"

But the dog kept barking, her barks echoing sharply through the house. She clearly thought somebody was outside.

"What is it?" Marybeth asked Lucy. "Was there a knock?"

"I thought I heard something hit the door," Lucy said, looking away from the television. "It sounded like a little rock hit it."

Joe slipped away and strode across the living room. It wouldn't be that unusual to have a night visitor; people often showed up late to report an incident or turn themselves in. But that usually happened in the fall, during hunting season, not in the spring.

He clicked on the porch light and opened the door. No one. He stepped outside on the porch, Maxine on his heels. The only thing he could see, in the distance, was a pair of red taillights growing smaller on Bighorn Road traveling east, toward the mountains, away from town.

"What was it, honey?" Marybeth asked.

Joe shook his head. "Nobody here now, but it looks like someone was."

"Dad," Lucy said, coming outside with her sister, "there's something on the door."

"Oh My God," Sheridan gasped, her hands covering her mouth. She recognized it.

So did Joe, and he was taken aback.

A small dead animal had been pinned to the front door by an old steak knife with a weathered grip. The creature was long and slim, ferretlike, with a black stripe down its back. It was a Miller's weasel, a species once thought extinct. It was the animal that had led to Sheridan being terrorized years before, and Marybeth being shot.

And somebody who knew about both had stuck one to his front door.

11

THE NEXT MORNING JOE WENT FOR A RUN, FED THE horses, retrieved the newspaper, walked the girls out to the school bus (via the back door, so they wouldn't have to see the Miller's weasel on the front), and paced back and forth from the living room to the kitchen, waiting for eight A.M., when he called headquarters in Cheyenne and asked for Randy Pope. He was angry.

"The director is in a meeting," Pope's receptionist said, her tone clipped. Joe didn't think he liked Pope's receptionist; there was something off-putting and chilly about her.

"Can you please get him out of it?"

"Is this an emergency?"

It is for me, Joe thought. So he said, "Yes," knowing Pope wouldn't agree.

Joe listened to Glen Campbell sing about the Wichita lineman while he held. The music was another addition since Pope had taken over, but the choice of songs belied not only another era, but another planet.

Pope came on. "Make it quick, Joe."

"Someone killed a Miller's weasel and stuck it to my front door last night," Joe said. "I tried the emergency number there in Cheyenne last night and they told me you were not to be disturbed."

"That's right, Joe," Pope said, an edge in his voice. "I was at a dinner at the governor's mansion. It was a get-to-know-you dinner, and I informed dispatch I was not to be interrupted."

Joe sighed. "Randy, if you're going to be my supervisor and require me to get authorization from you for every move I make, you need to be available. Either that, or loosen up the reins and let me do my job."

Marybeth passed by the doorway to his office holding the newspaper. She cocked an eyebrow, cautioning him.

"That would be *Director Pope*," Pope said, his voice flat. "Tell me again what happened and what you want to do?" Joe could discern he was measuring his words carefully. Joe vowed to try to do the same. Every time he talked with Pope he ran the risk of saying something that could get him reprimanded or suspended.

"There is a dead Miller's weasel stuck to my front door with a knife . . ."

"That house is Game and Fish property," Pope interjected. "It doesn't belong to you personally."

Joe stopped pacing and shut his eyes. This is what Pope did, his method—he'd say something so blatant and obvious that it killed the purpose of the conversation in the first place.

"I know who the house belongs to," Joe said wearily. "And since you own it, how about a new furnace? How about that? How about putting some insulation in the walls and sealing up all of the cracks where the wind blows through?"

Marybeth was hovering in the hall, listening and not trying to hide it. He could tell she was amused, but also concerned.

"Joe . . ."

"Right, you don't want to talk about that," Joe said to Pope. "So how about we talk about the animal on the front of my, um . . . *our* door. The Miller's weasel is an endangered species, as you know. But it's more than that. This is personal."

"So what do you want me to do about it?"

Again, Joe closed his eyes for a moment, contemplating whether or not he should count to ten, or resign immediately. Or drive to Cheyenne and shoot Pope in the heart, which would be the best alternative—or at least the most satisfying.

"I need your authorization to investigate it," Joe said quietly, trying to keep anger out of his voice. "You said in your memo that you want to be informed prior to me opening any new investigations, so I'm informing you. I want to ride to where the last colony of Miller's weasels are, and see if I can find any evidence of who was up there to kill one. Then I might need some help from our investigators to trace the knife. I can start interviewing people around here today to see if anyone saw the vehicle or knows who did it."

The line was silent for a moment. Joe could picture Pope sitting back in his chair, maybe putting his feet up on his desk.

"Joe?" Pope said.

"Yes?"

"There's a big difference between asking for authorization and telling me what you're going to do," Pope said. "This is a good example of the kind of problem I have with you and some of the other game wardens. You act as if you're the Lone Ranger in your district, that you and you alone decide what you're going to do and how you're going to do it. No other law-enforcement officer has that luxury, Joe. Everyone else has to get authorization to proceed. Can you imagine a sheriff's deputy showing up at work in the morning and saying, 'Gee, I feel like going out on the interstate highway today and catching speeders and playing highway patrolman instead of staying in the county and following up on all of these annoying complaints.' Can you imagine that, Joe? It's time you realized this isn't how things are done in the real world, where we have to justify our existence to the legislature and the public. Why is it you think you're special?"

"It's my problem," Joe said, opening the front door and staring at the animal pinned to it, the little body now starting to stiffen. "Like I said, it's personal. Whoever did this didn't just happen to find a Miller's weasel. He went looking for it, and left it here as a message. I haven't disturbed it since last night in case there are fingerprints or other evidence."

Pope said, "Do you plan to chase the culprit down and shoot him like you did that outfitter in Jackson? Like you're some kind of cowboy or gunfighter? That's not how we do things anymore, Joe. This is a new agency, and a new era."

A new agency and a new era. Another one of Pope's catchphrases.

Joe had trouble finding the right words to say. He knew he was turning red. When he looked up at Marybeth, she was gesturing frantically for him to "zip it" by sealing her own mouth with an imaginary fastener.

"Call the sheriff," Pope said crisply. "That's what you should have done last night. Ask him to investigate this. It's his jurisdiction, after all."

"Sheriff McLanahan is not competent to investigate this," Joe said.

Pope chuckled drily. "Now, I doubt that, Joe. I'm sure he can handle it. The good people of Twelve Sleep County would never have elected him if he was the buffoon you make him out to be. And this is part of the problem, too. It doesn't help with our community-relations outreach when our people refer to the locals as incompetents. We need all the support we can get, Joe. You need to learn to work with . . ."

Joe punched off and slammed the receiver down with so much force that the earpiece broke off. He couldn't listen to another word.

Marybeth obviously heard the end of the conversation and the crash and looked in the door as he tried to fit the pieces of the phone back together. Wires were still attached to the pieces.

"It's busted," he said, angry with himself.

"I see that," Marybeth said. "We can get a new phone. But it's not the phone I'm worried about."

As Joe pressed the pieces together, the handle shattered and covered his desktop with shards of plastic.

Joe said darkly, "Maybe I need a new job."

Marybeth said, "Phone repairman is definitely out."

SHERIFF KYLE MCLANAHAN arrived at Joe's house at ten-thirty that morning, driving the oldest pickup in the county fleet, his one-eyed Blue Heeler dog occupying the passenger seat.

Joe went outside to meet him.

The sheriff climbed slowly out of his pickup, as if he'd aged twenty years since he left town. The dog scrambled out behind him, and ran through the gate to Maxine so both dogs could sniff each other for a while.

That seemed to be McLanahan's intent with Joe as well, to sniff at him.

"That's it, eh?" McLanahan asked, pointing over Joe's shoulder at the Miller's weasel on his door.

"That's it," Joe said, watching McLanahan pull on his jacket.

"Happened last night, huh?"

"Yup."

"But you waited until this morning to call."

"Yes, I did."

"Woulda helped if you'd called last night," McLanahan

said, entering the yard and shuffling past Joe. "Before the blood dried and all the evidence was fouled up. I suppose you've touched the knife handle, and opened the fence, all of that."

"I'm afraid so," Joe said, embarrassed.

McLanahan turned to him stiffly. He moved as if he'd just dismounted after a long horseback trek. "D'you know who did it?"

Joe shrugged. "Someone who wants to send a message. You remember the history on that Miller's weasel."

McLanahan nodded. "Well," he said, reaching up and smoothing both sides of his mustache with a meaty index finger in a surprisingly effete gesture, "I ain't got much to go on, since you already fouled up the crime scene and you can't tell me anything."

"Nope, I guess you don't," Joe said, frustrated.

McLanahan ambled back toward his pickup. "You let me know if something else happens, all right? Or if you hear anything about who mighta' done this? You'll call, right?"

Joe sighed. "I'll call."

The sheriff opened the door of his truck to let his dog bound in, then stopped suddenly and looked up at the sky. Joe followed McLanahan's gaze, puzzled. A V of geese was outlined against a massive cumulous cloud.

"I like to watch the geese," McLanahan said, as if it were something profound. Then he looked back at Joe and squinted his eyes. "Next time, call me right away. Don't wait twelve hours, pardner."

12

"A MILLER'S WEASEL?" ROBEY ASKED, SITTING BACK in the booth at the Stockman bar. "No shit. Where would someone even find one?"

Joe sipped his beer, his third of the night thus far. It was Saturday night. The Stockman bar in downtown Saddlestring was a long, narrow chute of a place that stretched back the entire length of the city block. It was a classic, old-fashioned western bar with dusty big-game mounts on the walls, a dark knotty-pine interior, a mirrored backbar, and an entire wall of ancient black-and-white rodeo photos. Between the bar and the pool tables in the back was a pod of private booths with red-vinyl-covered seats and scarred tabletops emblazoned with local cattle brands, graffiti, and the initials of patrons dating back to the 1940s.

Joe said, "There's a small population of them in the Bighorns. I transplanted them there myself. Not many people know where they are, or how to find them."

Robey stared at Joe. "That's more information than I needed to know," he said, since what Joe had done was a federal crime. It was illegal to interfere with an endangered species.

The Miller's weasels were originally discovered in the proposed path of a natural-gas pipeline, shortly after Joe had been named game warden of the district. Their discovery resulted in the deaths of four outfitters and a local caretaker of mountain cabins, and a firestorm that destroyed friendships and relationships and ended about as badly as it could have with Marybeth being shot by Wacey Hedeman. Once the species had been verified, there followed a brief flurry of national and international publicity to Twelve Sleep County that had long been forgotten on a large scale but continued to burble under the surface in the county and the state.

"Odd news about Wacey Hedeman, huh?" Robey said, glancing at Joe and then away from him, as if he didn't want to press Joe for a reaction.

Joe nodded.

"Is Marybeth okay with that?"

"I think so," Joe said. "It brought everything back again, of course. The past never just goes away, does it?"

Robey shook his head.

"You couldn't see the vehicle, read a plate?" Robey asked.

"Just the taillights."

Robey whistled. "There were a lot of folks who weren't real happy with you back then. People on both sides of the issue. But it's hard to believe someone has held a grudge this long, someone you wouldn't know about."

"That's why it bothers me so much," Joe said. "Right in front of my girls too," he added, his voice rising. "It really shook up Sheridan. She recognized the animal right off. In fact, she even said she wondered if someone wasn't threatening *her*. And that pisses me off, to involve my family like that."

Robey sat back, his eyes searching Joe's face. "Let's hope this was an isolated incident. It's odd that whoever did this waited six years to get back at you, isn't it?"

"Yeah, the timing doesn't make sense," Joe said. "But what better way to get me right where I live? I mean, I'm the game warden. What worse kind of thing can someone do than stick a dead animal on my door? And especially that particular animal?"

"Stay alert," Robey said. "That's all I can say. I'll do the same. Maybe one of us will hear something."

Joe nodded.

"But, Joe, if you figure out who did it, please run it by me or call the sheriff before you do anything. Don't go trying to take care of it on your own, okay?"

Joe signaled for two more beers from the bartender, not answering yes or no.

"Joe," Robey said, "it's no secret the situation you're in with your new director. The word is out that he's watching every move you make. He's even made a couple of discreet calls to my office, and the sheriff's office, to try to dig something up on you. He doesn't know we're friends."

"I'm not surprised," Joe said. He'd suspected Pope might be investigating him on the sly. That was the way he operated. Again, Joe felt the politics of his job crushing down on him. It was not what he had signed on for. He was battling within a system he didn't like or respect anymore.

Robey said, "There are some things you've been involved in that probably won't help you if this Pope guy digs too deeply. Like about Nate Romanowski? Or a certain Forest Service district supervisor whose death was *remarkably* ruled a suicide a few years back?"

Joe knew it was true. Robey knew more than he probably wanted to. As county prosecutor, Robey was aware of things that he likely wished he wasn't. But as a good man, one who valued actual justice as opposed to process, Robey had chosen simply not to ask certain questions of Joe when he had a right, and a duty, to ask them. Because of that, Joe was fiercely loyal to his friend.

THE TOPIC TURNED to the purpose of the meeting in the first place.

"It's the curse of the third generation," Robey said, shaking his head and absently rolling the beer bottle between the palms of his hands. "I don't know if there is a worse thing in the West than that."

Robey paused and glanced up at Joe. His face looked haunted. "Did I ever tell you the main reason I left private practice and ran for county attorney?"

"Let me guess," Joe said facetiously. "Would it be . . . *the curse of the third generation*?"

"That would be it," Robey said. "It's a pattern you can pretty much predict. When I first got my license, I was involved in way too many of these cases, and it just about killed me. It works this way: A matriarch or patriarch establishes the original ranch, and passes it along to the firstborn. The heir inherits land and power, and it feels different to him because he didn't have to fight for it or earn it. It's his by birthright, but he's close enough to the founders that the initial struggle still resonates. But from then on, everything starts to get comfortable. This works the same way with family-owned companies. But if we're talking about ranches, and we are, it gets more personal than if it was a shoe factory, because on a ranch everyone lives together and eats together. Sometimes, the second generation is smart and appreciates what they've got and how they got it, and plans ahead. You know—they form corporations or partnerships or something." Robey paused to take a long pull of his beer before resuming, and Joe marveled at how engaged his friend was with the subject, how much he had obviously thought about it, how it concerned him.

"So," Robey continued, "the third generation inherits a going concern but they *really* don't give a shit about how they got it. The third generation splinters. A couple of the sons and daughters want to keep the place, and the others want to do something else. So when it comes time to figure out who owns what, the lawyers are called in to battle it out. It's like couples who divorce without considering the best interests of the children because they're so bitter. But instead of children, we're talking about the ranch itself. There is only so much land in the world, it's finite. Especially good, scenic, or productive land that can't speak for itself. The litigation gets so messy that sometimes it's unbelievable. Other people want that land, that asset. So we've got brothers against brothers and sisters against sisters. You can really see the worst in human nature in a situation like that, and you just want to grab those idiots and knock their heads together and say 'Wake up! Look what you're doing to a place your ancestors put all of their sweat and blood into!'"

Robey rose and pretended he was grasping litigants by their necks and smashing their heads together. Joe looked around to see if anyone at the bar was watching. Fortunately, they weren't.

Joe said, "And when it comes to our situation here with the Scarletts and the Thunderhead Ranch, we've got the curse in spades, right?"

"It's like the curse has gone nuclear," Robey said. "In this case, the original ranch was established in the eighteen-eighties, which was when most of the big ranches got going in our part of the country. Before statehood, and before homesteaders started spreading their wings. For the Thunderhead Ranch, a man named Homer Scarlett left West Virginia and used a small inheritance to buy what was then a small five-thousand-acre ranch on the river."

"That would be the original Thunderhead Ranch?" Joe asked.

Robey shook his head. "Nope, the Thunderhead was the ranch next door at the time. Homer Scarlett, the great-grandfather, acquired it through somewhat dubious means—I think he won a big chunk of it in a poker game or something—and added it to his own holdings. He picked up five or six other small ranches along the way, and kept adding on. He was ruthless, from what I've heard. But he was also a hell of a businessman, because he thrived when others around him were going broke. As he added property, he put them all under the umbrella of the Thunderhead Ranch, I guess because he liked the name. Pretty soon, Scarlett owned sixty thousand acres outright and another hundred thousand acres on long-term lease from the government. He used his influence to make Saddlestring the county seat, and for a while there they almost renamed this town Scarlettville. Did you know that?"

Joe shook his head. "No. How do *you* know all of this?"

Robey laughed wearily. "Because I'm on the museum board and a few weeks ago we took a tour through the new Scarlett wing that's scheduled to be dedicated next month. In fact, your mother-in-law was on the tour. It's a damned nice addition to the building, and there is a special room to honor the family. Opal insisted on the display, and provided the photos and documents.

"Anyway," Robey continued, "Homer had a son named Henry and two daughters named June and Laura. In those days, it was a lot simpler than it is now, and Henry assumed control of the ranch because he was the only male heir. There wasn't any squabbling about control, even though the daughters legally had the same claim to it. Henry Scarlett took it over in the mid-nineteen-thirties, and the two daughters got nice little cottages on the ranch. June and Laura never married, so they produced no heirs. Henry had a couple of sons, though, named Wilbur and Dub. Dub died in combat at Normandy, so Wilbur had a clear line."

"And Wilbur married Opal," Joe said. "Who eventually had three sons."

"Right."

"So when did Wilbur die?"

"Early 1970s," Robey said. "He was driving a truck across an old bridge over the river on the ranch when the bridge collapsed. I read about it. He was pinned inside the vehicle, and drowned in six inches of water."

"And Opal got everything?"

Robey signaled for two more beers. "The whole thing lock, stock, and barrel. If Wilbur specified which one of his sons got the place, or if he had plans to divide up the ranch—no one knows. There wasn't a will."

"So where are we now?" Joe asked.

"We are in limbo, ownership hell," Robey said. "Arlen claims Opal assured him the ranch would be his because he's the oldest. Hank says Opal told *him* the same thing, and that she never trusted Arlen. Opal has two lawyers here in town, and both thought the other took care of the estate planning, but it turns out neither did. The ranch is a corporation with Opal Scarlett as its sole owner, with no management agreement, no will, no nothing."

"What's it worth?" Joe asked, thinking of the vast acreage, the meadows, the buildings, the twenty miles of riverfront.

"Tens of millions," Robey said. "An appraisal will need to be done, but we know we're in the mid-teens. If it were put up for sale, there would be buyers from all over the country and the world. These days, all the rich corporate guys want to own a ranch."

Joe whistled.

"Until Opal's proven dead and there's a court order—or a will is found—nothing can be done to establish ownership or a succession plan," Robey said. "Those brothers just continue to live out there in conflict. They could decide to sell the place and pocket the money, or one could buy it outright from the other. But in order to do that, they'd need to sit down and talk like human beings. Instead, they've both hired lawyers, accountants, and soldiers of their own, and they're preparing for battle. My fear is that the war won't make it as far as a courtroom, that it'll start breaking out all over this valley."

In the meantime, Robey said, the case against Tommy Wayman was also in limbo. He told Joe that although Tommy had confessed to tossing Opal in the river, the lack of a body prevented him from filing charges. In a legal holding action, Robey had persuaded Judge Pennock to order Tommy to stay in the area and check in weekly until the situation could be resolved.

Joe said, "This is about a lot more than the money, isn't it?"

Robey looked quickly around the room to see who had entered since they started talking and that no one appeared to be eavesdropping. He leaned forward, lowered his voice, and said, "Joe, Opal was a damned monster. That's what I'm finding out, the more I dig into it. She played those two brothers against each other all of their lives, telling one he was the favorite and that he'd get everything, denigrating the other, and vice versa. No wonder Wyatt is nuts, if he grew up with all of that going on around him. Arlen and Hank each really, honestly believe it is his personal destiny to control the ranch, and to continue the Scarlett legacy. That's what they both call it, with a straight face, the 'Scarlett legacy.' Even Wyatt uses that term, easy as pie. According to Hank, Opal distrusted Arlen so much that she hired a third lawyer in secret to draw up a will giving Hank the whole place, but the lawyer was instructed not to come forward until Opal was declared dead. Hank says he'd rather 'Mother' show up than have her declared dead, of course, but if she doesn't, he's absolutely confident the ranch will be his. That's how crazy these brothers are."

"A *third* lawyer?"

Robey laughed, clearly not believing there was one. "Hank claims it's Meade Davis. You ever hear of him?"

Davis was one of Saddlestring's oldest and most prominent lawyers. So prominent, in fact, that Joe couldn't recall his ever taking a case. Davis was involved in real estate, convenience stores, and he owned the cable television company.

"Davis winters in Arizona," Robey said. "He isn't back yet. We've tried to track him down but his phone's disconnected and the registered letters we sent were returned. We've got a request in with the sheriff down there to find him, but so far no luck."

Joe sat back, sipped his beer, thought of the implications. Robey was clearly agitated.

"So Wyatt is out of it for sure?" Joe asked. "It's completely between Arlen and Hank? And Wyatt is okay with that?" He thought of Wyatt's tears on the floor of the sheriff's office; the heartbreak of a giant.

"As far as I can tell, Wyatt just wants Opal to come back and cook him his meals," Robey said. "He misses her. And he doesn't seem to care about the dispute either way. When I talked to Arlen, he actually referred to Wyatt as the 'turd in the punch bowl.' He has no respect for his youngest brother, but Wyatt adores Arlen. And Hank, for that matter."

Joe thought about that and wondered if anyone really knew Wyatt.

"I understand some anonymous tipster contacted the IRS and turned Arlen in for tax evasion," Robey said. "We were contacted by the feds about it earlier this week with a request to provide background."

"Hank," Joe said.

"Or one of Hank's people. But that's just the start of it. I got a visit this morning from Roger Schreiner. He was scared shitless."

"Roger Schreiner? The accountant?"

"Yup. He's working for Hank's side of the operation and he got a letter accusing him of playing a part in an illegal conspiracy to defraud Arlen. The letter even cited the RICO statutes, which means he's liable for triple damages if he's found guilty. Roger says he's innocent as the day is long, but he's scared to death of going to court because he's not sure how far his firm will back him."

"Arlen," Joe said.

Robey nodded.

Joe told Robey about the 1-800-POACHER tip he'd received earlier, naming Hank.

"Oh, man," Robey said. "What could that mean if it's true?"

Joe said, "Tens of thousands in fines, but that's not what would hurt Hank the most. What would hurt Hank would be the confiscation of the equipment used to poach the animals, meaning his airplane, vehicles, and guns. And even worse for him, his license to guide and hunt could be revoked. Since he runs a big hunting operation in at least three locations, it would put him out of business."

Robey shook his head. "Jesus," he said. "This is getting even nastier than I thought."

Joe snorted. "Of course, before investigating Hank I need proper authorization from my supervisor, which I'm still waiting for."

"You're kidding," Robey said flatly.

Joe just looked at him. He *hated* feeling the way he did. Pope's management of Joe stripped away both his independence and his confidence. But that was Joe's problem, not Robey's.

"And you know what?" Joe said, pointing the mouth of his bottle toward Robey. "I don't think we've seen anything yet in regard to Scarlett versus Scarlett."

Robey nodded. "We haven't, because the next stage in the war will be more of what Arlen started in going after the surrogates of the other brother, like Hank's accountant."

"Or," Joe thought out loud, "Arlen's future management consulting firm—MBP Management."

Robey sat back. "You think?"

"It fits," Joe said.

And the door opened and in walked Hank Scarlett with a ranch hand. Joe watched as Hank mumbled hellos to men seated at the bar and then took the stool at the end that used to belong to ex-sheriff O. R. "Bud" Barnum, before Barnum went away. Hank's tiny eyes, set close together in his thin face, burned like coals as they swept the room, settled for a moment on Joe, then moved on. He was doing inventory, Joe thought, seeing who in the Stockman was in his camp, and who wasn't.

"Speak of the devil," Joe said, his eyes narrowing. As he stared at Hank Scarlett, things started to tumble together and click. Six years before, Hank had been one of the most vocal opponents of calling in the feds when the Miller's weasels were discovered, and he publicly blamed Joe for the intrusion of biologists, endangered-species advocates, and environmental groups that came as a result. Hank felt the issue would be best resolved locally, meaning: *All the animals should be secretly killed.* That's how he'd always proceeded with endangered species.

In addition, Hank knew the Bighorns as well as anyone in Wyoming—even better than Joe, because he had hunted and explored every inch of them. If anyone knew where the colony of Miller's weasels thrived in the wilderness, it was Hank. The fact that Marybeth had chosen to work for Arlen in Hank's mind put Joe in his brother's camp, even though it wasn't the case.

"Joe, I don't like that look on your face," Robey said.

Joe didn't realize he had any look at all.

"If you think Hank had something to do with that Miller's weasel, you had best keep it to yourself until you can prove something," Robey said.

Joe thought about the animal on his door, the steak knife pinning it there, the single streak of dark red blood that coursed down and pooled in a crack. And of Sheridan's horrified expression when she realized what it was, what it meant.

"Excuse me," Joe said, and slid out of the booth.

"Joe . . ." Robey said, his voice hard, but Joe didn't turn around.

He approached the bar. Hank had his back to Joe, although the man Hank had come into the bar with watched Joe intently. Joe measured Hank's companion, met his eyes dead-on. *This one is a thug,* Joe thought. There was nothing cowboy about him. He was tight through the chest, and his rolled-up sleeves revealed enhanced forearms with coils of cablelike muscle writhing under tattooed skin. His face was thin and pinched, his mouth full and rubbery. He had a soul patch under his lower lip and a ponytail. He wore the wrong jeans and his boots were black Doc Marten lace-ups, not real working cowboy boots. The man's hat was Australian outback, not cowboy. And there was something about him, Joe thought, something familiar. When he looked at the man's face he saw somebody else he was familiar with, or the shadow of that person. But Joe couldn't remember if he had ever seen this man before.

The beer Joe had been drinking with Robey surged through him, deadening what should have been self-preservation warning bells going off like a prison break.

"Hank," Joe said, to Hank's back.

"Is there a problem here?" the man with Hank said in a low southern accent.

"I was talking to Hank," Joe said, looking from the

ranch hand to the mirrored back bar, to see that Hank saw him and was staring back with his dead sharp eyes.

The ranch hand spun on his stool and rose to his feet, but Hank said, "It's okay, Bill, he's just the game warden."

Bill relaxed, stepped back, sat down.

Hank took a long drink from his glass of bourbon, then swiveled around, not getting up. Joe was three feet away, and he tried not to let his face twitch as Hank frowned and leveled his gaze on him.

"What can I do you for, Game Warden?" He said *Game Warden* with detached sarcasm. Hank's voice was high and tinny. He bit off his words, as if speaking them were painful in itself.

"I wanted to ask you about something that happened at my house," Joe said.

Hank flicked his eyes toward Bill, then back. His voice was a low hiss. "I don't believe you've met our local game warden before, Bill. He's the one who arrested our last governor for fishing without a license, and shot and killed both Wyoming's greatest stock detective and our best out-fitter. He's sort of our own Dudley Do-Right. Joe, this is Bill Monroe, my new foreman."

Monroe snorted and squinted and showed his teeth, which were white and perfect replacements for teeth that had been knocked out sometime in his career.

Joe looked at Hank, felt his rage build. Hank's face was still slightly yellow—bruised from his fight with Arlen a month before. His nose was askew.

"Bill," Joe said, trying to stanch his fear, "why don't you take a walk? Go out and buy some new cowboy clothes, or something? I need to talk to Hank here."

"Fuck you," Monroe said.

"Settle down," Hank said without looking at Monroe. "What was that about your house? I'd like to have a drink in peace."

"Somebody stuck an animal on my door," Joe said. "A Miller's weasel."

Hank stared for a moment, then smiled with his mouth. "I'm not exactly sure why you're asking me about that, Game Warden. Do you think I had something to do with it?"

"That's why I brought it up," Joe said. "My daughter was pretty upset."

Hank said, "Her name is Sheridan, right?" Saying her name as if it were the first time he'd ever enunciated it. "She's Julie's friend, isn't she? I've seen her. She's a nice girl, from what I can tell. Not as damned goofy as her father. Why would I want to upset my daughter's best friend?"

Hank was enjoying himself at Joe's expense. And Joe felt humiliated. But it made Joe even angrier, because he sensed there was something Hank knew about the incident.

Joe said, "Hank, I don't care what you say about me to your rent-a-wrangler here. But don't screw with my family."

Hank smiled.

Monroe rose again, said, "'Rent-a-wrangler'?"

"Sit down," Joe said to Monroe, his voice harsh. "Or I'll make you sit down." As he said it he couldn't believe it had come out of his mouth. But it worked, and Monroe leaned back on his stool, poised on the edge, ready to lunge forward if necessary. His eyes bored into Joe's face like dual twin lasers, something was going on behind those eyes that was violent and seething. Joe thought, *I've got to watch out for this guy.*

Hank chuckled drily. "That sounded a lot like a threat, Joe. That's big talk from a state employee. Especially one who has sided with my brother. Or at least his wife has. I'd watch what you say, Game Warden."

"I haven't sided with anyone," Joe said. "Neither has Marybeth." He still couldn't believe that he'd threatened Monroe that way. "But if it was you, this is the end of it.

Don't come to my house again, or send any of your . . ." Joe thought about it for a second, then forged on. ". . . *wranglers* to my home. If you do, things are going to get real western, Hank."

Hank started to answer, then didn't. He looked away, then turned to Monroe and said, "Settle down."

Monroe seemed as if he were about to explode. He clenched his fists and glared at Joe as if trying to figure out whether to strike with his left hand or his right. If he did either, Joe thought, there would be trouble, and he'd likely come out on the worst end of it.

Hank said, "You've had a few beers, I can tell. And I can see you've been listening to Robey Hersig over there, hearing how Arlen should get the ranch and I shouldn't. So I'll let this go for now, and pretend you don't know what the hell you're talking about. Which you don't. But let me tell you something, Game Warden."

Hank paused, letting the clock tick. Eventually, Monroe turned his head to hear what he had to say. Joe was rapt.

"The Thunderhead will be mine," Hank said. "Nothing you, or your lovely wife, or anybody can do about that. So get used to it."

Then Hank leaned forward on his stool, looking up at Joe under scarred eyebrows, and said, "My family was here a hundred years before you were a gleam in your daddy's eye. We *own* this place. We *stuck*. The rest of you come and go, like lint. Goddamned *lint*. So don't poke your nose where it doesn't belong. This ain't your fight."

He swiveled on his stool, turned his back to Joe, and sipped at his glass of bourbon.

Joe felt Robey tugging at his sleeve, saying, "Let's sit down."

But Joe found himself staring at the back of Hank's sweat-stained Stetson, and thought of his daughter looking at the animal pinned to his front door. He said, "It better not

have been you, Hank. And by the way, we got a call on you.
I'll be out to see you soon."

For the first time, Joe saw a slight flicker of fear in
Hank's face in the mirror.

THEY FINISHED THEIR beers, and Robey spent most of the
time telling Joe not to react, not to get mad, but to cool
down and let the process work. Joe only sort of listened. He
was furious that Hank had gotten the best of him, and even
angrier that he'd opened himself up to it. He knew better
than to create a confrontation when he was unprepared. But
something in Hank's eyes and demeanor had told Joe that
he knew more than he let on. So if for no other reason than
knowing that, it had been worth it.

The night went on. Robey was drunk, and repeating
himself about the curse of the third generation. Joe called
Marybeth on his cell phone, woke her up, and said he'd be
home soon. She was groggy, and not happy with him.

Hank left the Stockman without looking back, although
Monroe paused at the door and filled it, glaring at Joe, letting cold air in, which normally would have resulted in
shouts from the patrons. But because Monroe was with
Hank Scarlett, no one said a word.

JOE LEFT WITH Robey, and they both marveled at the
night itself, how two grown men with families had drunk
the night away, how unusual it was for them. They blamed
the Scarletts for creating a situation where they felt it
necessary—even justified—to do so. Robey started in on a
soliloquy about drinking in general, and how intrinsic it
was to living in the mountain west, how *important* it was to
understanding the culture and isolation, but Joe said good
night and sent him home, wishing there were a cab he

could call for his friend, but taxis didn't exist in Saddlestring.

As he searched for the ignition key on his key ring in the dark in the tiny parking lot behind the Stockman, Joe had an almost disembodied reaction to the sound of approaching footfalls crunching through the gravel, each step gaining in volume, realizing at the last possible second that someone was upon him. He turned with a frown and glimpsed the flash of a meaty fist in the moonlight before it struck him full in the face, the blow so powerful that his world went red and spangling white and his head snapped back and cracked the driver's-side window of his pickup. He staggered to his left and felt his legs wobble, sidestepping furiously to regain his balance. The man who hit him mirrored his movements and snapped another blow out of nowhere. The explosion Joe felt on his cheekbone was tremendous— it seemed to make his brain erupt with sudden flashes of orange. Blood flooded his nose and filled his mouth from the back of his throat, tasting hot and salty. His legs gave out, and he was down on his hands and knees, gravel digging into the palms of his hands, pebbles under his skin. The attacker stepped back and delivered a kick to Joe's stomach as if kicking an extra point in football, and Joe felt himself momentarily lifted into the air. When he came down, all his limbs were rubbery and his bloodied face smash into the pavement. His ribs burned and he knew instinctively that a few of them might be broken. He thought: *Get under the truck.* Roll out of harm's way. But in his confusion he rolled the wrong way, his arms and legs askew, and he was farther away from his pickup than when he started. That apparently confused his attacker, who yelled, *"Stupid fucker,"* in exasperation as Joe found himself on the black Doc Marten lace-up boots, stopping Monroe from kicking him again. Monroe leaped back, getting clear, and Joe tried to rise but he couldn't get beyond a clumsy crouch because his bloodied head swooned, and he rocked back in slow motion and fell, splayed out like a gut-shot animal on the asphalt of the parking lot. Despite the booming pain in his head, Joe thought, *You've beaten me.*

He heard a shout from across the parking lot. Instead of another blow, he heard the slow crunching of gravel as Monroe walked away and Hank saying, in the shadowed distance, "Yeah, that's enough."

JOE WAS HELPED to a sitting position. He leaned back against his truck tire. His benefactor was Hank.

"Here," Hank said, handing Joe a bandanna from his pocket. "Use that to clean off your nose and mouth."

Joe took it.

"I called the sheriff a minute ago. Somebody ought to be here any minute."

"You called?" Joe asked.

"Damndest thing," Hank said, squatting down by him. "When I saw what Bill was doing, I told him to stop and he ran off. I don't know where he went."

"You said, '*Yeah, that's enough,*'" Joe said.

"Right."

"You said it like you ordered and approved of the damage so far."

Hank cocked his head to the side in an exaggerated way, said, "I have no idea what you mean, Joe. Bill was acting on his own there. If I could find that damned Bill, I'd be the first to testify at his trial that he attacked you for no good reason."

"Hmmm," Joe said, not believing Hank, but having no way to prove otherwise.

"'Hmmm,'" Hank mocked. "Maybe you shouldn't have called him a rental wrangler, or whatever it was you said. You must have really made him mad."

"Yup," Joe said, cringing against a headache that was barreling through his head from the base of his neck.

Deputy Reed pulled into the parking lot. He got out and bathed Joe in the light of his flashlight, said, "Who the hell did *this*?"

THE NEXT MORNING, a warrant for arrest was issued on Bill Monroe, age unknown, last known address Thunderhead Ranch.

13

ON FRIDAY EVENING, NEARLY A WEEK AFTER THE beating, Joe drove Sheridan to her sleepover with Julie Scarlett on the Thunderhead Ranch, his thoughts echoing what Marybeth had said: *This valley is getting too small.*

His body still ached each time he turned the wheel of the pickup, even though it turned out his ribs were bruised, not broken after all. But his right eye was still partially swelled shut, and his nose felt detached, as if it were floating around his face like a slow bird, trying to find a place to land.

Joe had spent the last week in the field, repairing fences and signage for public fishing access and walk-in areas. The maintenance needed to be done, but it wasn't urgent. The primary reason for keeping his distance from town was to avoid anyone seeing him and asking what had happened to him. He knew the beating was already a bit of a joke with McLanahan, who had worked long and hard on a description of what had happened, calling it, "The Fistfight at the KO Corral," which the sheriff thought sounded western and funny. In a response to an e-mail from Pope asking if Joe was, in fact, injured in a brawl, Joe wrote back: "It takes two to brawl. I'm fine."

While fixing signs and fence, he had seen no other people, which was how he wanted it. Instead, he stewed and thought about what had happened. He should never have challenged Hank without anything concrete to challenge him with. He had tipped his hand, lashed out because of the Miller's weasel. Hank was much too experienced in trench warfare, and Joe came off like a rank private. Looking back, he thought of the look in Bill Monroe's eye, a look of peeled-back hatred that still gave Joe the chills when he recalled it. And the humiliation of being beaten up hung over his head, darkening the sun. He was ashamed, humiliated, violated. The worst thing was when Lucy looked at him at the breakfast table and made a face similar to the one she had displayed when Maxine vomited a bag of jerky on the carpet. Or when Sheridan cocked her head to the side and asked, "Somebody beat you up? Jeez, Dad." It didn't help that Marybeth was quietly disdainful of what had happened, shaking her head and expelling a little puff of breath every time she looked at him.

EACH DAY SINCE the beating, Joe had called headquarters and asked for Randy Pope when his e-mails went unanswered. Joe wanted authorization to proceed on the 800-POACHER tip on Hank Scarlett. The director was out of state at a national conference in Cleveland, the receptionist said.

"They don't have telephones in Cleveland?" Joe asked.

That morning, before leaving his house for the field, Joe called again and got a message on the receptionist's phone saying she was "either on another line or away from her desk."

"Joe Pickett here," he said on her voice mail. "Again. Calling for Randy Pope. Again. Wondering if he realizes he has crossed over the line from bureaucratic micromanagement to obstruction of justice."

Joe had also called the sheriff's department throughout the week to check on the status of the investigation into Bill Monroe.

"That Bill done hit the highway" was how Sheriff Kyle McLanahan sized it up.

JOE GLANCED OVER at Sheridan as he drove. Her overnight bag and rolled-up sleeping bag were on the floor. She looked back with an expression that said, "What?"

"I'm taking you to the main ranch house, right?" he said.

"Uh-huh."

"And there will be other girls there?"

"A few."

"And the reason we're going to the main ranch house, not Julie's father's house, is that she actually lives at the main house, right?"

Sheridan nodded her head, as if she were engaged in a competition and speaking would make her lose points.

"Sheridan, I'm not crazy about this idea," Joe said.

"I know," Sheridan said.

"It was one of Hank's men . . ." He couldn't say *who beat me up.*

"I know," she said. "But I've never even seen Julie's father, Hank, on Uncle Arlen's side of the ranch."

Joe cringed inside. He didn't want his daughter to think he was scared of Hank, or Hank's man, and it wasn't just fright anymore. He knew he was capable of violence if he saw Hank or Bill Monroe again.

"I still don't see why you couldn't have had Julie to our house for a sleepover," he said.

"Because she invited me and some other girls," Sheridan said. "That's how it works."

Joe sighed. Recently, he had begun to encounter some

of the same intransigent behavior from Sheridan that Marybeth had been dealing with for the past year. Sheridan was closemouthed, sullen, and, more often than not, sarcastic. Where had that little chatterbox gone? The one who verbalized everything? The little girl who once provided play-by-play commentary of her own life in wild bouquets of words? Joe had to admit that her moods hadn't bothered him as much when they'd been directed at her mother. But now that they extended to Joe too he didn't like it. He always had a special relationship with his older daughter. Deep down, he thought it was still there. But they had to get through this early-teen thing. At the recent parent-teacher conference, Sheridan's English teacher, Mrs. Gilbert, asked him and Marybeth if they knew what was worse than an eighth-grade girl. They shrugged, and the teacher said, "Nothing on earth."

"ARLEN WILL BE around the whole time, right?" Joe asked.

Sheridan did a quick eye-roll, so fast he would have missed it if he hadn't been looking for it. "Yes. And so will lots of employees. Not to mention Uncle Wyatt."

"Maybe you *shouldn't* mention Uncle Wyatt," Joe said, trying to keep the impatience out of his voice. "He's kind of an odd guy, from what I can tell."

Sheridan said, "I'll avoid him. I always do."

"What about her mother?" Joe asked. He'd heard that Julie's mother, Hank's ex-wife, lived in a small cabin on the ranch in order to stay involved in Julie's life.

"I don't know. Probably."

"Sheridan," Joe said, exasperated, "what *do* you know?"

Which really made her clam up.

Joe said, "Sorry," and kept driving. He knew Marybeth had extracted enough information out of Sheridan to give the sleepover her stamp of approval. But he wanted to know the details too.

As he drove, the motor hiccupped and the check-engine light came on.

"What's wrong with the truck?" Sheridan asked.

"It's a piece of crap," Joe said.

THE MAIN RANCH house was a lumbering stone castle of a home with sharp gables and eaves and the look of a building that belonged not in Wyoming on a river but on some country estate in England. Towering hundred-year-old cottonwoods shrouded the home on all sides, the spring leaves having burst out just that week. Joe approached the home from the east on a firm graded and graveled three-track that snaked through heavy trees. He could see assorted outbuildings through the timber; old sheds, a tall barn that was falling down, an old icehouse built of logs.

As they crossed a bridge over a little stream made manic by snowmelt, Joe saw what looked like an old chicken coop tucked away in an alcove facing the road, and noticed the windows had glass in them and the roof had a new set of shingles. It puzzled him that the Scarletts would maintain a chicken coop, and he was about to say so when Sheridan said: "That's where Uncle Wyatt lives."

Joe stopped the truck.

"Wyatt lives in a *chicken coop*?"

"That's what Julie told me," Sheridan said. "He keeps odd hours, so instead of waking everybody up all the time, he lives in there. I guess he doesn't mind."

Joe looked at his daughter. "Are you sure you want to do this?"

Sheridan nodded grimly. She was of an age when the last thing she wanted to do was admit that her parents might be right.

"Julie's my friend," she said.

"We can still back out," Joe said.

"No. I'm not doing that."

. . .

ARLEN GREETED THEM in the ranch yard wearing an apron and cleaning his hands with a towel. There was a smudge of white flour on his forehead. He strode across the yard and stuck his hand out to Joe, who climbed out of his pickup. Julie was right behind Arlen, beaming at Sheridan and running around to her side of the truck.

"My God, your face," Arlen said, booming.

Joe looked over. Sheridan and Julie were packing the sleeping bag and overnight bag into the house and chattering. He wanted to talk to Arlen but didn't want the girls overhearing him.

For a few moments, Joe had forgotten about his injuries. After shaking Arlen's hand, he reached up and touched his closed eye with the tips of his fingers. Now that Arlen mentioned it, his face hurt again.

"That's what Bill did, eh?" Arlen asked, reaching out and cupping Joe's chin in his big hand so he could look closely at the damage. Joe didn't like another man touching him that way and turned away as if checking on Sheridan. That was something about the Scarletts that grated on Joe, he realized. These people thought they owned everything in the valley, even the game warden's face.

"Guess they haven't picked him up yet, huh?" Arlen said. "Does Sheridan know who did it?"

"Nope," Joe said. "Not by name."

Arlen said, "When Bill Monroe showed up a couple of weeks ago he came to me first to ask for a job. My impression of him was that he was trouble with a capital T. I turned out to be right. I guess when I sent him on his way he drove up the road and Hank hired him."

Joe nodded.

"I'm a pretty good judge of men," Arlen said. "Hank's got a couple of other new men over there I'd put firmly in the 'thug' or 'cutthroat' category. If I see Bill slinking around the ranch anywhere, I'll call right away."

"Arlen, let me ask you something," Joe said. "How safe is it here right now? I mean, with the problems between you and Hank, and Hank's new men? Do you feel okay about things?"

"Joe, it's perfectly safe around here," Arlen said, his voice low. "In fact, I'd wager it's safer than just about any-place I can think of. Safer than your own house, if you don't mind my saying so. I heard about that little gift on your door . . ."

Joe felt his face flush when Arlen said it. He'd never liked the implication that he couldn't protect his own fam-ily, and Arlen seemed to be implying that, if indirectly.

"Sure, Hank wouldn't throw me a rope if I were drown-ing," Arlen said. "But despite everything that's wrong with that guy, and it's a lot, he desperately loves his daughter. I don't blame him, the girl is a gem. Hank still pines for Doris, his ex-wife. Doris is in the kitchen in there now, helping me bake some nice bread," Arlen nodded toward the main house. "Hank wouldn't let anything bad happen to his wife or his daughter and by extension, to her friends. He wants them to think he's a good guy. He needs allies. He believes one of these days they'll all come to their senses and move back to his place." Arlen smiled at the absurdity of the notion.

"Besides," he said, arching his eyebrows, "not every man on Hank's payroll is loyal to Hank, if you know what I mean. If Hank was going to try something, I'd know about it well in advance."

Arlen's words had the ring of truth, especially that last bit of news. Arlen was a schemer, and he obviously had an informant in Hank's camp.

"What's the deal with Wyatt?" Joe asked, turning his head toward the road they had just come in on. "Sheridan said he lives in that chicken coop."

Arlen laughed. "It's much nicer than that, Joe. Wyatt's got it all fixed up now. You make it sound like he's sleeping in there with chickens. There are no chickens in there anymore."

"Still . . ."

"It's odd, I'll grant you that," Arlen said. "But Wyatt has always marched to the beat of his own drummer. The man just doesn't sleep, or when he does, it's for an hour at a time. He used to keep us up all night wandering around the house, puttering, doing his hobbies. Wyatt has a lot of interests, and almost all of them"—Arlen rolled his eyes, then settled them back on Joe—"stink. Everything Wyatt does stinks."

Despite himself, Joe smiled at the way Arlen said it.

"He's either making model planes and spacecraft, which smell of glue and oil paint, or he's tanning hides or reloading bullets. Taxidermy is his newest obsession. Those chemical smells can get to you."

JULIE AND SHERIDAN came back out through the front door with an adult woman in tow. She was dark and attractive, Joe thought, but there was something hard about her. Her eyes took him in. Her expression didn't reveal what her conclusion was about him.

"I'm Doris Scarlett, Julie's mother," she said, extending her hand.

"Joe Pickett." Her fingers were long and cool. She didn't wear a wedding ring.

"Nice to meet you," she said. "We're going to get these girls to bake some bread, and then some cookies. We thought we'd have a few more girls coming out, so we have more than enough dough to roll in there."

"Lindsay, Sara, and Tori can't make it," Julie told Sheridan, who had caught what Doris had said about the other girls.

Joe wondered if the other parents were concerned about

the situation at the Scarletts, or if it was happenstance that the other girls weren't there. He thought, as he often thought: *What would Marybeth do here?* He decided Marybeth would proceed with what they'd already decided, that Sheridan could spend the night with her best friend. Arlen had assured Joe things were fine. And they appeared fine.

"Nice to meet you too," Joe said to her. She smiled and nodded, and turned and went back into the house. Joe could tell the introduction was for his benefit, at Sheridan's instigation, to assure him that things were okay, that she and Julie were well supervised.

Arlen said, "When Hank and Doris started having trouble, Mother let Doris and Julie move across the ranch to the guest house. Hank doesn't like it one bit, but at least he can see his daughter from time to time. Mother really doted on that girl."

Arlen stood there, something obviously on his mind, making it awkward for Joe to turn and go.

Arlen said, "Now I've got a question for you, if you don't mind."

"Fire away."

"I heard someone called and reported my brother Hank had committed some pretty serious game violations. That he had illegal mounts and species displayed at his house. Do you know anything about this?"

Joe thought: *Now I know for sure who made the call.* But he said, "I got the report. I'm waiting on authorization to proceed." It embarrassed Joe to say that.

Arlen searched Joe's face. "Authorization?"

Joe knew he was on thin ice as he proceeded, Arlen being a new Game and Fish commissioner. But why protect Randy Pope?

"You might have heard," Joe said, as diplomatically as possible, "the agency director has assigned himself the job of being my immediate supervisor. He reserves the authority to okay my actions and duties."

"And he hasn't done so," Arlen said, his voice cold.

"No sir, in this case . . ."

Arlen turned on his heel and walked back to his house. "Wait here," he said over his shoulder to Joe. "I'll be right back."

Joe leaned back against his pickup, wondering what kind of trouble he'd just gotten himself in now.

SHERIDAN CAME OUT of the house to hug him good-bye. As he pulled her into him, he leaned down and whispered, "I can still take you home."

She stepped back and raised her eyes to him. "Dad, I'm the only girl who showed up. I can't leave. Don't you understand?"

Joe looked at her, wanted to insist she get her things and climb back in, but he saw his growing daughter in an admirable new light.

"Then at least promise to call immediately if you need anything, okay?"

"That would be easier to do if I had a cell phone," she said, her eyes triumphant.

"We'll talk about it later," Joe said, sighing.

Arlen appeared at a window on the second floor of the main house holding a telephone. He leaned out of the window, and gestured a thumbs-up to Joe.

"What's that about?" Sheridan asked.

"Hank," Joe said.

JOE SLOWED AS he cruised by Wyatt's chicken coop. The place looked dark and buttoned down, the window curtains pulled tight.

His cell phone burred and he plucked it from its mount on the dash and said, "Joe Pickett."

"Hold for Director Pope," said Pope's administrative assistant.

Joe smiled. That hadn't taken long.

"Pickett," Pope said brusquely, "I want you to proceed with that 800-POACHER tip as soon as possible."

"Gee," Joe said, "what's the hurry?"

Silence. Joe could imagine Pope gritting his teeth, having just concluded his call from Arlen.

"Just get right on it," Pope said.

"It'll have to wait until tomorrow."

"What do you mean it will have to wait?"

"I've got to get home and write up my daily report," Joe said. "My supervisor demands it by five P.M."

"Oh, for God's sake . . ."

"And you need to get me a new truck. This thing is ready to fall apart," Joe said, looking at the temperature gauge, which was in the red. "I don't think it'll last the month."

"*Another* truck!" he said, as if Joe were asking Pope to pay for it out of his own pocket instead of simply assigning another from the fleet. "We've had this discussion, I believe. You've damaged more government property than any other single game warden in the state, as you know. The damage case file we've got on you is . . ."

"I can't hear you. You're breaking up," Joe said, tapping the phone against the side of his head before punching off.

His visit to Hank would need to wait, Joe said to himself, until his daughter was off the Thunderhead Ranch.

14

THE WORD THAT POPPED INTO SHERIDAN PICKETT'S mind that evening, as the Scarletts sat down to dinner in the old dining room of the main ranch house, was *Gothic*. Ranch Gothic. Not the kind of Gothic she was used to, like those black-clad Goths in school who painted their nails and lips black and looked amazingly silly in P.E., but the older definition of Gothic, the kind she'd read about in novels. Until now, that definition had always been beyond her grasp, because she'd never encountered it. She never thought there was anyplace in Wyoming ancient enough or sinister enough to be considered Gothic. Until now. An image of Miss Havisham from *Great Expectations* wearing her wedding dress and riding a horse across the meadow outside popped into Sheridan's head. She almost giggled at the thought but she was too on edge.

· · ·

A ROILING BUT invisible cloud seemed to hang in the air of the dining room and throughout the house. She imagined the cloud to be made up of violent past emotions. The whole place, she thought, could use a good airing out.

The décor within the main ranch house had obviously not been changed—simply added onto—since it was built. The walls and wallpaper were dark and the trim ornate, the cornices were hand carved, each doorway a custom lark of intricate woodwork. Ancient wagon-wheel chandeliers hung from high ceilings on rough chains. The kitchen was big enough that when the cast-iron cookstoves were replaced by modern ovens there was no need to throw the old ones out. The dining room and sitting room were close and stuffy, with old paintings on the wall of Wyoming and Scottish landscapes. Sheridan had found herself staring at an entire wall of framed black-and-white photographs in the living room.

"This is the Scarlett Legacy Wall I told you about," Julie had said, sweeping her hand through the air. "There are pictures here of all of my relatives."

Sheridan had looked at her friend, expecting to see a smile on Julie's face when she said "the Scarlett Legacy." But she was serious, and much more solemn than Sheridan had seen her before. It was as if Julie had been schooled to be solemn in front of that wall the way a good Catholic would cross herself in midsentence as she passed by a cathedral.

Julie pointed out the photos of her great-great-grandparents who had founded the ranch, then her great-grandparents. Prominent within the display was a portrait of Opal Scarlett as a girl, the photo tinted with color to redden her cheeks and bring out her blue eyes. Even then, Sheridan thought, she looked like a tough bird. Her eyes, even through the blue tint, were sharp and hard and gave off a glint, like inset rock chips. In the photo, though, Opal had smiled an enigmatic smile that was disarming. Sheridan had only met Julie's grandmother a couple of times before and had never seen the smile.

The high school portraits of Arlen, Hank, and Wyatt were fascinating, she thought. It was telling seeing Julie's dad and uncles at ages more closely resembling her own, so she could look at them more as contemporaries than old men. Arlen looked then as he did now: handsome, confident, full of himself, and a little deceitful. Hank wore a fifties-style cowboy hat with the brim turned up sharply on both sides, his face sincere, serious, earnest, dark. It was the face of a boy who looked determined to stake a claim, a hard worker who would not be stopped. Wyatt looked big and soft, eager to please, proud of a mustache that was nothing to be proud of. Something about his face seemed wounded, as if he'd already met great disappointment. He was not a guy, Sheridan thought, you would pick first for your team if you wanted to win. Arlen would be, though, if the competition was a debate. And Hank would be the choice if there was a chance a fight might break out.

"Your dad looked cool," Sheridan said.

Julie nodded. "He can be," she said simply.

"But you live here with your uncle."

"I moved to be with my grandmother and my mom." Julie shrugged. "But my grandma, well, you know . . . she's gone."

AS SHE SAT across from Julie at the massive table that at one time fed twenty "strapping ranch hands," as Arlen put it, Sheridan felt as if she were in a place and with people who shared a mutual faded glory that she wasn't a part of.

She tried not to stare at Arlen or Wyatt as they ate, but she did observe them carefully. Wyatt tore into his food as if he were a starved animal. He pistoned forkfuls of food into his mouth with a mechanical fury, as if he couldn't wait to complete his meal and punch off the clock. Arlen was leisurely, urbane, continuously refilling his wineglass before it was empty.

Julie appeared to be oblivious to both of them, picking at her food. She seemed put out by something. She kept stealing glances at Sheridan, and Sheridan had the feeling she was somehow disappointing her friend.

Sheridan was uncomfortable. It wasn't the food, which was very good: steak, salad, fresh hot rolls with butter, garlic mashed potatoes, apple cobbler for dessert. Uncle Arlen was a great cook, and he told both girls so repeatedly.

It was interesting when Julie's mother, Doris, returned from the kitchen with a plate filled with the cookies Julie and Sheridan had baked. As she served Sheridan, Doris leaned down and spoke in a tone so low the others at the table couldn't hear her.

"This place used to weird me out as well," she said. "But you eventually get used to it."

Sheridan nodded but didn't meet her eyes.

BEFORE THEY WATCHED a DVD movie and went to bed, Uncle Arlen told them stories with a fire crackling in the fireplace. He was a good storyteller. He knew how to use words and inflection and would look right into Sheridan's eyes as he made a point, as if it were the most important thing in the world that she hear him and hear him now.

Sheridan had been seated next to Julie on a bear rug at Arlen's feet. The way Julie walked over, collapsed on the rug, and turned her immediate attention to her uncle suggested to Sheridan this Story Time was a very common occurrence.

"Tell about Grandpa Homer," Julie had asked her uncle. And he complied. About how Homer had to confront a bear ("You're sitting on it," Arlen said). How he fought with the Indians. When Homer stood up to the ranch hands—there

were dozens of cowboys living on the ranch back then—
and told them either to get out or shape up when they
threatened to walk off the job unless they got more pay and
better food.

To hear Arlen tell it, the Scarlett family had been involved in everything that had ever happened in the valley,
and in Twelve Sleep County, Wyoming. While haughty
newcomers either tried to overreach and failed or panicked
and ran, the Scarletts provided the grounding force. When
locals ran around like "chickens with their heads cut off"
about a drought, fire season, flash floods, or the fact that the
world seemed to have passed Saddlestring by, the Scarletts
were there to provide context, experience, and wisdom.
Sheridan was aware of how Julie kept looking over at her
as Arlen talked, as if to say, "See how lucky you are that
I'm sharing this with you?"

Arlen called it "oral history," and said he repeated the
stories to Julie over the years so she could continue the tradition when she got older. "It's sad that families don't hand
down stories anymore," Arlen said. Then, shaking his head
and clucking, he said, "Of course, maybe they don't have
much to tell."

That stung Sheridan, because at the time he said it she
was thinking she didn't really know much about her own
parents, where they came from, and therefore where she
came from. Well, there was Grandma Missy, but she reminded Sheridan of some of the popular girls in her school.
Missy was whatever she was at the time, but there wasn't
much more to her than that. Sheridan remembered her
grandmother being the aristocratic wife of a real estate de-
veloper turned politician in Arizona whom they'd never
seen. That's when she first knew her, when her grandmother insisted she and Lucy call her "aunt." Then Grandmother Missy moved to Wyoming, and now she was on the
huge Longbrake Ranch. She'd done okay for herself, but
Sheridan had no idea where she'd come from.

And she didn't know much about her dad. Until that moment, when Arlen said it, she hadn't given it much thought. Her dad didn't talk much about growing up, but Sheridan always felt that it couldn't have been too good. Once, when she asked him about his mom and dad, her grandparents whom she'd never met, he said, simply, "My parents drank."

She had looked at him, waiting for more that never came.

"That's one reason I wanted to be a game warden," he said at the time, gesturing toward Wolf Mountain, as if he were explaining everything. There was also a hint about a younger brother, who would have been Sheridan's only uncle. Something had happened to him. A car accident.

Unlike the Scarletts, who passed down everything, Sheridan's family seemed to be starting anew, creating their own legacy and tradition. She didn't know which was better. Or worse.

However, the longer Arlen talked, the happier Sheridan was that the family oral history in her household seemed to have started when her dad met her mom. What Arlen presented seemed to be too heavy a burden for a girl as shallow and frothy as Julie to carry on. It would be nice, though, to know more.

AS SHERIDAN AND Julie had gone upstairs for bed, Sheridan had noticed the pair of binoculars on a stand near a window in the hallway and had asked about them.

In response, Julie parted the curtain and pointed out across the ranch yard into a grove of trees, where Uncle Wyatt's chicken coop could be seen in the distance.

"That way Uncle Arlen can check to see if Wyatt is around," Julie said, as if it were the most natural thing in the world.

"My grandma used to tell me stories," Julie said to Sheridan when both girls were in Julie's room for the night.

"She'd tell me about my great-grandfather Homer, and my grandfather, her husband. And about my dad and my uncles. She had this really pretty voice that would put me to sleep. I really miss her, and that voice."

Sheridan didn't know quite how to respond. The Julie she knew from the bus and school—impetuous, fun loving, charismatic—was not the Julie she was with now. This Julie was cold, earnest, arrogant, superior—but at the same time very sad. She didn't think she liked this Julie much, although she did feel sorry for her. This Julie just wanted to tell Sheridan things, not have a conversation. Although Julie's monologues had, at first, been interesting, Sheridan had reached a point where she wished her friend would not make it so completely about *her.*

"You probably don't know what it's like to be a part of a famous family," Julie said. "I mean, if it weren't for the Scarletts, there would be no Saddlestring, and no nothing out there. Like, without us, you wouldn't even be here. No offense, of course."

"Of course not," Sheridan said, sarcastically.

"You don't have to be like that," Julie said, sounding insulted. "I'm just telling you what is, you know? That's what my grandma used to do. She made sure I knew I was special, and that my dad and uncles are special too. We have the Scarlett Legacy and nobody can take it from us. I'm the sole heir, that's what she told me from the time I was little, how special that is."

Sheridan simply nodded. This was going to be a long night.

"I miss her," Julie said.

SHERIDAN LAY WIDE awake in her sleeping bag on the floor of Julie's bedroom. Julie was next to her in a sleeping bag of her own. It was one of the rules of sleepovers: both the guests and the host slept on the floor, so there would be no jockeying or fighting over the bed. Sheridan could hear Julie's deep, rhythmic breathing. Her friend was asleep.

Sheridan felt both scared and guilty. The house itself frightened her, and she felt silly about it. What Julie's mom had said about "getting used to it" helped a little, but not much. The house was so big, so dark, so creepy. There were sounds, the soft moaning of old boards in the roof, the pop or squeak of a floorboard. She thought of what Julie had told her once about Uncle Wyatt rambling through the hallways in the middle of the night because he couldn't sleep. She wondered if he was out there now.

And there was something about how Julie, Doris, Arlen, and Wyatt looked at one another, as though they were sharing a secret. It was probably just intimacy, she knew. Her own family probably displayed the same thing to strangers, a familiarity so comfortable that others could only wonder what was going on. But in this case, she felt remarkably like an outsider.

Jeez, she thought, her dad had given her a chance—more than one chance, actually—to back out of this sleepover.

Now, though, she tried to persuade herself there was no need to be scared. It had been years since she had felt this way. She wondered if it was the house, or the odd way Julie had acted, those photographs, the dinner, what? Maybe a combination of all of them. She wished she had a cell phone. *Really* wished it. If she had one, she could call her dad to come get her.

Then the guilt came in. Where she once saw Julie and thought of royalty, it seemed what Julie had inherited was a kind of genetic disease. The poor girl had been reared by relations who disliked one another, a kind of parents' committee made up of her separated father and mother, her uncle, grandmother, and a number of domestics and ranch employees who treated her with barely disguised contempt simply for who she was. She grew up isolated from other kids, in the middle of a simmering stew of anger and resentment. That

she'd turned out halfway normal was a testament not only
to her mom but also to Julie herself. And it wasn't as if
Julie had lots of friends, even though it seemed like it at
school. When it really mattered, like tonight, Julie had only
one friend: Sheridan. No one else showed up.

Julie needed Sheridan's friendship and understanding.
Sheridan vowed to try harder to give it to her. She only
wished she didn't have the feeling Julie needed much more
than Sheridan could provide.

SHERIDAN HAD TO go to the bathroom but didn't want to
get out of bed to do it so she lay there in the dark, studying
the ceiling, wondering if she could hold out all night. And
deciding she couldn't.

She slid out of her bag wearing her pajama pants and a
T-shirt. Julie didn't wake up, even when Sheridan stepped
over her and took a thin fleece blanket from Julie's bed to
wrap herself in against the chill in the house. Opening the
bedroom door, Sheridan stuck her head out and looked
both ways in the hallway. It was dark, although there was
some kind of light coming from the first floor, down the
staircase. There was a bathroom at the end of the hall next
to Arlen's bedroom. Although his door was closed and
there was no light under it, Sheridan thought it best to go
downstairs to use the guest bathroom.

SHERIDAN PADDED DOWN the stairs in her bare feet,
wrapping the blanket around her. She found herself drawn
to the Scarlett Legacy Wall, and specifically to the tinted
photo of Opal she had seen earlier that night. It was one of
those portraits that drew you in, she thought. Something
about that woman's eyes and that confident but mysterious
half-smile. She broke away and quickly used the bathroom,
washed up, crept out, and shut the door. Since the bathroom

didn't have a cup near the sink and she wanted a drink of water, she followed the light.

The kitchen was empty and stark, and she had the feeling the light hadn't been left on by mistake. Then she saw the loaf of bread and a knife on a cutting board on the counter, the cold cuts near it, and wondered who had been up making a sandwich but wasn't there now. And she decided she was in the process of scaring herself silly, so she must stop it. The main house of the Thunderhead Ranch wasn't simply the home for Julie and Uncle Arlen. It was also the business headquarters of a large enterprise. Employees could come and go. Maybe one of them wanted a midnight snack, she thought. There was nothing frightening in *that*.

Nevertheless, when she heard a set of deep men's voices outside approaching the house, Sheridan reached out, grasped the handle of a steak knife from a collection of them near the cutting board, and pulled it inside the blanket. As the front door swung open and heavy boots scraped the hardwood floor in the living room, Sheridan had a choice to make: either dash through toward the stairs and be seen by the men, run out the back door into the ranch yard, or stay where she was.

She quickly reasoned that just as there was nothing wrong with making a snack in the middle of the night, there was nothing wrong with her getting a drink of water from the kitchen sink. But she would also keep the knife under her wrap, and return it later when the coast was clear.

She recognized one of the voices as Arlen's. The other was unfamiliar, a guttural but syrupy southern drawl. They were coming toward the kitchen. She would be caught unless she made the decision—*now*—to run out the back door into the ranch yard. She froze.

Arlen was saying, "So he's got all you boys building fence . . ." when he swung the kitchen door open and saw Sheridan standing there by the counter. He was obviously startled, and what Sheridan took as genuine anger flashed across his face for a brief second. Then his semiauthentic smile returned.

"Sheridan, what are you doing up?" he asked.

"I wanted a drink of water," she said as boldly as she could.

The man with Arlen squeezed into the kitchen behind his host, his eyes fixed on her. He was medium height, rangy, with pinched-together eyes, a taut skeletal face, and thin lips stretched over a big mouthful of teeth. His brown ponytail spilled down his back from beneath his hat over the shoulders of his denim jacket.

Arlen stepped aside stiffly, as if embarrassed by the situation he was in. "Sheridan, this is Bill," he said.

"Bill Monroe," the man said. "It's a pleasure to meet you, Sheridan Pickett."

His voice, Sheridan thought, chilled her to the bone—and the way he looked at her, with familiarity even though she was sure she had never seen him before. She was glad she had the knife hidden under the blanket in her fist.

Then it hit her. "How'd you know my name is Pickett?" she asked.

The question made the man blink, as if it startled him. Uncle Arlen looked over, intrigued.

"Why, everybody's heard of Sheridan Pickett," the man said, making a lame joke as if he were saying the first thing that popped into his mind while trying to think of something better. "Actually, I believe Arlen here might have said your name."

Sheridan didn't reply, and felt threatened the way Monroe looked at her, with a kind of leering familiarity.

"I don't remember saying anything," Arlen said. "But whatever . . ."

"Or maybe I heard it from Hank," the man said with sudden confidence, as if he liked this version much better. "Yeah, I heard it from Hank. You're a friend of Julie's, right?"

"Right," Sheridan said.

Bill Monroe nodded knowingly, then tilted his head to the side without once taking his eyes off her. "That's what it is," he said. There was an awkward silence. Sheridan wanted to leave, but the men crowded the door. Obviously, Arlen expected her to go back to bed. Bill Monroe—who knew what he wanted? Whatever it was, he wouldn't stop staring at her, sizing her up. He scared her to death.

Then she thought: the man knows both Arlen *and* Hank, and knows them well enough that he could say Hank's name in Arlen's house without retribution. What did that mean?

Finally, Arlen said, "Well, Sheridan, did you get your drink? You can take a glass of water upstairs with you if you want. I was about to make a couple of sandwiches for Bill and me while we talked a little business. Can I make you one?"

"No, thank you," Sheridan said.

"Good night," Arlen said, stepping aside as she sidled around the counter and headed for the doorway.

" 'Night," she replied. She was close enough to Bill Monroe as she passed to smell him—tobacco smoke, dust, and bad sweet cologne.

"Pleasure to meet you," Bill Monroe said to her back.

As she went up the stairs, she looked over her shoulder to see him watching her carefully, a hint of a smile on his lips, and for a second it felt as if a bolt of electricity had shot through her.

WHEN SHE AWOKE she could hear Julie still sleeping beside her, a burr of a snore in her breathing. Her dreams had been awful, once she finally got to sleep. In one, a vivid dream, Bill Monroe was outside their house, on the lawn, looking through the window at Lucy and her as they slept.

In another dream, Sheridan went back out into the hallway in the dark to where the window was and parted the curtain. A yellow square could be seen through the distant trees, the light from Wyatt's chicken coop.

She raised the eyepieces of the binoculars to her eyes and adjusted the focus tight on the square. Then something or somebody passed by the window inside, blocking out the light like a finger waved in front of a candle flame. And when the person passed, she could see the slightly smiling face of a woman, her expression paused in mid-conversation.

It was Opal Scarlett.

15

EARLY THE NEXT MORNING, IN THE CHILLED HIGH-altitude predawn, J. W. Keeley labored up a rocky hillside on the western slope of Wolf Mountain with a bucket full of creek water in each hand. He walked carefully, the soles of his Docs slick in the dew on the grass, trying not to slosh water on his pant legs.

When he reached his pickup he lowered the buckets to the ground, then rubbed his gloved hands together hard, trying to work the soreness out of them from the bucket handles. It would be a little while before the sun broke over the mountain and he could see well enough to finish up.

While he waited, he leaned over the hood of his pickup and raised the binoculars to his eyes. Over a mile away were the house, the garage, the little barn, the single blue pole light. As the sky lightened, the white picket fence around the front lawn began to emerge. He couldn't see much behind the place yet. He knew there was a steep hill, and a red-rock arroyo back there.

Inside the house, the family slept. Except for the oldest girl, of course. She was still at the Thunderhead Ranch.

Keeley lowered the field glasses and used the back of his glove to soak up the snot running out of his nose. He would never get used to the cold, he thought. Even when it should be nearly summer, when the grass was coming up and the trees were budding, it still dipped below freezing most nights. Sure, it got warm fast once the sun came out. In fact, it heated up so quickly and with such thin-air intensity that he found himself short of breath at times. It felt as if there were nothing between him and that sun, nothing to mute the heat and light. Like *air,* for example.

He wished it weren't so far down the slope to the little creek. He'd need to make a few more trips with those buckets. He had a mess to clean up. The bed of his pickup was wet and sticky with blood and clumps of hair.

MORE THAN ONCE since he'd been in the Bighorns, he thought about that cowboy in the Shirley Basin, the one he'd shot. When he recalled that morning, he shook his head and looked at the ground, not out of remorse but because an act like that was such a bold and reckless chance to take. A smile would break across his face and he had to make sure no one was looking, because he was infused with the kind of raw dark joy that he'd felt only once before in his life, with that hunter from Atlanta and his wife.

But that cowboy, well, maybe that had not been the smartest thing. There was a highway within view, and someone could have seen him. Hell, there could have been someone in the cowboy's truck, waiting for him. Keeley hadn't checked out that possibility at the time.

That he had just raised the rifle and shot the way he did, as easy as it was, as slick as it was, man . . .

Maybe it was smart after all, he figured. Anyone investigating the shooting would look at the cowboy's friends and family, try to figure out who didn't like him, whom he owed money to, that sort of thing. The randomness of the act accomplished a couple of things. It reminded Keeley that he had ultimate power over those who fucked with him. Anybody could get angry, or let himself be insulted. But it took someone with big brass balls to do anything about it. Recalling that morning made him think harder about what he was doing, and what he was about to do. He couldn't be impulsive again, for one thing. No more lashing out, no outbursts. He had to be cool and smart.

That was the difference, after all, between him and those assholes in Rawlins, even the late Wacey Hedeman. Damn, he wished he'd been there to see *that,* when Wacey took his last chew. It wasn't quite the same thrill when it happened offstage, even though in the end the result was the same.

LUCK WAS HIS lady, though. Luck and cool and a purpose. They'd all come together, like whiskey, ice, and water to form something perfect. For five long hot years at Parchman Farm, Mississippi's only maximum security prison, he'd had to just fucking sit there and stew. The more the rage built inside, the colder he got on the outside. He'd learned about what happened to his brother Ote through a letter from their mother. Two years later, after Mama died, he found out about Jeannie and April from his shit-for-brains lawyer. While he cooled his heels at Parchman Farm, what remained of his family was being taken from him one by one and there was nothing he could do about it. His frustration and anger was white-hot, and in some ways it was the purest emotion he'd ever felt. But he channeled it, tucked it inside himself. And waited. His reward for holding his emotion in, he felt, was coming now. Events were finally breaking in his favor. Getting hired by Hank Scarlett within a day of hitting town, what was the likelihood of that? Plus, Keeley knew how this small-town stuff worked. Normally, he would have attracted a little bit of attention, being so different and all. But two things were happening. One, the coal-bed methane companies were hiring just about any warm body they could find, so there were lots of new faces in town. Hard men, like himself. Many were from the South, like him. Second, the feud between Hank and Arlen took center stage in Twelve Sleep County, and the new men Hank was hiring were lumped into the category of thugs. No one cared about the individual makeup of Hank's private little army, just the fact that the army existed.

Keeley couldn't imagine any other scenario in which he could have been hired as a ranch hand with practically no ranching experience. The closest he'd ever come to cows, he thought, was eating a cheeseburger. But Hank had looked him over the way a coach evaluates on-field talent, said the word *sinewy,* then asked his name.

"Bill Monroe," Keeley had said, thinking of the first name that popped into his head.

"Bill Monroe," Hank repeated, "you've got yourself a job."

One of these days, Keeley thought, somebody was going to be a bluegrass fan and ask him twice about his name. But so far it hadn't happened.

THERE HAD BEEN that morning two weeks ago, Keeley recalled, when he watched Joe Pickett through the scope of his rifle and nearly pulled the trigger. Hank had sent him out to drive the fence line and check the locks. The game warden was out counting deer when Keeley saw the familiar green pickup. Hunkering down in a tangle of brush, Keeley placed the crosshairs of the rifle scope on Joe Pickett's nose.

The game warden seemed to sense he was being watched, the way he looked around. But he never saw Keeley.

It would have been simple. Easier than the cowboy. The

game warden would never even know what hit him. Keeley had flipped the safety off, pressed his cheek harder into the stock of the rifle, and begun to squeeze the tigger . . .

Then he thought better of it. That was the problem; it was way too easy. He didn't want to kill him from a distance, without Pickett knowing who had done it or why. The why was important.

Even the week before, when he had Joe Pickett down on the pavement behind the Stockman bar, it would have been easy to stomp him to death. Hank couldn't have stopped him.

But he didn't want to just kill the man. He wanted to destroy him first. That would take more time.

IT HAD BEEN quite a surprise to meet Joe Pickett's daughter the night before, Keeley thought. She was kind of a little cutie, he had to admit. Too bad he couldn't see her better, but she was all wrapped up in that blanket that way.

How old did Arlen say she was? Fourteen? That would be about right.

Then he thought: April Keeley would be twelve if she were alive today.

But she wasn't.

And he knew who was responsible for that.

IT HADN'T TAKEN Keeley long to size up the situation on the Thunderhead Ranch. It was Hank versus Arlen, and Hank was hiring. Hank's employees would be expected to do a hell of a lot more than ranch work if it came to it. There were standing orders to confront any of Arlen's men if they were stupid enough to cross over to the east side of the ranch for anything. There had already been a few spitting contests of sorts, with Hank's men threatening Arlen's men and vice versa. Keeley had taken out some dumb Mexican irrigator who was working for Arlen. The Mexican never even knew what hit him. He just woke up in Twelve Sleep County Medical with a concussion from a two-by-four.

Keeley was lying low since he'd thumped the game warden. By working for Hank in the open and Arlen behind the scenes, Keeley had assured himself he would be in the middle of anything that happened between the two brothers, and he might be able to use his unique position to manipulate the outcome. He knew he had stumbled upon a great opportunity. And not only was he smarter than those dickweeds down in Rawlins, Keeley thought, he was also smarter than those two brothers.

NATE ROMANOWSKI. KEELEY had heard the name spoken in quiet tones enough times around the ranch and in the bars in town that he was concerned. This Romanowski guy was a friend of Joe Pickett's and he wasn't someone to screw around with. He was rumored to be behind the murders of two men, one being the former county sheriff. Hank said he'd heard Romanowski carried a .454 Casull handgun made by Freedom Arms, the second-most-powerful pistol on earth, and he could hit what he was aiming at up to a mile away.

But Romanowski was nowhere to be found. No one had seen him in six months, and with the outlaw falconer gone or missing, Keeley knew it would be easier to get to the game warden.

KEELEY WAS RINSING off his knife and bone saw in one of the buckets when he noticed movement at the house on Bighorn Road. Yup, someone had turned on the porch light.

He put the saw and knife on the tailgate of his truck, wiped his hands dry on his jeans, and picked up the binoculars again. He focused on the front door.

. . .

AT THE SAME moment on the Thunderhead Ranch, there was a shout.

"Girls, time to get up," Arlen called from downstairs. "What do you want for breakfast?"

Julie moaned and rubbed her eyes. "Are you hungry, Sherry?"

"No," Sheridan said, rolling over, feeling the hardness of the steak knife under the sleeping bag where she'd hidden it the night before. "I had a really bad dream. I just want to go home."

Which was true.

As Julie dressed, Sheridan peeled back the bag and looked at the knife in the morning light, feeling suddenly sick. She let the flap drop back over it before Julie could see what she had been doing.

"You don't look good," Julie said, looking over while she brushed her hair. "Your face is completely white."

"I don't feel very good all of a sudden."

"What's wrong?"

Sheridan hesitated. Should she tell her? She knew at that moment that no matter what, things would never be the same between her and Julie Scarlett.

No, she decided, she couldn't tell her that the knife she'd taken from the kitchen matched the one that had pinned the Miller's weasel to her front door.

16

"I'LL GET THE PAPER IF YOU'LL MAKE COFFEE," JOE said to Marybeth as he yawned, snapped on the porch light, and looked outside through the window on the front door.

"You've got yourself a deal," Marybeth said from the kitchen. Then: "You're up early."

"Couldn't sleep," he said, sitting on a bench to pull on his boots.

"What were you worried about?" she asked.

He smiled. She knew him so well. If he couldn't sleep it was because he was concerned about something. Nothing else ever kept him awake.

"I hope it wasn't Sheridan's sleepover," Marybeth said.

Joe had to proceed cautiously here. In fact, it had been about Sheridan's sleepover. He kept thinking his daughter was in over her head with the Scarletts, but that she would never admit it. Something was brewing besides coffee, he thought.

"Just a lot of things," Joe said.

He clamped on his cowboy hat and cinched the belt on his bathrobe against the morning chill and was three strides down the cracked concrete pathway in his front yard when he realized he was being watched. He froze, and felt the hair on his neck stand on end.

He looked quickly at the road. There were no vehicles on it, and no one was parked. Wolf Mountain, still in shadow, loomed to the north, dominating the view. Then he felt more than saw something in his peripheral vision. Something big and black, hanging above the ground. Joe snapped his head to the side.

Then to the other side.

For a moment, he thought he was surrounded and he wished he'd brought his weapon.

He realized what it was, and his stomach surged and he felt sick.

Four elk heads—the Town Elk—had been mounted on the posts of his picket fence, facing inward toward his lawn. Toward him. The tongue of the big bull elk stuck out the side of its mouth, pink and dry. All eight cold black eyes were open.

Joe tried to swallow, but couldn't.

Whoever had done this had hit him where he lived in more ways than one. Not only had he killed and beheaded four popular animals in Saddlestring that he was responsible for, but he'd brought the heads out to his own home and stuck them on posts to taunt him. To humiliate him. To frighten him and his family. He was telling Joe nothing was off-limits, and that he didn't fear or respect him. He was bringing it right to him, and shoving it in his face in front of his family.

He was disgusted as well as angry. Who in the hell was he up against who would do something like this?

"Joe?" Marybeth was at the door.

His first impulse was to run back and physically turn her around before she could see the heads.

"Oh My God," she whispered. "Joe . . ."

He was too late.

In the distance, above the thumping of his own heart and Marybeth's gasps, he could hear an engine start up. They were being watched by someone, all right.

Unfortunately, Wolf Mountain was covered by a spider's web of old logging roads. Unless he knew specifically where the vehicle had been parked, he would never be able to track the driver or drivers down.

"Who is doing this to us?" Marybeth asked.

"I don't know."

"Joe, what can we do about it?"

"I don't know that either," he said.

"I hope you get rid of those things before Lucy gets up and sees them."

Joe nodded.

"This is awful," she said. "It's getting worse."

"Yup."

"What if he doesn't stop?"

Joe went to Marybeth and took her in his arms.

"Joe, what if he doesn't?" she said into his shoulder.

"He'll stop," Joe said, with no confidence in his words.

A FEW MINUTES later, Marybeth came out the front door again to find her husband walking across the lawn in his robe, cowboy hat, and boots, holding a severed elk head aloft by the antlers.

"Come in and get dressed, Joe," she said, distressed. "Look at yourself. What if someone drives by and sees you?"

Instead of answering, Joe held the head up. "This really pisses me off, Marybeth."

"Come in, Joe . . ."

. . .

JOE WAITED FOR the dispatcher to patch him through to the sheriff, who was having morning coffee with the rest of the "morning men" at the Saddlestring Burg-O-Pardner.

He drawled, "Sheriff McLanahan. What can I do you for, Joe?"

"Somebody cut the heads off of four elk and stuck them on my fence," Joe said. "They were the Town Elk. All four of them."

"Jeez," McLanahan said. "I was beginning to really like those critters."

"They're all dead now. You want to come look at them?"

"Naw," McLanahan said. "That ain't necessary. I seen plenty of elk heads before. Shoot, they're on just about every wall in town!"

"Now they're in my yard."

"That's not very neighborly."

"No, it's not very *neighborly*," Joe said, loud enough for Marybeth to hear. She looked up and grimaced. "Sheriff, it wasn't neighbors. It was the same guy who pinned that Miller's weasel on my door. He's upping the ante."

"Are you sure it was the same guy? How do you know that?"

"It has to be."

"So you're speculating," McLanahan said, pronouncing it "speck-u-late-un."

"Who else could it be?"

"I don't rightly know."

"You 'don't rightly know,'" Joe repeated, feeling his neck flush hot.

Marybeth stood in the doorway, listening to Joe, shaking her head as if to say, *This valley is getting too small for us.*

KNOWING HE WOULD need a front-end loader to dig a hole deep and wide enough to dispose of the massive elk heads,

Joe angrily carried three of them into the back of his truck and drove them deep into the timber of Wolf Mountain, where he disposed of them. Although insects and predators would make short work of the hide, flesh, and soft parts, leaving only the skulls and antlers, the act of dumping the heads like bags of garbage went against everything he stood for. The last head he'd dragged behind his garage and covered with a tarp to ship to state forensics. It was possible, although not probable, that they could find a human hair or fiber that could lead them to the killer.

He was not in the mood for a cell phone call from Randy Pope. When Joe saw who was calling on the display, he considered not answering. But it was early Saturday morning. The headquarters office in Cheyenne was closed. It could be something important.

"Yes?"

"I'm at home, Joe," Pope said, not trying to disguise his indignation, "when I get a call from a sobbing reporter from the Saddlestring *Roundup*. She asks me if I have any comment on the slaughter of four elk in the middle of town. She says the bodies are in the park for all to see, but the heads are gone. She says little kids are bawling."

Joe closed his eyes. On the underside of his lids, he saw red spangles.

"She also tells me the sheriff said the local game warden says the heads turned up at his place."

"That's true," Joe said.

Pope hesitated a moment before shouting: "What in the hell are you doing up there? Can't you even protect wildlife *in the middle of your goddam town*?"

Joe couldn't think of how to answer that. He opened his eyes to the sky, hoping for a sign of some kind.

"This will hit the wires, Pickett. It's the kind of juicy story the press loves. Four poor innocent animals. And it will all come down to the fact that the local game warden can't seem to do his job. But they won't call you, Joe, they'll call *me*!"

"Somebody is trying to destroy me," Joe said, not liking the paranoid way the words sounded as they came out.

"I'd say that somebody is you!" Pope shouted. "Have you been out to Hank Scarlett's place yet?"

"No."

"Just what in the hell are you doing?"

Joe sighed. "Cleaning up the mess."

Pope was so angry he sputtered, not making sense. Joe didn't ask him to repeat himself. Instead, he closed the phone and threw it as far as he could into the trees.

Before he left the timber, though, he reluctantly walked back and retrieved it. He felt like leaving his own head in the brush. Pope, and most of the people in town, would probably endorse that concept.

FROM WOLF MOUNTAIN, Joe drove to the Thunderhead Ranch to pick up Sheridan. He was used to how Sheridan looked after sleepovers—wan and exhausted—but he quickly perceived there was something more to her demeanor. That's when she told him about meeting Arlen and Bill Monroe in the kitchen, and about the bad dreams she had when she went back to bed.

"Who?" Joe asked suddenly, startling her.

"Bill Monroe."

"He's the man who beat me up," Joe said.

"Oh, Dad . . ."

It tore him up inside, the way she said it. He wished he hadn't said anything. At that moment, he hated his job, hated what had happened in that parking lot, hated that Sheridan even had to know about it. And he hated Bill Monroe.

He thought: What was Bill Monroe doing in Arlen's

house? Wasn't Bill Hank's man? Then he remembered what Arlen had said about having an informer in Hank's camp. He also knew Arlen had misled him about Monroe's role.

When she showed him the knife she had taken from the Scarlett kitchen and hidden in her overnight bag, Joe pulled to the side of the road to examine it.

"It looks like the one that was stuck in our door, doesn't it?" she asked.

"Pretty close," Joe said, turning it over. The length and design were the same. The dark wood handle seemed more worn, though.

He looked up at her. "Sheridan, what are you thinking about this?"

She shrugged. "I don't know. I'll feel really bad if the knives are from the same set, but I'll feel bad if they aren't and I took the knife. I already feel bad about being suspicious of my best friend's family. Do you know what I mean?"

Joe nodded. "I know what you mean, darling." At that moment, he was proud of her for what she'd thought about and done, and profoundly sad for her what she'd discovered.

Joe asked about the dreams, hoping to change the subject. "So you dreamed you saw Opal Scarlett alive, huh?"

"Um-hmmm."

"What did she look like?"

"Are you going to make fun of me?" Sheridan asked, raising an eyebrow at her father.

"Nope," he said. "Remember when I promised to pay more attention to your dreams no matter how goofy they seem at the time?"

"Yes."

"I'm doing that. Just don't give me any woo-woo stuff," he said.

"She looked kind of pleasant, actually," Sheridan said. "Like a nice old lady. Nicer than I remember her. But I didn't *really* see her, you know."

"You're sure?"

"I'm sure. I just spent too much time last night staring at a portrait of Julie's grandmother on the wall. It's a pretty interesting picture. I let her eyes get to me, I guess, so when I finally got to sleep that's what I dreamed about."

"Bill Monroe is the name of a famous bluegrass singer and bandleader," Joe said. "Some people called him the Father of Bluegrass. Ever hear of the 'high lonesome sound'?"

Sheridan looked at him as if he'd swallowed a bird.

"Really," Joe said. "Dig in the glove box. I think I've got *The Very Best of Bill Monroe* in there."

She opened it and rooted around and brought out a CD case with a black-and-white photo of a man playing a mandolin in a suit and tie with a cocked cowboy hat on his head. "This looks awful," she said. "And it isn't the Bill Monroe at the ranch either."

"I didn't think it was."

"I wonder if they're related in some way?" Sheridan asked, turning the case over and reading the back. The look of distaste remained on her face. Joe was pleased they had digressed somewhat from their earlier discussion. He didn't like seeing Sheridan troubled.

"Listen to it before you decide," he said.

"Have you been listening to the CD I made you?" she asked.

"A little, not much," Joe confessed.

"You need to get with it," she said. "You need to know what's good."

"So do you. Put that on."

"Hmmpf."

Joe thought it was odd Hank had hired a man with a southern accent named Bill Monroe.

"Footprints in the Snow" filled the cab.

Sheridan said, "Ew!"

. . .

WHEN THEY GOT home, Joe wrapped both the steak knife he had found stuck in his door and the knife Sheridan had brought home and sent them to the state forensic lab. He attached a note asking the staff to confirm that they were the same brand and lot number.

17

BY LATE MORNING, JOE WAS CRUISING EAST ON THE state highway that bordered the Thunderhead Ranch all the way to the Bighorn Mountains. It was one of those schizophrenic spring/summer/winter May days when storm clouds shot across the sky in fast motion dumping both slashing rain and wet snow as if ditching their payloads in a panic, then darting away leaving sunshine and confusion, only to be followed by a second and then a third wave of clouds doing the same thing. There was something wildly adolescent about days like this, Joe thought, as if the atmosphere were supercharged with hormones and just didn't know what in the hell to do next.

There were five entrance accesses to Thunderhead Ranch from the state highway. Two were on the western half of the ranch, Arlen's side. The other three were on the eastern half, Hank's. The difference between the sets of entrances was Hank's gates were closed and locked with heavy chains and multiple combination locks. To get to

Hank's lodge, one either needed permission to enter via the state highway, or went through Arlen's side, where there were three different access roads. Joe didn't know the status of those roads, but assumed they had locked gates as well.

After his frustrating conversation with Pope, Joe had done a quick inspection and review of the gear and paperwork he might need to search Hank Scarlett's home. He put fresh evidence vouchers and envelopes in his briefcase, and made sure his digital camera and microcassette recorder were fully charged. He tossed two clean legal pads into his case for taking notes and making sketches, if necessary.

His plan was to call Hank and inform him that he wanted to come to his home for the purpose of doing a cursory inspection to determine if there was evidence of illegal mounted game animals. If Hank could produce documentation that the animals had been taken legally, Joe's investigation would be over. If not, Joe would proceed with issuing citations or, if the infractions were serious enough, arresting him outright and taking him to the county jail. *That* would certainly raise some eyebrows in town, Joe thought.

In Joe's experience, the only people who denied him permission to search were those who had something to hide. Simple as that. Not once had anyone refused him entrance who hadn't violated the law. In that case, Joe had always been able to obtain a search warrant signed by Judge Pennock in Saddlestring within the day and come back.

Pulling off the highway onto the gravel two-track that led to the second of three locked gates on Hank's side of the ranch, Joe parked, snatched his cell phone from the dashboard, and called.

The phone rang only twice before a voice answered and said, "Thunderhead East."

The voice sounded familiar, Joe thought. Deep, southern.

"Is this Bill Monroe?"

"Who wants to know?"

"You're answering a question with a question. Let's stop that right off. Again, is this Bill Monroe?"

Hesitation. Joe guessed Monroe had recognized his voice.

"You aren't supposed to be around anymore, Bill," Joe said. "Both Hank and the sheriff claim you left the state after attacking me. You pounded me pretty good, Bill. What I want to know is if it was your idea or if Hank put you up to it? Not that it'll matter in the end, when I arrest you and put you in jail, but I am wondering."

Silence.

"And what are you up to with Arlen? What's that about?"

Joe hoped Monroe wouldn't hang up on him.

"If you tell Hank about me meeting with his brother, there'll be blood on your hands. I'm the only one keeping them from going at each other."

Joe heard the truth in that. If Bill was Arlen's inside man, it was not a good idea to expose him. Yet.

"I'm making a deal with the devil," Joe said.

"Call it whatever you want."

"Bill, let me talk with Hank, please."

A beat, three beats, then a mumbled "Hold on."

Joe heard the handset clunk down on a table. He felt a wave of sweat break over his scalp. There was no way to prove it was Bill Monroe, he thought, unless he caught him outright. But the behavior of the man who answered was evasive enough that he thought he had his man.

He could hear voices in the background, then the heavy sound of boots on hardwood.

"Hank Scarlett," Hank said.

"Hank, this is Wyoming game warden Joe Pickett. We have an anonymous tip alleging you have game mounts in your home that were taken illegally. The tip also alleged evidence of violations that might have occurred in Alaska at your outfit up there. I'd like to come out to your place and have a quick look around to assure the department there is no merit to this tip."

"That's interesting," Hank said. "I bet I know who called."

"I have my suspicions as well," Joe said. "But it doesn't matter. The call was placed with some pretty specific details in it, and my director has authorized me to come out and take a look. Mind if I check it out?"

Hank didn't hestitate. "Yes, I mind."

Joe said, "Look, Hank, I'm at the gate to your place. If you'd send one of your men out here or give me the combination of the locks, I could be at your place in fifteen minutes and we can get this all cleared up."

"This is private property," Hank said, his voice flat. "Don't that mean anything to you?"

"Yes, it does. That's why I'm calling."

"Every entrance is locked. You can't come out here unless you bust the locks and enter illegally. And if you do that, I'll have *you* arrested, Mr. Game Warden."

He said it with such calm assurance, Joe thought. It unnerved him, but he continued. "Hank, is Bill Monroe still out there? I thought that was him who answered."

"Nope," Hank said. "Just somebody who musta' sounded like him."

"I can get a search warrant and be back out within a few hours. Are you really going to make me do that?"

Joe could almost feel Hank smile on the other end, that cold smile he had, the one he reserved for people beneath him. "Yes, Mr. Game Warden, I'm really going to make you do that."

And he hung up.

JOE SPEED-DIALED Robey Hersig and got his voice mail.

"Robey, I'm on my way down from the Thunderhead Ranch. Hank refused access, so I need a warrant drawn up as soon as possible and signed by Judge Pennock. And when I come back, I may need a couple of deputies to help look around, if you don't mind coordinating that with the sheriff."

Robey came on the line, saying he had just stepped into his office. Joe repeated what he'd left on the voice mail.

"I'm meeting with the judge this afternoon," Robey said. "Will that work?"

Joe said it would.

"I wonder why he's being so cantankerous," he said, then chuckled, "but I guess that's just Hank."

"Or he's guilty as sin," Joe replied. "And his friend Bill Monroe is out there too, answering his phone for him."

"Really?"

"That's another reason why I might need the deputies."

"So you don't do something over-the-top to the guy?"

"No," Joe said. "So he doesn't beat me up again."

JOE SPENT THE afternoon at his home trying to put epoxy over all the cracks and holes in his drift boat. He kept his cell phone on and in his front breast pocket. He was ready to drop everything on a moment's notice and meet the deputies at the entrance to Thunderhead Ranch.

Robey didn't call until a few minutes to five.

"The judge won't sign the warrant until he sees the documentation for probable cause."

"What?"

"That's what he said, Joe."

"He's never asked for documentation before. What does he want, the transcript of the tip? That's all we can provide him."

"I guess so."

"But a tip is a tip. I told you everything in it."

"Joe, I'm just the messenger here."

"Oh, I thought you were the county prosecutor," Joe said, immediately feeling bad that he'd said it.

"Fuck you, Joe."

"I'm sorry. What is it, is the judge hooked up with Hank? Or is he just shy about doing anything if the name Scarlett is involved?"

"Why don't you ask him?"

"I said I was sorry."

"I don't want to talk to you right now," Robey said.

"Robey . . ."

He hung up.

Joe angrily tossed his phone into the boat, where it clattered across the fiberglass bottom.

June

As is the generation of leaves, so is that of humanity. The wind scatters the leaves on the ground, but the live timber burgeons with leaves again in the season of spring returning. So one generation of men will grow while another dies.

—HOMER, *ILIAD*

I wished to possess all the productions of nature, but I wished life with them. This was impossible.

—JOHN JAMES AUDUBON

18

ARLEN SCARLETT WAS DISTRACTED. MARYBETH COULD tell. Though he was looking at her across her desk with the well-practiced face of an eager-to-please canine, his mind was clearly elsewhere. Even as she explained that she had broken Opal's code when it came to her record keeping for the ranch, something Arlen *should* have been ecstatic over, his mind was elsewhere.

The previous week, Arlen had shown up at Marybeth's office with five banker's boxes full of paperwork—envelopes, statements, invoices, files. He complained he could not make hide nor hair of them. Opal had kept the books on the ranch, he said, and she'd never explained to anyone how she did it. Arlen claimed he had no true idea if the ranch made money and if so how much, or if they were in trouble.

Marybeth had reluctantly agreed to take a look at the contents of the boxes to see if she could find a method in Opal's madness.

"It didn't really take me as long as I thought it would," she explained to Arlen, who looked at her but not really. The antenna of a cell phone extended out of a snap-buttoned breast pocket of his white cowboy shirt. Even though he never looked down at it or reached up for it, Marybeth got the distinct feeling the phone was what he was concentrating on, even as she spoke. He was waiting for a call.

"At first," Marybeth said, "I couldn't figure out why she filed things the way she did. It seemed like random collections of paper held together with rubber bands. Some of the papers went back years and some were as current as two months ago, just before she . . . went away. All in the same bundle. It was obvious she wasn't using monthly P and Ls, or any kind of cash-flow records to keep track of things. But we know Opal was not the type of woman to maintain haphazard records, so I figured there must be some kind of formula she was using. It came to me last night," she said, widening her eyes, trying to engage Arlen. "I realized she grouped records by season and category. It kind of makes sense, when you think about it. For example, you grow and sell grass hay, correct?"

Arlen nodded.

"Well, Opal's approach was to start a file with a receipt from the first hayseed purchased for a specific meadow and go from there. She's even put the purchase of a new tractor in that hay file if the tractor was used for cutting and baling. If one of your employees fell off the hay wagon and busted his arm, the workers' compensation hearing materials would be put in the hay file."

"We paid workers' comp?" Arlen asked, surprised his mother had been so progressive.

"No, of course not," Marybeth said, shaking her head. "Opal fought every single claim to the death. My point is that the only way to figure out what you've got here is to understand how Opal kept track of everything. It was her own system, and I still don't have everything figured out yet, but I'm getting there. There are a few bundles of invoices I can't assign to a specific project or category yet."

"You've done a great job," Arlen said. "I looked at that stuff for a month and couldn't make anything out of it. My lawyer looked at it for ten hours, which he charged me a hundred dollars per hour for, and handed it all back and said there was no logic to it. But you figured it out. Damn, you're good."

Marybeth thought, *Yes, I am.*

"So?" Arlen said.

Marybeth arched her eyebrows, not sure what he was asking.

"Are we making money?"

"You're making a ton of money."

"Did you find anything that will help me in my battle with Hank?"

"Actually," Marybeth said, "Hank's side of the ranch seems to make more money than yours. It's more efficient."

Arlen said dismissively, "You mean he's more ruthless."

"If that's possible," Marybeth said, thinking of the workers' comp claims.

Arlen's cell phone rang and he jumped in his chair, clawing for it. Marybeth sat back and observed. He plucked the phone out of his pocket and stared at it for a moment while it rang. She realized he was unfamiliar with it, and didn't know for sure how it worked.

"New phone," he mumbled to her. "The buttons are so damned small . . ."

But he pushed one and held it up to his face, tentatively saying, "Yes? This is Arlen?"

From where she sat, Marybeth could hear a loud, deep voice on Arlen's phone. As he listened, Arlen peered around her office. His expression was anticipatory.

"You're here *now*?" Arlen said, looking at Marybeth as if she should be as amazed as he was at the identity of the caller. "You're right outside on the street?"

Arlen signed off, dropped the phone in his pocket, and stood up. His face had drained of color.

"Meade Davis is outside," Arlen said, referring to the lawyer Opal was rumored to have worked with to develop an updated will. "He just got back from Arizona today and he says everybody he meets tells him we've been looking for him. He said someone broke into his office while he was away and stole a bunch of records. But he says he's got some news for me." Arlen was clearly excited.

Marybeth said, "You'd better go meet with him, then. Maybe we'll actually see a resolution to the dispute. Please let me know how it goes."

"I will," Arlen said, acting more nervous than Marybeth had ever seen him.

When he left her office his Stetson and barn coat were still on her couch, so she knew he would be back.

She stood up and watched him through blinds. He bounded outside and approached the dusty black Lincoln Continental that belonged to Meade Davis. Davis got out. He was portly, avuncular, with thinning hair and a white mustache and a quick smile. Arlen and Davis were of the same generation. Marybeth watched Davis shake Arlen's hand, then place his other hand on it as well, as if offering condolences. Then he shook his head from side to side, and Arlen looked momentarily distraught.

It looked to Marybeth as if Davis was delivering bad news. Marybeth was surprised, but not as surprised, it seemed, as Arlen.

But Arlen quickly recovered. He spun Davis around, threw an arm over his shoulder, and they started walking away, Arlen bending his head toward Davis, putting his face in Davis's ear, his jaw working, talking up a storm.

AN HOUR LATER, Arlen burst through her door. His eyes blazed.

"There *was* a secret will," Arlen said excitedly. "Meade Davis drew it up last fall. Mother gave me the entire ranch, as I knew she would. Hank gets nothing."

Marybeth was taken aback. But when she watched them it had looked like . . .

"Congratulations are in order, I guess."

"You can say that again," Arlen said, beaming.

"When I saw you outside, it looked as though Davis was telling you something awful. You looked unhappy with what he said."

Arlen stared back at Marybeth as if frozen against a wall by a spotlight. He regrouped quickly, and fully, threw back his head and laughed too loudly for the room. "When he told me his office had been broken into and the will stolen, I thought Hank had beaten me once and for all. That's probably what you saw. Then I realized that if Meade testifies to what it said, and what Mother's wishes were, it's as good as finding the will in the first place! You must have seen me before I figured that out."

"That must be it," she said, rising and holding out her hand. "Again, congratulations." She said it not so much for Arlen but for the rest of the valley.

19

AFTER THE DINNER DISHES WERE CLEARED AWAY, Marybeth and her mother, Missy Vankueren-Longbrake, sat down at the kitchen table with cups of coffee. Joe had called from somewhere in the mountains to say he would be late and he would have to miss dinner because someone had reported a poacher allegedly firing at a herd of deer. Marybeth found it suspicious that the night her mother came to visit was the night Joe happened to be late.

Missy had retained her previous name and added the "Longbrake" after marrying local rancher Bud Longbrake six months before, saying she liked the way it sounded all together. Sort of patrician, she explained.

Sheridan and Lucy were in their room, ostensibly doing their homework. Missy favored Lucy, and Lucy played her grandmother like a musical instrument. Sheridan seemed to hold both of them in disdain when they were together because she claimed they fed off each other and thrived in a place she called "Girlieville."

Marybeth had just told her mother about the Miller's weasel stuck to the front door and the elk heads on the fence the week before. Missy shook her head in disgust while she listened. Marybeth knew Missy's ire was aimed at Joe as much as the incidents themselves. It was no coincidence that Missy and Joe were rarely in the same house together. She tried to time it that way. The two of them had been operating under a kind of uneasy truce borne of necessity: they had to live in the same county and there were children and grandchildren involved, so therefore they couldn't avoid each other. But they did their best.

"SO WHERE ARE the elk heads?" Missy asked, raising her coffee cup and looking at Marybeth over the rim.

"Joe buried them somewhere out in the woods. I think he was ashamed of them."

"My God. You can't imagine some of the things people are saying in town," Missy said. "They loved those elk. The people can't understand how someone could just shoot them right under the nose of the local game warden."

"Mom, Joe's district is fifteen hundred square miles. He can't be everywhere."

"Still . . ." Missy said, sighing. That "still" seemed to hang in the air for quite some time, like an odor. Then Missy leaned forward conspiratorially. "I can't help but think it has something to do with the situation on Thunderhead Ranch. Your husband must have done something to make one side or the other angry."

Missy said *your husband* instead of using Joe's name when she was making a point.

"My guess is he angered Hank," Missy continued. "Hank would do something like that. I've heard he's hired a bunch of thugs to do his dirty work. I know Arlen pretty well and he's a good man at heart, a good man. He's the majority floor leader in the Senate, for goodness sake! We serve together on the library board."

"I know you do," Marybeth said, looking away.

"You don't have to say it like that. I've had several long conversations with Arlen."

"Mom, Joe and I have been here for six years and we can't figure out all the history in this valley with the Scarletts. No one can who hasn't grown up here. There's just so much to know. Yet you've been here two and a half years and you're an expert?"

Missy raised her eyebrows and narrowed her eyes. She had a glass doll-like face that belied her age. It tightened with arrogance. Marybeth hoped she hadn't inherited that particular look.

"Some of us have the ability to get to the bottom of things quickly." Her eyes flicked in the direction of Joe's tiny office, then her voice turned to ice: "Some of us don't."

SHERIDAN INTERRUPTED THEM when she brought her math book and work sheet out of her room and asked Marybeth to help her with a problem.

"Don't ask me," Missy said, raising her coffee cup to her lips with two hands. "Math is like Greek to me."

"That's why I didn't," Sheridan said brusquely.

SHERIDAN RETURNED TO her room with her homework and closed the door. There was a long pause as Marybeth felt her mother assessing her, wearing the most profound and concerned expression. It was a look Marybeth knew always preceded some kind of dire statement. It was another look Marybeth hoped she didn't share.

"I'm just thinking about the children when I say this," Missy said, "so don't take it wrong."

Marybeth braced herself. She knew what was coming by the tone.

"But given what's been happening here, with the dead animals and the severed heads and all, and the fact that whoever is doing this seems to be able to come and go as he pleases, I would strongly suggest—for the sake of your children and my grandchildren—that you pack up and move out to the ranch with me for a while."

Marybeth said nothing.

Missy put down her cup, leaned across the table, and stroked Marybeth's hand. "Honey, I don't want to have to say this, but you're putting your children in danger staying here. Obviously, there isn't much *your husband* can do to stop it. Whoever is doing this has no qualms about coming right to your home, literally, and doing these things. What if they get worse? What if whoever is doing this gets worse? Can you live with that?"

Marybeth sighed, started to speak, then didn't. Her mother had a point, and one she'd considered herself.

"I've got a five-bedroom ranch house," Missy said, "meaning we've got four empty rooms. You and the girls would be safer there."

"What about Joe?"

Missy made a face as if she'd been squirted in the eye with a lemon. "Your husband would be welcome, of course," she said without enthusiasm.

Marybeth nodded, thinking it over.

"You deserve better. My granddaughters deserve better."

"I thought this was about our safety," Marybeth said.

"Well that too," Missy sniffed.

MISSY LOOKED AT her watch and prepared to go. "Thanks for dinner, honey," she said, pulling on her jacket. "Please think seriously about what we spoke about. I'll talk to Bud to make sure it works with him."

"You haven't discussed it with him?"

Missy smiled and batted her eyes coquettishly. "It's not a problem, dear. Bud doesn't argue with *me*."

"Right."

"Right."

Marybeth nodded. She planned to raise the issue with Joe when he got home that night. It should be about an hour or so, she figured.

Sheridan and Lucy were now in their pajamas and they came out so Grandmother Missy could kiss them good night. Lucy was dutiful; Sheridan shot a glance at her mom about the good-bye ritual that Marybeth pretended she didn't catch. Missy turned to go.

Marybeth was behind her mother and snapped on the porch light as Missy opened the front door.

Missy froze on the porch.

"Marybeth, who is out there?" she asked.

Marybeth felt her legs almost go limp. Oh, no, she thought. What now? The way her mother asked . . .

She looked over her mother's shoulder. The porch light reflected back from the lenses of a pair of dark headlights as well as the windshield of a vehicle parked and pointed at the house in the dark.

"Someone's just sitting there," Missy said, backing up into Marybeth, "staring at us."

"Come back in the house," Marybeth said, stepping aside, thinking of the loaded lever-action Winchester rifle in the closet in Joe's office.

When she looked at the profile of the vehicle in the darkness, she recognized the squared-off roofline and toothy grille.

"*Oh my,*" Marybeth said, pushing past her mother onto the pathway that led through the lawn toward the gate.

She heard Sheridan come to the door behind her and say, "Who is it out there?"

"Nate!" Marybeth said over her shoulder.

"That's not Nate's Jeep."

And it wasn't, Marybeth realized as she went out through the gate and practically skipped to the driver's-side window. It wasn't Nate at all, and in an instant her fear returned, canceling out the surprisingly strong burst of elation. Instead of Nate Romanowski, a man she couldn't see well slumped against the window from the inside, his cheek pressed against the glass in a smear of drool.

Marybeth felt foolish for jumping to conclusions. She rapped against the driver's-side window with one knuckle.

Tommy Wayman sat up with a start, then turned and looked at her, his eyes wide for a moment until he seemed to recognize where he was, who she was.

She opened the door. "Tommy, are you all right? Why are you here?"

"Is Joe here?" the river guide gushed. She could smell the fetid smell of alcohol. As he spoke he moved in his seat and Marybeth could hear empty bottles clink at his feet.

"No," she said, stepping back.

"I saw her," Tommy said, his eyes comically widening, as if he'd suddenly remembered why he came in the first place and everything was just rushing back to him as he sat there. "I fucking saw her today!"

"Who?" Marybeth said coolly. "And please watch your language at my home."

"Opal Scarlett!" Tommy hissed.

"What?"

"Opal. *I saw Opal.*"

"I doubt that," Marybeth said to Tommy, then turned back to the grouping of her mother, Sheridan, and Lucy on the porch looking out. "It's all right," Marybeth said. "It's Tommy Wayman. He's drunk."

Missy gestured "whew!" by wiping her brow dramatically.

"I really did see her," Tommy said, reaching out and grasping Marybeth's arm, imploring her with his eyes. "I need to tell Joe! I need to tell the world she's alive!"

"You can wait for him out here or in his office," Marybeth said, hoping Tommy would chose the former. "He should be home anytime now. I'll call and tell him you're here."

"Tell him who I saw!"

Marybeth went back into the yard. This was the kind of thing she hated, these late-night adventures with drunken men who wanted to talk to Joe. Add this to the fact that someone was harassing them, and Missy's idea about moving to the ranch sounded better all the time.

"Watch out for that guy," Marybeth heard Sheridan telling Missy. "He throws old ladies in the river."

"I'm not an old lady," Missy said icily.

As Marybeth passed her daughter, trying not to smile at the exchange, Sheridan leaned toward her mother and said under her breath, "Nate, huh?"

Marybeth was grateful it was dark, because she knew she was blushing.

20

"SO YOU CLAIM YOU SAW HER EXACTLY *WHERE*?" Robey Hersig asked Tommy Wayman, who was drinking his second cup of coffee.

"I told you three times," Tommy said, raising his mug with two hands but not successfully disguising how they trembled. "At that big bend of the river before you get to the old landing. Closer to Hank's side of the ranch than Arlen's. She was just standing there in the reeds looking at me as I floated by. Scared me half to death."

Joe had been home an hour. When he heard what Tommy had to say, he called Robey and Sheriff McLanahan. McLanahan claimed he needed his "beauty sleep" and sent Deputy Reed, who was preferable anyway. The three of them sat around Joe's kitchen table because there were too many big bodies to fit in his office. Marybeth went upstairs to read and the girls were in bed. Tommy was at the head of the table, nursing black coffee. He had asked Joe for a little shot of hooch in the coffee to "cut the bitterness," but Joe had refused.

"She said something to you," Robey asked. "What was it she said?"

"No," Tommy said, shaking his head, starting to get angry at the repetition of the questions. "I said I *thought* she was telling me something, but I couldn't hear the words over the sound of the river."

Reed checked his notebook. "Earlier, you said she smiled at you. Are you serious? Is that *really* what you meant, that she *smiled* at you as you floated by?"

Reed looked from Joe to Robey and back to Tommy. He was clearly skeptical. "What kind of smile?" he asked. "A Hi-Tommy-happy-to-see-you-again smile? Or a Get-over-here-and-pay-me-my-fee smile?"

"Damn it," Tommy said, thumping the table with the heel of his hand, "that's what she was doing. And yeah, I guess it was sort of a, um, *pleasant* smile. Like she was, you know, happy."

Reed rolled his eyes toward the ceiling.

Although small details kept changing, which was very disconcerting if one wanted to believe Tommy Wayman's story, the basic tale was the same: The outfitter took his fifteen-foot Hyde low-profile drift boat out on the Twelve Sleep River to do some fishing of his own after a pair of clients canceled. He brought along his cooler, which had been filled with beer for three. Fishing was good. The beer was cold. Tommy landed nothing smaller than twenty-two-inch rainbows on dry flies. He lost track of how many beers he had drunk after counting eleven, and how many fish he caught after twenty. He may have even dozed off. Yes, he *did* doze off, which wasn't a good thing, generally.

Luckily, he thought to drop the anchor off the back of the boat before he settled back between the seats on a pile of life vests and took a little nap. No, he wasn't sure how long exactly. Maybe a whole hour. When he awoke he didn't know where he was at first. He raised the anchor and started to drift downriver, picking up speed. That's when he saw her. Opal Scarlett, right on the shore, standing in thick brush. But close enough that he could see her face, even if he couldn't hear what she was saying over the river sounds. He had drifted too far and was picking up too much speed to row back upstream to hear her words. Nevertheless, he had hollered back at her. "Turn yourself in, Opal, for Christ's sake! Everybody thinks I drowned you in the river!"

"You said she was closer to Hank's place than she was to her own house," Robey said to Tommy. "Doesn't that strike you as odd?"

Tommy was getting annoyed with the questions, and a hangover of industrial strength was starting to settle in, which made him even tougher to deal with.

"The whole fucking thing strikes me as odd, Robey," Tommy said. "What has she been doing out there for a month when she knows the whole county is wondering what happened to her?"

Reed reviewed his notes, sighing loudly. Tommy looked over at him.

"What?" he asked.

"When I first got here and wrote down your story, you said you were fishing and you looked up and there she was," Reed said. "Then, an hour later, you say you passed out in your boat, and when you woke up there she was. Now you say you were drifting downriver and picking up speed, and you didn't see her until you looked back and by then it was too late to go back. That's three different versions of the same event, Tommy. Which one are we supposed to believe?"

Joe had noted the discrepancies as well. Tommy was turning red. Beads of sweat were breaking out on his scalp.

"The last one, goddammit," he said. "It was the last one. The last version."

"That doesn't sound too credible," Robey said, sounding more sympathetic to Tommy than Joe expected him to be.

"And what exactly was she wearing?" Reed asked, not kind at all. "You say she was in jeans and a plaid shirt. What color was the shirt?"

"Huh?"

"What color was it? You said earlier it was a certain color. Do you remember now?"

Tommy looked down at his coffee cup and mumbled something.

"What was that?" Reed asked.

"He said 'light yellow,'" Joe repeated.

Reed rolled his eyes again. "Light yellow is the color of the shirt he originally claimed Opal was wearing that day he threw her into the river. Are we supposed to believe she's been wearing the same clothes for a month?"

"Yeah," Robey said, rubbing his jaw. "And I think you said earlier she was wearing a dress, didn't you?"

"If I did, I didn't mean it," Tommy said.

"Tommy Wayman," Deputy Reed said, snapping his notebook closed and shoving it in his shirt pocket, "you are full of shit."

Tommy moaned and sat back in his chair.

"I did see her, you guys," he said thickly. "I just can't remember all of the little details 'cause I'd been drinking."

Robey said, "Of course, it would just be a coincidence that if Opal were actually seen on her ranch then you'd be completely off the hook, right?"

Tommy looked from Reed to Joe to Robey and said, "Really, guys . . ."

"I'm out of here," Reed said. "You want me to give Tommy a ride back to his house?"

"Really, guys," Tommy said again as Reed helped him to his feet.

. . .

JOE AND ROBEY sat at the table. It was midnight, and Tommy Wayman and Deputy Reed had been gone for fifteen minutes. Joe had poured a bourbon and water nightcap for both of them.

"That was interesting," Robey said. "I thought for a minute there we had something."

Joe nodded.

Robey said, "I think he wanted to see her alive, so he did. She's probably on his mind all the time, since he could wind up in Rawlins because of her. He probably dreamed she was there while he was passed out, and when he woke up he convinced himself she was there. Tommy is losing it, is what I think. I hope he holds together long enough to go to trial. He's a good man, Joe. He drinks too much, but he's a good guy."

Robey looked up for a response. Joe stared at his drink, which was untouched.

"What? Something is bugging you."

"Sheridan said she had a dream about something similar to Tommy's. She said Opal was alive out on the ranch."

Robey stared. "A dream, Joe?"

"Hey," Joe said, raising his hand. "I know. But Sheridan's had some dreams that turned out to be pretty accurate. She's like Nate Romanowski that way," he said, wishing immediately he hadn't brought Nate into it.

"Speaking of . . ."

"Nothing," Joe said. "Honestly. Not a word."

MARYBETH CAME DOWN the stairs in her robe. Her blond hair was mussed. Joe could see one bare foot and ankle and she looked particularly attractive standing there. He was suddenly ready for Robey to head home.

"Are you guys about finished?" she asked.

Joe said, "Yup." He was glad he was the one staying. He wondered if Robey had the same thought and guessed that he did. *Go away, Robey,* Joe thought.

"Did Tommy have anything interesting to say?"

Robey chuckled. "That was the problem, Marybeth. He had so many interesting things to say—so many versions—that in the end he had nothing. It was a waste of time."

"Maybe I should have called Nancy to come get him," she said.

"You did the right thing."

"He scared us when we saw him out there," she said. "With all the things that have been happening around here, we're a little jumpy."

"I understand," Robey said.

Joe said nothing. It made him angry to think about it.

He saw Robey to the door. As they passed his office, Joe said, "I've been meaning to ask you about that search warrant for Hank's place. Do we have it yet?"

Robey turned, his face wary. "You haven't heard?"

"Not a thing."

"Judge Pennock refused to issue it."

"What?"

Robey nodded. "I'm sorry, I thought you knew. The judge said we needed probable cause, that the anonymous tip wasn't enough to search a man's home. Even though you transcribed the call real well."

Joe was confused. He'd never had a search warrant refused before.

"Judge Pennock and Hank are friends," Joe said.

"I'm afraid so. I didn't realize it before. They must be pretty close."

Joe snorted. "If they are close, Pennock would have recused himself. It's got to be more than that."

"I don't even want to speculate, Joe," Robey said cautiously. "I have to appear before Judge Pennock all the time. I can't push this one too hard or he could make my life miserable."

"Can't we go over his head?"

Robey suddenly looked very uncomfortable. "We could, but I hesitate to do so."

"You 'hesitate to do so'?" Robey's choice of words was so formal and bureaucratic that Joe repeated them.

"Look, Joe," Robey said, "there are things I will go to the mat with, as you know. There are some subjects, for example, I won't discuss with you because I don't want to know the answers. But this fight between Hank and Arlen . . . I don't know. It's so dirty, and so . . ." He searched for a word. ". . . *epic*, you know? I'm not sure how hard I want to come down on either side. And we're just talking about what? The possibility someone may have taken some animals out of season? That's not even a felony."

As Robey talked, Joe felt his anger rise.

"How about if we try to enforce the law," Joe said. "You know, on a lark?"

"Joe . . ."

"Enforcing Game and Fish regulations is what I do, Robey. I take it seriously, because I've learned if a man will do something illegal or unethical out in the field when no one is looking, he's capable of anything, no matter who he claims to be, or how big a man he is in the county."

Robey sighed, reached out, and put his hand on Joe's shoulder to calm him. "Joe, sometimes I think you take things a little too far, you know? It seems like you think bad character is a crime. Again, we're talking about some game animals that might have been poached."

"No," Joe said. "We're talking about looking the other way because we don't want to appear to take sides in a conflict. Well, I'm not taking sides, and I'm not looking away. I'm doing my job."

Robey shook his head. The silence grew uncomfortable.

"I'll run it by Tucker Fagan in Park County," Robey finally said, sighing, referring to the new judge there. "Thunderhead is so big it's in Park also, right?"

"Right."

"I'll do my best."

"Thank you, Robey."

"Good night, Joe. Sometimes you piss me off."

JOE AND MARYBETH lay in bed facing each other. They talked softly so the girls wouldn't hear them. Marybeth's reading lamp was on low and the light cast a buttery glow on the side of her face and softly illuminated her blond hair. As they talked she stroked his forearm, rubbing it with her thumb.

She had broached the subject about moving the girls to the ranch. Joe had grunted at the idea.

"I know you don't like it," Marybeth said. "Frankly, neither do I. But if this continues . . ."

Joe started to argue, but caught himself. There was no reason to think it wouldn't continue. And get worse. The sheriff's department had done nothing he was aware of to investigate the incidents. His hands were tied by Pope to investigate himself. But enough was enough. This was his family, and his wife was talking about *moving*.

SHE HAD TURNED off her light and shifted to his side of the bed in the dark, her hands moving over him under the covers, her lips brushing his neck and ear. Joe liked it. He smiled in the dark.

They both froze when they heard the sounds.

A two-beat noise, a sharp *snap,* then a tinkle of glass downstairs.

"What was that?" Marybeth whispered.

Then the roar of a vehicle racing away on Bighorn Road.

Joe shot out of bed, naked, and cast back the curtain on the window. There were no lights outside, and no moon. The starlight was shut out by cloud cover.

He looked right on the road, the way to town. Nothing. Then left, nothing. But he could hear the motor, so how could it be?

Then he saw a flash of brake lights in the distance. Whoever had been outside was fleeing without his lights on, and revealed himself when he had to tap on his brakes at the turn that led to the foothills and the mountains beyond.

But aside from the brief flash of brake lights, he could see nothing about the vehicle itself, whether it was a car or pickup or SUV.

He cursed for two reasons: he could never catch who had been out there, and whoever had been out there had destroyed the mood in bed.

"What do you think that sound was?" Marybeth asked.

"I'll go check."

"Put some clothes on . . ."

JOE SNAPPED ON the lights in the living room. He had pulled on his robe, and he carried his .40 Glock loosely in his hand. He could see nothing amiss. He might have to get Marybeth to come down, he thought. It was one of those male/female things, like his inability to notice a new couch or when his daughters got a haircut unless it was pointed out to him. Conversely, he could see a moose in a faraway meadow on Wolf Mountain when it was a speck and Marybeth wouldn't see it unless it charged her and knocked her down.

But when he walked near the front window, he felt slivers of glass dig into his bare feet and yelped in pain.

Then he saw the hole in the glass, like a tiny star. Someone had shot into their home.

He turned, visualizing the trajectory. The shot originated on the road and passed through the glass into the family portrait. Marybeth had arranged for it the previous summer. They had stood smiling against the corral fence rails so the mountains framed them in the background. In the photo, Joe thought they all looked a little uncomfortable, as if they were dressed for a funeral, and the smiles were forced. Except for Lucy, who always looked good. The portrait was slightly askew.

Joe limped across the living room, his feet stinging, and stared at the photo. The bullet had taken off most of his face and lodged into the wall behind the frame. Beneath the hole, his mouth smiled.

A chill rolled through him. Followed by a burst of rage.

Again, whoever was doing this had come right to his house and this time, in his way, he had entered it. The bullet hole in his face in the portrait was no coincidence. Joe thought, if Nate were around he'd ask for help now. But Nate *wasn't* around, and Joe was officially prevented from investigating.

Screw that.

Marybeth came down the stairs looking at the bloody footprints on the floor. She followed them to where Joe stood.

Joe said, "You're right. Let's get the kids. We're moving to the ranch."

"Joe . . ."

"I'm going to get this guy."

IT WAS ALMOST dawn when he felt her stir beside him. He was entangled, spooning, skin against skin, his leg thrust between hers, pulling her so tightly into him that he could feel her heart beat from where his hand cupped her right breast. His feet were bandaged. She was wide awake, as he was.

"It's so personal," she said in a whisper, "it scares me to death."

"I'll find him, Marybeth."

She didn't speak for a long time. As the minutes lapsed, he started to fear what she would say. He thought she might mention Nate Romanowski. That she wished Nate were there to protect them, instead of him. If she said Nate's name, Joe wondered if he could go on, because he would feel that he had lost everything. Their tight little family was the only thing that anchored him to earth, the only constant. A breach could tear them apart and unmoor him to a degree he didn't even want to imagine.

The sun slowly rose and backlit Wolf Mountain and fused the blinds with soft, cold gray light.

He was deep into melancholy when Marybeth said, "I love you, Joe Pickett. I know you'll protect us."

Despite the situation, Joe was suddenly filled with joy and purpose. He rolled over and kissed her, surprising her.

"What was *that* about?" she asked.

He tried to answer. The only thing he could come up with was "It's about everything."

But as he rose, the thought that they were running away came rushing back at him. And he hated to run.

21

SATURDAY BROUGHT THE GRAND OPENING OF THE SCAR-
lett Wing of the Twelve Sleep County Historical Society.
The day was fresh with early summer, aching with sun-
light, character provided by the new wildflower smells and
the first bursts of pine pollen drifting down from the mountains.

Joe sat next to Marybeth on metal folding chairs set up
in the parking lot of the museum. It seemed as if most of official Saddlestring and the county was there, including
Missy and Bud Longbrake, who sat in the row in front of
them and had saved seats for the girls. Although no usher
greeted each arrival with an extended hand and whispered
"Arlen or Hank's side?" the effect was the same, with
Hank's backers on the right facing the podium and Arlen's
on the left.

On the raised podium itself, Arlen sat comfortably in a
chair looking out at the audience, waving and winking at

his friends. There was an empty seat on the other side of the podium. The chair was for Hank, as both brothers were supposed to speak at the event. The closer it got to ten A.M., when the wing was to be dedicated, the emptier the seat seemed to be.

JOE HAD AWAKENED in a foul mood that continued to spiral downward as the day went on. It had started when he opened his eyes in bed, looked around, and realized once again that his family was on the Longbrake Ranch instead of in their own home. It continued through breakfast, as Missy held court and pointed out repeatedly to his daughters how many fat grams there were in each bite they were taking. His black mood accelerated and whipped over into the passing lane when he started to contemplate just how ineffectual he had become; how useless, how he was no better than the bureaucrats he worked with.

Then there was the message on his cell phone from Randy Pope: "You left your house? Don't you realize that is state property? What if it is vandalized even more while you're gone? Do you plan to take responsibility for *that*?"

Joe seethed as he drove.

He was tired of following procedure, asking permission, seeking warrants, waiting for instructions, hoping for help.

No one, except him, was going to get him out of this.

As he drove his family to the grand opening, Joe made a mental list of things that were driving him mad. While he did so, he vaguely listened to Sheridan tell Lucy about the incredibly boring English literature class she was in. They were now reading Shakespeare, she said. Suddenly a thought struck him with such force that his hands jerked on the wheel and Marybeth said, "Was there a rabbit in the road?"

"No," Joe said. "Something just occurred to me."

"What?"

"About Opal. Something I never thought of before."

"So . . . ?"

"Sheridan," Joe said, looking up into his mirror so he could see her face, "would you please repeat what you just told Lucy about the play you're reading? The one about the king?"

AS THEY WAITED for the ceremony to begin, Marybeth said, "I've been thinking about your new theory."

"Yes?"

"I'm not sure I buy it. Is Opal really capable of something that mean? With her own sons?"

Joe nodded. "Opal is capable of anything. Remember, she didn't have any qualms about stretching a neck-high wire across the river. And you untangled her books. You know how secretive she could be."

Marybeth shook her head slowly. "Joe, if you're right . . ."

"I know," he said.

Marybeth started to say something to him when she was distracted by the fact that most of the people in the crowd had turned in their seats and were craning their necks and pointing.

"Well, look who's here," Marybeth said.

"Who?"

Marybeth pointed at the black new-model Yukon that had entered the lot with a license plate that said simply ONE.

The driver's door opened and a big man with stooped shoulders and an easy smile swung out. He began instantly shaking hands and slapping backs. He moved through the crowd with a slick expertise, never stopping long enough to be engaged, but making eye contact with each person and calling most by name.

Marybeth said, "He looks like he's headed this way."

In a moment, he was right in front of them.

"Joe Pickett?"

"Yup."

"I'm Spencer Rulon."

"Hello, Governor."

"Call me Spence. C'mon, let's go for a little ride. Is this your wife?"

"Yes. Marybeth."

"Lucky man. Come along, Marybeth. We'll be back before the hoopla begins."

WYOMING GOVERNOR SPENCER Rulon drove and spoke with a kind of daredevil self-assurance that came, Joe thought, from being pretty sure all his life he was not only the smartest but the cleverest human being in the room.

"We've got ten minutes before I need to be back at the opening," the governor said, roaring out of the parking lot and onto Main Street, making the turn on what felt to Joe like two wheels. "Then I've got to take the plane back to Cheyenne right afterward. A pack of snarling Feds are coming to meet with me at four o'clock about the wolf issue. They're like hyenas when they smell blood, and since we lost that court case they're circling what they think is a dying corpse. But we're not dead yet. We'll win." He shook his head in disgust. *"Feds,"* he spat.

Joe fumbled for the seat belt and snapped it on securely. He shot a glance back at Marybeth in the back seat, who was doing the same thing.

Rulon looked over at Joe and flashed on his full-blast smile. "It's a pleasure to meet you, Mr. Joe Pickett."

"Likewise," Joe said, shaking the governor's proffered hand while, at the same time, glancing out the windshield as they drove through a red light. Luckily, there was no cross traffic at the moment.

"I've been wanting to meet you."

Joe couldn't think of how to respond, so he didn't.

"How is that Scarlett situation going up here?"

"Not well," Joe said.

"You know Arlen's the majority floor leader, right?"

Joe nodded, trying to keep up.

"He explained everything to me after the session. About his brother and all. What a clusterfuck that is, eh?" Then he glanced in the rearview mirror and said, "Sorry for the inappropriate language, ma'am."

"It's quite all right," Marybeth said. "It's a perfect description."

"JESUS CHRIST!" the governor howled, hitting the brakes. "Did I just drive through a red light back there?"

Joe said, "Yes. It's our only one."

"Then why the hell didn't you say something?" Rulon asked. "Why did you just sit there and watch me do it? And when did Saddlestring get a light?"

"We were through it before I could say anything."

"Don't let me do that again."

Joe snorted. "I'll do my best, sir."

"I'm still getting used to my new ride," Rulon said, patting the dashboard as if it were the head of a dog. "Pretty nice, eh? It gets twelve miles a gallon, a real gas-guzzler. A couple of my supporters asked me how I could drive a car like this when I'm a Democrat and I'm for energy conservation and the like. I explained to them I'm a *Wyoming* Democrat, which means I'm a Republican who just wants to be different and stand out from the crowd, and we've got a hell of a lot of oil in this state we want to sell at high prices. Besides, it's comfortable, ain't it?"

Joe nodded, wishing the governor had not fired his driver.

"You should see the state plane. It's really a dandy. I didn't think I'd use it much, but this state is so damned big it's really a blessing."

"I can imagine."

"So, I've got a question for you," Rulon said. "An important question I've been wanting to ask you since I got this job."

Joe was surprised the governor even knew of him, much less actually thought about him.

"What's it like working for Randy Pope?"

Joe thought, *uh-oh*. He did not want to be put in the position of talking about his boss to the governor. Besides, what Joe thought was no secret. His allegations about Pope were in the report he had submitted after he returned from Jackson Hole.

"Actually, that's not *the* question," Rulon continued. "That's *a* question. *The* question is still to come."

As he said it, he rolled down his window again and shouted at a woman carrying groceries from her car toward the door of her town house.

"Hey, you want some help?" he shouted at her. "I can send over a trooper if you do!"

She turned on the walk and grinned. "I'm fine, Governor," she said.

"Hell, I can give you a hand myself. Do you have any more bags in the car?"

"No."

"You're sure you're okay?"

"Yes, I'm fine."

"Have a good day, then, ma'am."

He powered the window back up. "I do enjoy being the governor," he said. Then: "Where were we?"

Joe gestured toward the digital clock on the dashboard of the Yukon. "We all probably ought to get back."

"You're right," Rulon said.

And he stopped in the middle of the road, did a three-point turn through both lanes, and roared back down Main toward the museum.

"That was an illegal turn," Joe said.

"Screw it," Rulon said, shrugging, picking at something caught in his teeth. "I'm the governor."

RULON STOPPED PARALLEL to Joe's pickup in the parking lot.

"What a piece of crap," Rulon said, looking at Joe's vehicle. "They give you *that* to drive around in? It's an embarrassment!"

"My last truck burned up," Joe said, not wanting to explain.

Rulon smiled. "I heard about that. Ha! I also heard you shot Smoke Van Horn in a gunfight."

Joe paused before opening the door. "You said you had a question for me."

Rulon nodded, and his demeanor changed. He was suddenly serious and his eyes narrowed as if he were sizing up Joe for the first time.

"I've followed your career," Rulon said.

"You have?" Joe was genuinely surprised.

Rulon nodded. "I'm endlessly fascinated by the kind of people I have working for me all around the state. I'm the biggest employer this state has, you know. So when I see and hear something out of the norm, I latch on to it."

Joe had no idea where this was going. He shot a glance at Marybeth in the back seat, which she returned.

"So, here's my question," the governor said. "If you caught *me* fishing without a license, what would you do?"

Joe paused a beat, said, "I'd give you a ticket."

Rulon's face twitched. "You would? Even though you know who I am? Even though you know I could get rid of you like this?" he said, flicking an imaginary crumb off his sleeve.

Joe nodded yes.

"Get out then," Rulon said abruptly. "I have to say hello to the rest of the people here."

Joe hesitated. That was it?

"Go, go," Rulon said. "We're going to be late."

"Nice to meet you, Governor," he said, sliding out.

"You have a lovely bride," Rulon said.

JOE AND MARYBETH returned to their seats.

Missy had been waiting for them and turned completely around in her chair.

"What was *that* about?" she asked.

Joe and Marybeth exchanged glances.

"I have no idea," Marybeth said. "But I'm suddenly exhausted."

TEN MINUTES BEFORE ten, when the grand opening was to begin, a dirty pickup rattled into the parking lot and disgorged Hank. Joe saw that the driver of the pickup was Bill Monroe.

"There he is," Joe said, sitting up straight and pointing out the driver to Marybeth. "Just driving around wherever he wants to go. He's not worried about McLanahan, and he's not worried about me."

"That's Bill Monroe?"

"Yup."

"Why does he look familiar?"

Joe snorted. "I thought the same thing at first. I told you that. But there is no way in hell we've ever met him or run into him before."

"Still there's something about him," Marybeth said, and he knew she was right. He waited for her to recall where she'd seen him. She was good at those kinds of things.

As the pickup drove away, Joe searched the crowd for Sheriff McLanahan, who stood on the side of the podium talking to some ranchers on Hank's side about the state of alfalfa in the fields.

Joe left his seat and strode over. "Hey, Sheriff."

McLanahan looked up with his eyes, but didn't raise his chin.

Joe said, "Did you see who was driving that truck? That was Bill Monroe. Aren't you supposed to be looking for him? Isn't there a warrant out for his arrest? That was him right there."

Pink rose from under McLanahan's collar and flushed his face. He looked away from Joe for a moment.

"Didn't you see him?" Joe demanded. "He was right here in this parking lot. He dropped Hank off. Aren't you supposed to be on the lookout for him?"

Joe stepped closer to the sheriff, talking to the side of McLanahan's turned face, to his temple. "I know what you're doing. You're playing both sides, keeping your head down until it's resolved between the brothers. But don't you think it's time you started *doing something* around here? Like arresting people who commit crimes, no matter what their name is or who they work for?"

McLanahan stared ahead, angry, his mouth set tight.

"How long can you sit back and watch geese fly? Or waste your time calling my boss and telling him I'm not doing my job?"

That made McLanahan's face twitch. Yup, Joe thought, it was McLanahan after all.

"I've got an idea what might be going on with Hank, Arlen, and Opal," Joe said. "You want to hear it?"

McLanahan hesitated, said, "Not particularly."

"I didn't think you would."

With that, the sheriff turned on his heel and walked away, past the podium, around the corner of the museum.

Joe returned to the chairs and sat down next to Marybeth, who had seen the exchange.

"What are you doing, Joe?"

He shrugged. "I'm only half sure. But damn, it feels good."

. . .

JOE WAS INTERESTED to note the differences between the pro-Arlen and pro-Hank contingents. Arlen's backers tended to be city fathers, professionals, merchants. Hank's crowd looked much rougher than Arlen's, consisting of some other ranchers, bar owners, mechanics, outfitters, store clerks. If it were a football game, Joe thought, Arlen's folks would be cheering for the Denver Broncos and their upstanding players in their clean blue-and-orange uniforms. In contrast, Hank's crowd would have spiked their hair and painted their faces black and silver and would be waving bones and swinging lengths of chain rooting for their Oakland Raiders.

Joe and his family sat on Arlen's side, but Joe didn't feel completely comfortable about it. Especially after Marybeth told him about Arlen's meeting with Meade Davis. And even more so after the cell-phone message he had received that morning from forensics at headquarters. He wished there were seats in the aisle between the two factions.

THE NEW WING, called the Scarlett Wing, was actually larger than the rest of the building it was attached to, which was how Opal had wanted it. The museum itself was like every little town museum Joe had visited throughout Wyoming and the mountain west: a decent little collection of wagon wheels, frontier clothing, arrowheads, rifles, tools, old books. The new addition had state-of-the-art interactive exhibits on the founding families of Twelve Sleep County, the historic ranches, the bloodlines that flowed through the community from the first settlers. In other words the Scarlett Wing was about the Scarlett family, and was simply a much larger version of the Legacy Wall in their own home that Sheridan had told him about.

The addition had been completed that week. An earth-mover and a tractor still sat behind it. Grass turf had been so hastily rolled out to cover the dirt that the seams could be clearly seen. The manufacturer stickers on the windows had yet to be removed.

ARLEN TALKED FOR twenty-five minutes without notes, his melodious voice rising and falling, his speech filled with thunderous points and pregnant pauses. It was the speech of a politician, Joe thought, one of those stem-winders that, at the time you were hearing it, seemed to be all profundity and grace, but as soon as it was over, there was nothing to remember about it, as if the breeze had car-ried the memory of it away.

Despite that, Joe focused on what Arlen said about his mother:

"Opal Scarlett was more than a mother, more than the matriarch of Thunderhead Ranch. She was our link to the past, our living, breathing bridge from the twenty-first cen-tury to the pioneers who founded this land, fought for it, made it what it is today. And we celebrate her now with the opening of this museum . . ."

As Arlen spoke, Joe looked for Wyatt. Finally, he spot-ted the youngest brother, sitting off by himself, behind the podium. Arlen's words had obviously touched him, be-cause Wyatt's face was wet with tears.

THE MAYOR INTRODUCED Hank Scarlett next.

Hank sat hunched over on the other side of the podium, leaning forward in his chair so his head was down and all that could be seen of it was the top of his cowboy hat. He was studying his notes with fervor. The paper shook in his hands. Nervous, Joe thought.

"Now would be a good time to go out to his place and

see all of his poached game on display," Joe whispered to Marybeth, "while he's here and not there."

"But you need a warrant," she said.

HANK SHUFFLED TO the podium. There was something dark, mumbly, James-Dean-in-*Giant* about him, Joe thought. Hank followed Arlen with a crude but somehow more sincere and affecting message: "I ain't much of a speaker, but when Mother asks you to say something you say 'okay' . . ."

While he spoke he read from his notes, which were wrinkled and dirty in his hands. Joe guessed he had been reading them over and over for days.

"Mother lives and breathes the ranch and this valley," Hank said. "It's like the Twelve Sleep River runs through her veins instead of blood . . ."

He talked less than five minutes, but his tinny, halting delivery was more riveting than Arlen's speech. Never, in the entire time they were there, did either brother acknowledge the other, even with a nod.

When he was through, Hank folded up his notes, stuffed them into the back pocket of his Wranglers, and walked off the stage. While Arlen came down into the crowd to shake hands, Hank walked away through the parking lot toward the street. The pickup driven by Bill Monroe appeared and took him away.

Joe looked around for McLanahan and saw him in the parking lot talking heatedly with Robey Hersig.

THE CROWD MILLED around after the speeches. Groups formed to take tours of the new Scarlett Wing, others headed toward the snacks and drinks set up near the museum entrance. A few made their way to their vehicles.

Robey, his face red and his eyes in a snake-eyed squint, marched up to Joe and stabbed a finger into his chest.

"What are you trying to do? Burn every damned bridge behind you?"

"Stick around," Joe said, smiling. "I've got a few more to go."

Robey turned on his boot heels and strode away from Joe toward the parking lot.

22

"JOE, I DON'T KNOW IF YOU'RE DOING THIS RIGHT," Marybeth said. "This isn't like you. You seem to be a little out of control."

"You're probably right," Joe replied. "But it's time to shake things up."

She had lured him away from the crowd to a secluded place on the side of the addition. Joe felt his boot heels sink into the brand-new sod. There was real concern in her eyes.

"Joe, I see these people every day. I work for some of them. We have to *live* here."

He tipped his hat back and rubbed his forehead where the sweatband fit. "I hate to give any credit to Randy Pope," he said, "but he may be right about one thing, and that's the tendency to go native if you stay somewhere too long."

"I'm not following."

"Think about what you just said. You're starting to weigh my job and my duty against who we may offend. If that's a problem, Marybeth, maybe we've overstayed our welcome here."

Her eyes got wide, then she set her face. She put her hands on her hips and leaned forward. Joe rocked back and thought, *Uh-oh.*

"Listen to me, Joe Pickett," she said. "Don't you *ever,* for one second, think I would want you to compromise your principles or your oath in order for us to get along better here. I have *never* done that to you. If that was in my mind, I would have insisted on it years ago, before you and your stupid job put us in harm's way again and again and AGAIN."

Marybeth took a step forward and Joe took one back. She was now jabbing him in the chest. He wished she hadn't said "stupid job." But he didn't point that out.

"Don't you dare blame this on me," she said. "I think your problem is *your* problem. You're working for a man and an agency you don't believe in anymore. You're frustrated. You're finding out that everything you based your career and your validation on might be built on a foundation of sand. It kills you that you're thinking you're just another government employee working for a government agency. And instead of admitting it or dealing with it, you're lashing out. Am I right?"

Joe glared at her.

"Am I right?"

"Maybe," he conceded. "Just a little."

"Okay, then."

"It kind of pisses me off that you're so smart," he said, chancing a smile. "I must drive you crazy sometimes."

She punched him playfully in the chest. "It is a burden," she said.

AS THEY WALKED back toward the parking lot and the people, Joe said, "I'm still mad, though."

"You don't get mad very often, so I suppose you're allowed to every once in a while."

"There's a lot going on here," he said, gesturing toward the museum and the Scarlett Wing, but meaning the county in general. "We can't see it happening because we're too close. I think it's right there in front of us, but we're not seeing it because we're looking for something else."

Marybeth stopped and searched his face. "What are you talking about, Joe?"

"Where does Bill Monroe fit into all of this?" Joe said. "I can't figure out his role in it. He's Hank's thug, but he seems to be working with Arlen too. How do you square that deal?"

"I don't know."

"Something struck me during those speeches," Joe said. "I was wondering if you picked up on it."

"What?"

"Think back. What was the biggest difference between how Arlen spoke and Hank spoke?"

"Arlen was articulate and Hank was not?" Marybeth said.

"Hank spoke of his mother in the present tense," Joe said. "He said, 'When Mother asks you to say something you say "okay."' Remember that?"

"Yes." The realization of what Joe was getting at washed across her face.

"But Arlen spoke of his mother in the past tense: 'Opal Scarlett was more than a mother, more than the matriarch of the Thunderhead Ranch. . . .'"

"So what does it mean?"

Joe shrugged. "I'm not sure. But clearly, when Hank thinks of his mother she's still around. That's not the case with Arlen. As far as he's concerned, she's gone."

JOE GLANCED UP and saw Arlen making his way through the crowd straight for them.

"Here he comes now," Joe said, trying to get a read on what the purpose of Arlen's visit might be.

Arlen ignored Joe and greeted Marybeth. "It's so good you could come," he said. He threw an arm around her shoulders and gave her a squeeze, then stepped back. "Thanks to your wife," he said to Joe, "we are now within sight of making the ranch rightfully ours. She cracked the code in regard to Mother's accounting system on the ranch." Arlen gestured with his fingers to indicate quote marks around "cracked the code."

"I heard," Joe said.

"She's quite a woman," Arlen said.

"I agree."

"You should be proud of her."

"I am."

Arlen stepped away from Marybeth, who had been grinning icily the entire time he was next to her. Arlen's face was suddenly somber, the look he showed just before he commenced with a speech.

"I heard what happened at your home," Arlen said. "I heard about those town elk. It's a damned shame."

Joe nodded, eyeing him carefully. "I decided this morning to involve myself in the investigation of your mother."

"Oh?"

"Yup," Joe said. "My boss said stay away from it, but I'm going to anyway. I have this idea that maybe things aren't what they seem, Arlen. While I've been sitting on the sidelines, no progress I'm aware of has been made on the case. And at the same time, somebody has targeted my family. I think everything that's happened is connected to Opal's disappearance."

Arlen had listened with hooded eyes and a blank expression, offering no encouragement. "Really," he said. Arlen looked at Marybeth to gauge her opinion, and she stared back impassively. Joe noted the exchange.

"Really," Joe said.

"Are you telling me this in the hope that I won't inform Director Pope?"

"I don't care what you do," Joe said. "Pope knows about everything I do. The sheriff makes sure of that. Maybe someone else does too."

"I see." Arlen's expression hardened, as if he were concentrating on giving nothing away.

"So I hope you can clear up a couple of things for me."
Arlen didn't respond.

"It would help if you told me what your relationship with Bill Monroe is," Joe said. "I'm trying to figure . . ."

"That's confidential," Arlen interrupted.

Joe sighed. "He seems to work for Hank, but Sheridan saw him . . ."

"It's confidential," Arlen said in his most stentorian voice, cutting off debate, looking around to see if anyone had overheard them. No one appeared to be listening.

Joe stared at Arlen, taking new measure of the man. At his chiseled profile, his silver hair, his big lantern jaw and underbite, his darting eyes.

"You see that earthmover behind me?" Joe asked.

Puzzled, Arlen glanced over Joe's shoulder. Marybeth looked at Joe.

"Yes, what about it?"

Joe said, "If I find out you're playing me, which I'm beginning to believe you are, I'm going to get in that thing and knock this building down. And then I'm coming after *you.*"

Arlen's mouth dropped open. He was truly surprised.

"I got a message on my cell phone this morning," Joe said. "From forensics. The knife that was stuck in our front door matches the collection of knives in your own kitchen. Same model, same manufacturer. 'Forged German CrMoV steel, ice hardened and glass finished,' forensics said."

Arlen said, "Many people have access to my home—employees, ranch hands . . ."

"Right," Joe said. "And it appears Meade Davis seems to have changed his story to one you liked better. Anything to that? Do you think Meade Davis would stick with the latest version if I brought him in?"

It was amazing how icy Arlen's eyes had become, Joe thought, how frozen the expression on his face. This was a different Arlen than the glad-handing speechmaker. This was the Arlen Joe had glimpsed in the sheriff's office baiting his brother into violence, but acting as if he didn't know what he was doing.

Jabbing his finger at Joe, Arlen said, "You have crossed the line making accusations like that. Do you realize who you're talking to?"

"I realize," Joe said. "It's getting old."

Arlen shook his head, contemplating Joe, but saying nothing. As if Joe was no longer worth his words.

Arlen turned to Marybeth. "You've lost my account. If you can talk some sense into your husband, you might have a chance to get it back."

Marybeth's eyes were fiery. "He has plenty of sense, Arlen. We can live without your money."

ON THE WAY back to the Longbrake Ranch, Marybeth broke the silence.

"So you really think she's still alive," she said to Joe as they drove past the town limit toward the Longbrake Ranch. Sheridan and Lucy were touring the museum with Missy, so Joe and Marybeth had the truck to themselves.

"Yup," Joe said. "I think she's holed up somewhere on the ranch, just sitting back and watching what goes on. I can imagine her seeing what lengths her sons will go to to get the ranch. Seeing how much they love it and therefore how much they love *her.* Everything she's done over the years fits the theory—the secret wills, the internalized accounting, her obsession with her legacy. It came to me when I thought about Tommy Wayman claiming to have seen her, and Sheridan's dream. Maybe it wasn't a dream after all. In both cases, they described the same thing. They said she was *smiling*."

Marybeth was lost in thought for a few moments, then she asked, "Do you think Hank knows?"

"No."

"Arlen?"

Joe shook his head. "Maybe, but I can't be sure. I was hoping to smoke him out back there, but he's too damned wily for me."

After a few miles she turned to him. "There's only one thing about your theory that might be wrong."

"What?"

"I don't think it's about love at all," she said. "I think it's about hate."

Joe said, "I don't understand."

"Look at them," she said. "She raised them to hate each other and love her. What kind of mother does that?"

23

ON MONDAY MORNING, JOE PULLED ON HIS RED UNI-
form shirt and jeans for perhaps the last time, called Maxine, and drove out into the breaklands to finish up the
mule-deer trend count he had started weeks before.

As he cruised down the state highway, he kept a close
watch on the blunt thunderheads advancing over the
Bighorns. The clouds looked heavy and swollen with rain.
"Come on," he said aloud, "keep on rolling this way." By
his count, it had not rained in twenty-five days. Maxine
thought he was talking to her and got excited.

He had one more quadrant to go before submitting his
report. The area butted up against the property line of the
upper Thunderhead Ranch, Hank's half.

When his cell phone rang, Joe opened it and expected to
hear "Hold for Director Pope."

But it was Tony Portenson. "Hello, Joe."

"To what do I owe this pleasure?" Joe asked, keeping

the sarcasm out of his voice and wishing that years before he hadn't given his phone number to the FBI agent.

"We got a call from a contact in Idaho," Portenson said. "Someone matching the description of Nate Romanowski was spotted at a Conoco station in Victor, headed east toward Wyoming. I was wondering if perhaps you'd seen your old friend recently."

Joe felt himself smile, but kept the grin out of his voice. "No, I haven't seen or heard from him."

"You wouldn't lie to me, would you, Joe?"

"Nope, I don't do that."

Portenson sighed. "I guess you don't. But you'll keep me informed if he shows up, right?"

"Nope, probably not."

"At least tell him I want to talk with him, okay?"

"I'm sure he knows that."

"You're not very helpful, Joe."

"He's my friend," Joe said. Then he quickly changed the subject. "Did you ever find that guy you were looking for? The one who shot the cowboy?"

Portenson's voice dropped. "He's still at large. We faxed the information to the sheriff's department but haven't heard anything from him."

"I'm not surprised," Joe said.

Portenson said, "Tell Romanowski I haven't forgotten about him."

BY THE TIME Joe found the southeast corner of the quadrant, the dark clouds had redoubled in scale and continued their advance. Thirty miles away, he could see spouts of rain connecting the clouds to the earth, an illusion that made it look though it were raining *up*. Rain in any form was a revelation.

"Keep on rolling," he said again, wishing he could see

the secrets and motivations of the people in the valley with the same long-distance clarity.

Instead of mule deer, he happened first on a herd of thirty pronghorn antelope grazing and picking their way in the distance across the tabletop flat of a butte. Their brown-and-white camouflage coloring, which worked for eight months of the year, failed them miserably against the pulsing green carpet of spring grass and made them stand out like highway cones.

Joe fixed his spotting scope to the top of his driver's-side window and surveyed the pronghorn. Antelope almost always had twins, and the little ones were perfectly proportioned, despite their size, and within days were capable of running as fast as the adults. He loved to watch them play, chasing other newborns around, scampering between the legs of their mothers like shooting sparks.

Joe swung the telescope and found the lead buck. As always, he stood alone facing his herd, prepared at any moment to wade into the throng to enforce his will on them or punish transgressions. As Joe admired the buck through the scope a puff of dust and hair shot out of the buck's neck and the animal crumpled and dropped. A rifle shot followed, *pow-WHOP,* the sound of a hit, echoing across the sagebrush. In the bottom of his scope view, Joe could see the buck kicking out violently, windmilling his legs in a death dance.

"Man!" Joe shouted, amazed at what had happened right in front of his eyes.

The rest of the herd ignited as one and were suddenly sweeping across the top of the butte leaving twenty-nine streams of dust that looked like vapor trails in their wake.

Angry, Joe jumped out of his pickup with his binoculars. Antelope season was four months away. Before raising the glasses to his eyes, he swept the hills, trying to see the shooter. Was it possible the poacher didn't know the game warden was in the vicinity? No, Joe thought, the odds were totally against it. In a district of fifteen hundred square miles, the chance of his actually being there to see the kill in front of his eyes were infinitesimal. The act was a deliberate provocation, a direct challenge.

He followed the long line of three-strand barbed-wire fence that separated the public Bureau of Land Management land from the Thunderhead Ranch. The fence went on as far as he could see. But behind it—on a ridge, partially hidden by a fold in the terrain—was a light-colored pickup he didn't recognize.

He raised the glasses and focused furiously.

The pickup came into view.

It was an older model, at least ten years old, light yellow, rust spots on the door. The description was familiar to him, but from where? He didn't take the time to figure it out. The driver's-side door was open, and the window was down. A rifle rested on the sill, still pointing in the general direction of the butte.

A man stepped out from behind the door and waved.

Bill Monroe.

He waved again at Joe in a goofy, come-on-y'all wave.

Then Monroe stepped away from the pickup, set his feet, and pulled out his penis: a flash of pink against blue jeans. He urinated a long stream into the dirt in front of him, then leaned back in an exaggerated way, pointed at Joe with his free hand, and Joe could read his lips as he shouted: *"This is what I think of you, Joe Pickett."*

A THUNDERCLAP NOT unlike the sound of the rifle shot boomed across the breaklands followed by a long series of deep-throated rumbles. Joe could feel the temperature dropping even as he drove, as the clouds pulled across the sun like a curtain shutting out the light, muting light and shadow.

He had plunged his truck over the rise into the saddle slope of a valley in pursuit of Bill Monroe. There were no established roads that would get him from where he had seen the shooting, across the top of the butte, to the border of the Thunderhead Ranch, so Joe kept his left front tire in a meandering game trail that pointed vaguely toward Monroe's pickup and let the right tires bounce through knee-high sagebrush. He was driving much faster than he should have, the engine straining. Maxine stood on the bench seat with her front paws on the dash, trying to keep balanced.

Damn him, Joe thought.

Joe hated poachers, and not simply because they were breaking the law he was sworn to enforce. He hated the idea of poaching—killing a creature for sport with no intention of eating the meat. Joe took poaching as a personal affront, and to see it happen this way, to be mocked by Bill Monroe in this way . . .

And Bill Monroe was not yet running. He was still up there, outside of his pickup, on the far ridge, outlined against the roiling dark clouds. Monroe had plenty of time and distance before Joe got there, and he was in no hurry.

Maybe he wouldn't run at all. Maybe he would wait for Joe, and the two of them could have it out. Joe thought that sounded fine to him.

He was halfway across the saddle slope when three things happened at once:

His radio came to life, the dispatcher calling him directly by his code number, saying he was to call Director Randy Pope immediately off the air.

The check-engine light on the dashboard flickered and stayed on while the temperature-gauge needle shouldered hard into the red.

And the clouds opened up with a clash of cymbals and sheets of rain swept across the ground with such force that the first wave of rain actually raised dust as if it were strafing the ground.

. . .

BILL MONROE WAS still on the ridge, standing in the rain as if he didn't know it was soaking him. Joe was closer now, close enough to see the leer on Monroe's face, see his hands on his hips as he looked down at Joe climbing up the slope, aimed right at him.

A moment later, there was a pop under the hood of the engine and clouds of acrid green steam rolled out from under the pickup, through the grille, and into the cab through the air vents. The radiator hose has blown.

Joe cursed and slammed the dash with the heel of his hand. He stopped the truck and the engine died before he could turn the key.

JOE OPENED THE door and jumped out of his crippled pickup. Despite the opening salvos of rain, the ground was still drought dry; the moisture had not yet penetrated and was pooling wherever there was a low spot. The rainfall was steady and hard, stinging his bare hands.

Joe looked up the slope at Monroe.

"What's wrong with your truck?" Monroe shouted down.

"You're under arrest," Joe shouted back.

"For what?"

"For killing that buck. I saw the whole thing."

Monroe shook his head. "I didn't kill no buck."

"I saw you."

"I don't even own a rifle."

"I saw you."

"Your word against mine, I guess."

"Yup."

"I understand you're pretty convincing when it comes to Judge Pennock," Monroe said.

Joe felt a pang in his chest. So Monroe was well aware of the rejected search warrant.

The rain hammered the brim of Joe's hat and an icy

stream of it poured into his collar and snaked down along his backbone.

"Good thing your truck blew up," Monroe said. "You would have been trespassing on private property."

The fence line was just in front of Monroe, Joe saw.

Then Joe realized Monroe wanted him to come over there onto the Thunderhead, where access had been previously refused by Hank. What would Monroe have done when Joe crossed the line? What had been his plan?

IT WAS AN odd thing, how sometimes there could be a moment of absolute clarity in the midst of rampant chaos. With the rain falling hard, his vehicle disabled, the dispatcher calling for him, and Bill Monroe grinning at him from behind the fence, at least part of the picture cleared up. Portenson's call had reminded him of something.

The truck Monroe was driving was light yellow, ten years old, with rust spots on the door. Where had that description come from? Then it hit him.

Joe looked up at Bill Monroe, who wasn't really Bill Monroe.

"You know who I am now, don't you?"

Oh, God. Joe felt a chill.

"You're John W. Kelly," he shouted, dredging up the name Special Agent Gary Child had told him.

Monroe snorted. "Close," he said.

"You shot a cowboy in the Shirley Basin," Joe said, suddenly thinking of the .40 Glock on his hip and the shotgun in his pickup. Up there on the ridge, Monroe had the drop on him.

Monroe laughed. "I didn't shoot no cowboy, just like I didn't shoot no antelope buck."

"I saw you."

"It's just too damned bad your truck blew up," Monroe said. "Another two hundred fifty feet and you woulda' been on private property. Who knows what would have happened."

Joe started to answer when Monroe backed away from the top of the ridge. In a moment, Joe heard an engine flare and the grinding of gears before the truck drove off, leaving him there.

JOE STOOD IN the rain, thinking, running scenarios through his mind. They kept getting worse.

He got back inside the cab with Maxine. Even though the motor wasn't running the battery still worked, as did his radio. He even had a cell-phone signal, although it was weak.

BEFORE CALLING RANDY Pope, Joe reached Bud Longbrake on the ranch. Bud had a one-ton flatbed with a winch and he was much closer to where Joe was stranded than any of the tow-truck drivers in town. Bud agreed to come rescue Joe, bring his truck back, and even lend Joe a ranch vehicle in the meantime. Bud was positively giddy when Joe talked with him.

"This rain just makes me happy," he said. Joe could tell Bud was smiling by his voice. "It hasn't rained this hard in three years."

ROBEY WASN'T IN his office when Joe called. His secretary said he was trapped in his house because a flash flood had taken out the bridge that crossed over to the highway from Robey's property. She told Joe that Robey's phone was down now as well, as were most of the telephones in the valley, because lightning had struck a transformer and knocked the service out.

"What about his cell?" Joe asked.

"You can call it, I guess," she said. "But I can see his cell phone sitting on his desk in his office. He must have forgotten to take it home with him last night."

Joe rolled his eyes with frustration. "Please have him call me the minute he makes contact," Joe said. "It's important."

"Will do," she said. "Isn't this great, this rain? We really needed it."

"Yes," Joe said.

THE NEXT CALL was to the FBI office in Cheyenne. Joe asked for Tony Portenson and was told Portenson was away from his desk.

"Tony, this is Joe Pickett," he said on Portenson's voice mail. "Can you please fax or e-mail me the file on John Kelly? I may have a lead for you."

FURTHER DELAYING THE inevitable, Joe speed-dialed the Twelve Sleep County Sheriff's Department and asked for McLanahan.

"McLanahan." He sounded harried, high-pitched, and out of breath.

"Joe Pickett, Sheriff. I'm broken down on the border of the Thunderhead Ranch where I just had an encounter with Bill Monroe, although I don't think that's really his name."

"I'm lost," McLanahan said.

You sure are, Joe thought. He outlined his theory and told McLanahan about the yellow pickup and the investigation by the FBI.

McLanahan was silent for a moment after Joe finished, then said, "Are you sure you aren't just obsessed by the guy?"

"What?"

"He's the one who pounded you, right?"

"What difference does that make? You've got a warrant out for his arrest, even if I'm wrong about the rest of it. Why don't you drive out there and take the guy down?"

McLanahan sighed. "Have you looked outside recently?"

"I *am* outside."

"It looks like a cow pissing on a flat rock, this rain. We're in a state of emergency right now. You can't dump three inches of rain on a county that's dry as concrete and expect it to soak in. We've got flash floods everywhere. Bridges are out. In town the river has jumped the banks in at least three places. We've got a mess here, Joe. I've got truckloads of sandbags on the way from Gillette. I can't do anything until we get it under control."

Joe thought, *Man, oh man.*

"I've gotta go," McLanahan said. "Somebody just saw a Volkswagen Beetle float down First Street."

JOE BREATHED IN and out, in and out, then direct-dialed Randy Pope's office. He got the evil receptionist. The gleeful tone in her voice when he introduced himself told Joe all he needed to know.

"I told you I needed a new truck," Joe said when Pope came on the line. "Because of this lousy equipment you gave me, a poacher and murder suspect has gotten away."

Pope's voice was dry, barely controlled. "Joe, when I ask that you call in immediately, I mean immediately. Not when you get around to it."

"I was in pursuit of a murder suspect," Joe said. "I couldn't stop and call in at the time."

"That was an hour ago."

"Yes, and I called as soon as I could. I need to get this broken-down truck towed out of the middle of nowhere."

Pope sighed, then said, "I got a call from Arlen Scarlett, Joe."

Joe sat back. "I figured you would."

"We've now got official protests lodged against you from both Arlen and Hank Scarlett. Think about it. The only thing those two seem to agree on is that you are completely out of control, and that reflects on me. You're wasting time on a case totally out of our purview while game violations are going on in the middle of town."

"And you're only too happy to side with them," Joe said.

"You're fired, Joe," Pope snapped.

He heard the words he had been expecting to hear. Nevertheless, Joe still had trouble believing it was actually happening.

Pope's voice rose as he continued. "As of today, Joe, you're history. And don't try to fight me on this. You'll lose! I've got documentation stretching back six years. Threatening a legislator and Game and Fish commissioner with property destruction and bodily harm? WHAT WERE YOU THINKING?"

"Do you really want to know or is that a rhetorical question?" Joe asked, his mouth dry.

"I won't miss your cowboy antics," Pope said. "This is a new era."

"I've heard," Joe said. He was tired of arguing with Pope. He felt defeated. The rain lashed at the windshield.

Pope transferred Joe to someone in personnel who outlined, in a monotone, what procedural steps were available for him to take if he wanted to contest the decision. Joe half listened, then punched off.

IT WAS THREE hours before Bud Longbrake showed up in his one-ton. The rain had increased in intensity, and it channeled into arroyos and draws, filling dry beds that had been parched for years, even rushing down the game trail in what looked like a river of angry chocolate milk.

Joe watched the one-ton start down the hill, then brake and begin to slide, the wheels not holding. Bud was driving, and he managed to reverse the vehicle and grind back up the hill before he slid to the bottom and got stuck. Bud flashed his headlights on and off.

Joe understood the signal. Bud couldn't bring the one-ton all the way across the basin to pull the truck out.

"Fine," Joe said, feeling like the embodiment of the subject of a blues song as he slid out of the truck into the mud carrying his shotgun, briefcase, and lunch and walked through the pouring rain to the one-ton with Maxine slogging along, head down, beside him.

"Fine!"

24

WHEN BUD PULLED INTO THE RANCH YARD, HE splashed through a small lake that had not been there that morning and parked the one-ton in his massive barn.

Joe saw Marybeth's van in there also. She was home early. As he entered the house through the back door they used to access their new living quarters, Marybeth looked up, saw his face, and sat down quickly as if her legs had given out on her.

"We need to talk," he said.

"Let's go into the bedroom and shut the door," she said.

HE TOLD MARYBETH he'd been fired, and her reaction was worse than he anticipated: stunned silence. He would have preferred that she yelled at him, or cried, or locked herself in their room. Instead, she simply stared at him and whispered, "What are we going to do now, Joe?"

"We'll figure something out," he said, lamely.

"I guess we knew this would happen."

"Yes."

"When do we tell the girls?" Marybeth asked. "*What* do we tell them."

"The truth," he said. That would be the hardest part. No, it wouldn't. The hardest part would be that Sheridan and Lucy would expect him to say not to worry, that he would take care of them as he always had. But he couldn't tell them that and look them in the eye.

DINNER THAT EVENING was one of the worst Joe could remember. They sat at the big dining room table with Missy and Bud. Missy's cook, a Latina named Maria, had made fried chicken and the pieces steamed in a big bowl in the middle of the table. Bud ate as if he were starved. Missy picked at a breast that had been skinned and was made specially for her. Joe had no appetite, even though it was his favorite meal. When he had been employed, that is. Marybeth was silent. Sheridan spent dinnertime looking from her mom to her dad and back again, trying to figure out what was happening. Lucy was oblivious.

The rain roared against the roof and sang down the downspouts. Bud said a half-dozen times how happy he was that it was raining.

AFTER THE DISHES were cleared, Joe asked Bud if he could borrow a ranch pickup.

"Where are you going?" Missy said. Now that they were under her roof, Missy felt entitled to ask questions like that.

"I've got birds to feed," Joe said.

"Have you looked outside?" Missy said with an expression clearly meant to convey that he was an idiot.

"Why? Is something happening?" Joe said. He really didn't have the patience to deal with his mother-in-law tonight.

Marybeth shot him a cautionary look. Sheridan stifled a smile.

"I hope Bud doesn't have to come out and rescue you again if you get stuck," Missy said, and turned away.

"I don't mind," Bud said. "I kind of like driving around in the rain. It makes me feel good."

"I'll try not to get stuck again," Joe said as he headed to the mudroom for his still-damp boots and coat. Marybeth followed him there.

"Sheridan knows something is up."

"I know," Joe said, wincing as he pulled on a wet boot.

"Maybe when you get home we can talk to the girls."

Joe sighed. "I guess." He'd been putting it off all night.

"Joe, it's nothing to be ashamed of."

He looked up. "Yes, honey, it is."

"My business is doing well."

"Thank God for that," Joe said, standing, jamming his foot into a boot to seat it. "Thank God for your business, or we'd be out on the street."

"Joe . . ."

He looked up at her and his eyes flashed. "I brought it on myself, I know that. I could have played things differently. I could have compromised a little more."

She shook her head slowly. "No you couldn't, Joe."

He clammed up. Anything he said now would make things worse, he knew. His insides ached. How could she possibly know how it felt for a man to lose his job, lose the means of taking care of his family? He kept pushing the crushing reality of it aside so that he was only contemplating the little things: that he would no longer wear the red shirt, that he would no longer carry a badge and a gun, that he would no longer perch on hillsides watching deer and antelope and elk. That he would no longer bring home a monthly pay- check.

"Be careful," she said, taking his face in her hands and kissing him. "I worry about you when you're like this."

He tried to smile but he knew it looked like a pained snarl.

"I've got to get out for a while" was all he managed to say. God, he was grateful she was his wife.

Missy swept in behind Marybeth and stood there with her eyes sparkling above a pursed mouth. "This is interest- ing, isn't it?"

"What are you referring to?"

She opened her arms toward the window of the mud- room, a gesture designed to take in the whole ranch. "Three years ago, I was camped out on your couch in that horrible little hovel you made my daughter and my grandchildren live in. And you wanted me *out*."

Joe didn't deny it.

"Now look where we are. You're a guest in my home and your family is comfortable and safe for the first time in their lives."

He felt his rage build, but was able to stanch it. He didn't want this argument now, when he felt quite capable of wringing her neck.

"It's interesting, is all," she said, raising her eyebrows mockingly, "how situations can change and things that were thought and said can come back to haunt a person?"

SHERIFF MCLANAHAN WASN'T kidding. The rain had transformed everything. It wasn't like other parts of the country, where rain could fall and soak into the soil and be smoothly channeled away. This was hardpan that re- ceived only eleven inches of rain a year, and today had al- ready brought four. The water stood on top of the ground, forming lakes and ponds that hadn't existed for years. Tiny draws and sloughs had turned into funnels for raging brown water.

Joe drove slowly on the highway, water spraying out from under his tires in rooster tails. The sky was mottled greenish black and the rain fell so hard he couldn't hear the radio inside the cab of the ranch truck. He had no business going out, and especially going to Nate's old place to feed the falcons, but he needed something to do. If he stayed at the ranch contemplating his complete failure while Missy prattled on about fat grams and social clubs, he didn't know what he might do. Plus, he wanted to put off the talk with Sheridan and Lucy. Would Marybeth warn them? he wondered. Tell them to reassure their father, not to get angry or upset? He hoped she didn't. The only thing he could think of that was worse than being a failure was to have his girls pity him for it.

THE ROAD TO Nate Romanowski's old place was elevated enough that he was able to get there in four-wheel-drive high. On either side of the road, though, long lakes had formed. Ducks were actually sitting on ponds that hadn't existed eight hours ago. And he could hear frogs. Frogs that had been hibernating deep below the surface for years were coming out, croaking.

It was amazing what renewal came with water in the mountain west. Joe just wished that somehow the rain could renew *him*.

JOE CRESTED THE last rise near Nate's home to see that the river had not just jumped the bank, but had taken Nate's falcon mews and was lapping at the side of his house. He had never seen the river so big, so violent. It was whitewater, and big rollers thundered through the canyon. Full-grown cottonwood trees, cattle, parts of washed-out bridges were being carried downstream. The rickety suspension footbridge across the river downstream from Nate's home was either gone or underwater.

Joe parked above Nate's house on a rise. There was less than an hour of light left, and he wanted to feed the birds and get out before nightfall. He climbed out and pulled on his yellow slicker. Fat raindrops popped against the rubberized canvas of his slicker as he unwrapped road-killed rabbits from a burlap bag in the bed of the truck. This was a foolish thing he was doing, he conceded. The birds could probably wait. But he had made a promise, and he would keep it.

The sound of the river was awesome in its power. He could feel the spray from it well before he got to its new edge.

He laid the rabbits out on a sandy rise so they could be seen clearly from the air. In the past, it took less than ten minutes for either the peregrine or the red-tailed hawk to see the meat. Joe never had any idea where the falcons were, or how they always knew he was there. But they did, and they came to eat.

Joe could never get used to the relationship—or more accurately, the lack of a relationship—he had with Nate's falcons. It was something Nate had once told him about, how different and unique it was with birds of prey compared to other creatures. The cold partnership between falconer and falcon was primal and unsentimental. Quite simply, the birds never warmed up to the falconer and certainly not to Joe. To *anyone*. Raptors weren't like dogs, or horses, or even cats. They didn't pretend to like humans, or show even a flicker of affection. They simply coexisted with people, using them to obtain food and shelter but never actually giving back anything but their own ability to hunt and kill. The falcon could fly away at any time and never come back. There was nothing a falconer could do to retrieve a bird. It was a relationship based on mutual self-interest and a kind of unfeeling trust.

After twenty minutes, Joe saw a dark speck dislodge from the gunmetal clouds. He stood and wiped the rain from his face and watched as the speck got larger. It was the peregrine, the ultimate killer. The red-tail appeared shortly thereafter.

The peregrine buzzed Joe twice before flaring and landing on the edge of the rise. The red-tail made two false landings, close enough to see the meat, then climbed back up into the sky and disappeared.

He looked at the peregrine closely. The bird wasn't the least bit interested in the rabbits. And there was something else: the bird's gullet was swelled to bursting and there were blood flecks and bits of white down on its breast. It had already eaten.

Joe squatted and looked into the falcon's eyes, which were as impenetrable as shiny black stones.

"Who fed you?" Joe asked. "Or did you kill something yourself?" Then he thought about the red-tail. "Did you *both* make a kill?"

Something made him turn and look at the stone house that had stood empty for half a year.

Fresh lengths of pine boarded up two of the windows. The front door had been replaced. And half a row of new shingles were laid out on the roof.

Despite the drumming of the rain, Joe felt his heart whump in his chest.

He called out, "Nate, where are you?"

Then he saw him. Downstream, where he'd been hiding and watching in a thick stand of reeds. The reeds were dancing around him with falling rain. Nate rose from them, naked, holding his huge .454 Casull in his right fist. Joe didn't even want to ask.

"Have you come to kill me?" Nate called out.

"No."

"I deserve it."

"I know you do."

"I wouldn't blame you if you did," Nate said.

They stared at each other for a minute. Nate was slick with rain and his white skin was mud streaked from hiding in the bog. His long blond hair stuck to the tops of his shoulders. His eyes bored into Joe.

Nate had once vowed to protect Joe's family. Joe had promised to keep Nate's birds fed. Despite everything that had happened, both had lived up to their obligations, something greater than mere friendship.

Joe said, "Why don't you put on some clothes?"

25

J. W. KEELEY DIDN'T LIKE THE WAY HANK SCARLETT was talking to him. He didn't like it at all.

The rest of Hank's men had been dismissed from the dinner table—only he and Hank remained. The men had gone back to their bunkhouse a mile from Hank's lodge. They had grumbled through a huge steak dinner about the rain, how it had knocked out their telephone service in the bunkhouse and how the lights kept going on and off. Especially annoying was the fact that the cable was out for television and they would miss the third game of the NBA playoffs. And the worst thing of all was the news that the river had jumped its banks and was flooding the roads to the highway. The men would be trapped on the ranch until the water receded, so they couldn't even go to town to see the game. They had complained without quarter until Hank finally pushed away from the table, threw his napkin onto his plate as if spiking a football, and said in his loudest and most nasally voice,

"Why don't you boys just get the hell out of my house and go bitch somewhere else?"

That had shut them up, all right.

"Not you, Bill," Hank had said. So Monroe sat back down at the table.

Because the electricity was out again, the dining room was lit by three hissing Coleman gas lanterns. The light played on Hank's face, making the shadowed hollows under his cheekbones look skull-like and cavernous. The glass eyes on the head mounts of the game animals on the walls glowed with reflection.

That's when Hank began to annoy him, chipping away with that damned high voice, each word dropping like a stone in a pond, *plunk-plunk-plunk.*

"You need to stay away from that game warden," Hank said.

Keeley had told Hank and the boys the story over their thick steaks: how he'd dropped the buck right in front of the game warden, then watched the warden's truck break down in an aborted hot pursuit. The boys had laughed. A couple of them had laughed so hard that Keeley considered spilling the beans on the other things he'd done to get under the warden's skin. Luckily, he held his tongue, because that would have led to too many questions. Hank had appeared to be smiling, but now Keeley understood that it hadn't been a smile at all. It was too damned tough to tell if Hank was smiling or not. That was just one of the things wrong with the man.

Keeley glared at Hank. "That's my business," he said in response. "It ain't no concern of yours."

"The hell it ain't!" Hank snapped back. "I didn't make you my foreman so you could draw the cops in here because of your fucking antics with the local game warden. Joe Pickett knows for sure you're out here now, and I would guess he's told the sheriff."

Keeley gestured toward the ceiling at the sound of the rain thrumming the roof. "That sheriff couldn't get out here right now even if he wanted to. Didn't you just tell the boys the river's over the road?"

Hank nodded. "Except for one little two-track on high ground down by Arlen's place, my guess is there is no way in or out."

"Where's that?"

"About a mile downriver," Hank said. "I'd guess that road is still dry. But if the river gets any higher, that one'll be underwater too."

Keeley filed away the information.

"What's your problem with him, anyway?" Hank asked.

"Personal."

"That's what you always say," Hank said. "But since what you do could bring the wrath of God down on my ass, you need to tell me just what it is between you two."

"The wrath of God?" Keeley said, thinking, from what he had observed, that it was an odd way to describe Joe Pickett.

"Him and his buddy Nate Romanowski," Hank said. "Didn't I tell you about them?"

Keeley nodded.

"Why don't you grab that bottle of bourbon from the kitchen?" Hank said. "I'd like a little after-dinner snort. You can join me."

Keeley hesitated for a beat as he always did when Hank asked him to do something that was beneath him. He wasn't the fucking kitchen help, after all. He was the new ranch foreman. But Keeley sighed, stood up, and felt around through the liquor cabinet until his hand closed around the thick neck of the half-gallon bottle of Maker's Mark. A $65 bottle. Nice.

Hank poured two water glasses half full. He didn't offer ice or water. Keeley sipped and closed his eyes, letting the good bourbon burn his tongue.

"This thing you've got with the game warden," Hank said again, "it's time you dropped it."

"I ain't dropping it," Keeley said, maybe a little too quickly. Hank froze with his glass halfway to his lips and stared at him.

"What do you mean, you 'ain't dropping it'?"

"I told you." Keeley shrugged. "It's personal."

Hank didn't change his expression, but Keeley could see the blood drain out of Hank's cheeks. That meant he was getting angry. Which usually meant someone would start hopping around, asking what Hank needed. *Fuck that,* Keeley thought. Enough with Hank and his moods.

"Since you got here, you've been asking me questions about him," Hank said. "You've been kind of subtle and clever about it, you know, not asking too much at once and not tipping yourself off to the other boys. But I observed it right out of the chute. You got me to talking about those Miller's weasels, and what happened up there with the Sovereigns in that camp. You asked me where the game warden lived, how many kids he's got, what his wife is like and where she works. Don't think I haven't noticed, Bill. You're obsessed with the guy."

Keeley said nothing. Hank was smarter than he thought.

"There was that Miller's weasel stuck to Pickett's front door," Hank said. "Then what? The elk heads? I didn't like that one very much. It reminded me of what those fuckin' towelheads do over there in the Middle East, cutting off heads. Plus, I like elk. Now I hear somebody put a bullet through their picture window," he said, his eyes on Keeley like two flat black lumps of charcoal. "I'd say that's going too far. That's too damned mean, considering there are children in the house. Made that family move, is what I hear.

"So my question is," Hank said, leaning forward, "just what in the hell is wrong with you? Why do you hate Joe Pickett so much? I know if I hadn't found you and stopped you that night outside the Stockman you would've beat him to death."

"There ain't nothing wrong with me," Keeley said, resenting the implication. Feeling the rage start to surge in his chest and belly.

Joe Pickett was all he had left, Keeley thought. After five years in prison they raided his hunting camp and tried to find the bodies of that Atlanta couple, after Keeley was forced to run away. The only thing he still had of value was his hatred, and that was still white hot.

Damn, he hated to be judged by any man.

Then he realized what Hank was leading up to. He was going to fire him. That wouldn't do. Not yet.

"People think I'm a hater," Hank said, refilling his glass. "But I'm not. I'm just not. Not like you. I don't even hate Arlen. He hates me, and my defense just looks to some like hate. No one has ever been as mean, as low, as my brother Arlen. There's a hole where his feelings should be. I've always known that, because I saw it up close and personal when we were little boys. He puts up a damned good front, damned good. Hell, I admire him for it, the way he can prance around and shake hands and act like he gives a shit about people. But he doesn't. He doesn't care for anyone but Arlen. Arlen is his favorite subject, and his only subject. He hates me because I know him for what he truly is. Did I ever tell you about the time he cut the hamstring tendons on my dog? When I was six years old and he was ten? He denied it, but it was him. Damn, I loved that dog, and I had to shoot it."

Keeley was speechless. He had never heard Hank talk so much before. Why was the man opening up this way? Didn't Hank realize who he was talking to? That Keeley was much more like Arlen than Hank? That instead of invoking sympathy or a bond or a mutual understanding, Keeley listened simply so he could look for an opening where he could strike?

Hank *wasn't* so smart after all, Keeley thought.

"Mother knew, but she wouldn't admit it," Hank said. "She didn't want to think her oldest boy was a fucking sociopath—although that's exactly what he is. She didn't want the town to know, or anybody to know. That's why she stayed down there at the ranch house, so she could keep an eye on him. And that's why I think he got rid of her."

Keeley poured himself more bourbon. This was getting rich.

"That's why Mother had that will drawn up with Meade Davis giving me the ranch if something happened to her," Hank said. "She told me about it but kept it a secret from Arlen. But then he broke into the law office and found out what the will really said."

Hank looked up, and his eyes flashed with betrayal. "I shoulda' fucking known that a lawyer like Meade Davis would change his story if he was offered enough money. That's what Arlen did, that son-of-a-bitch. He got to Davis and either threatened him or sweetened the pot. Or both. Now Davis claims the ranch was supposed to go to Arlen after all.

"I can't keep up with the guy. All I can do is fortify my bunker," Hank said morosely, gesturing around his own house.

"He even convinced my daughter I was a bad man," he said, his eyes getting suddenly misty. "That may be the worst thing he's ever done."

"At least you have a daughter," Keeley said flatly.

Hank didn't follow.

"I had a daughter once," Keeley said. "Her name was April. My brother thought she was his, but she wasn't. She was mine. April was the result of a little fling I had with my sister-in-law, Jeannie Keeley. My brother, Ote, never knew a damned thing about it."

Hank's face went slack. "Keeley . . ." he said. "The Picketts had a foster daughter named Keeley."

"That's right."

"Ote Keeley was your brother? Jeannie was your sister-in-law? Jeannie, who died in that fire with April?"

"That's right," Keeley said, his teeth clenched.

"Jesus," Hank said.

"Joe Pickett was responsible for the death of my brother, my sister-in-law, and my daughter," Keeley hissed. "And he don't even know why I'm here. I'm an avenging angel, here to take out the man who destroyed my family."

Hank sat back. "Joe didn't kill anyone," he said. "You're full of shit, Bill."

Keeley felt his face get hot. "He was in the middle of everything. He was responsible."

Hank shook his head. "I've been here a long time, Bill. I know this country, and I know what happened. Joe Pickett tried to save your daughter, if that's who she was. He didn't . . ."

"My name ain't Bill."

That stopped Hank.

"My real name is John Wayne Keeley."

Hank stopped and swallowed. Keeley liked the look of confusion on Hank's face.

"You know," Keeley said, standing up and pacing, "when I first heard about what happened to April I was in prison. I went along for a year or so, not really thinking about it. Things that happen on the outside don't seem real. Then one day I looked up and I realized I had no family. Nobody. No one was still alive to connect me to anyone else. My folks were dead, my brother, my sister-in-law, now my little daughter. I tried to forget all that when I started a guide service. But this fucking arrogant asshole client from Atlanta was there with his wife. They treated me like dirt, especially him. So I fucked her just to piss him off, and he walked in on us, and . . ."

Hank's eyes were wide.

"You remember Wacey Hedeman?" Keeley asked, still pacing, although he now circled the table.

Hank nodded, following Keeley's movement with his eyes.

"That was me."

Keeley left out the cowboy. He would never tell anyone about it. That was his secret, like a sexual fantasy, the way that cowboy had tumbled off his horse after the shot.

He was behind Hank now, and the rancher would have had to turn completely around in his chair to keep his eyes on him. But before he could do that, Keeley snatched a dirty steak knife from the table with his right hand while he clamped Hank's head against his chest with his left hand and he cut the rancher's throat open from ear to ear.

Hank tried to spin away, but all he could manage was to stand and turn around, facing Keeley while his blood flowed down his shirt. Keeley used the opening to bury the knife into Hank Scarlett's heart. It took three tries.

Hank looked perplexed for a moment before his legs turned to rubber and he fell to the floor. Keeley stood above Hank's gurgling, jerking body, watching blood stream across the floor like the Twelve Sleep River jumping its banks outside.

THE LIGHTS FLICKERED on. Keeley had no idea how long it would last, but he used the opportunity to walk across the dining room and pick up the phone. He left bloody footprints on the Navaho rug.

There was a dial tone, so Keeley punched in the numbers out of memory.

Arlen picked up.

Keeley said, "You owe me big-time now, Bubba . . ."

"Who is this?"

"You know who it is."

"Bill? What are you talking about?"

"You know who it is. The problem is solved."

"Again, I don't know what you're talking about."

"Knock it off, Arlen. You know what we discussed. You said you'd make it worth my while in a big way if I helped you out with your problem. That night in your kitchen, remember? That's what you said."

"Who did you say is calling?"

Keeley held the phone away from his ear, trying to figure out what kind of man Arlen really was to suddenly play this dangerous game with him.

"Arlen, goddammit," Keeley said, his voice cracking, "you know who this is and you damn well sure know what I'm talking about when I say your problem is solved . . ."

"Bill," Arlen said, his voice flat, "you must be having a bad dream. We've never discussed anything of consequence I can think of . . ."

And then the lights went out, plunging the room into darkness except for the lanterns.

"I'VE BEEN BETRAYED," Keeley told Hank's lifeless body as he poured another half glass of bourbon. "You were right about him. He has no conscience, that brother of yours."

Keeley sipped. The bourbon had long since stopped burning. Now it was just like drinking liquid warmth. The aroma of the alcohol drowned out the copperlike smell of fresh blood. That was a good thing.

Cut the body up, Keeley was thinking. Scatter the pieces all over the ranch. What the predators don't eat, the river will wash away.

But he'd need more fortification before he could start *that* job, he thought. Keeley had butchered hundreds of animals over the years. He knew how to do it. But this would be his first man.

He'd retrieved the skinning knives and bone saws he used on the Town Elk from the shed. Now all he needed was nerve.

After draining the glass, Keeley managed to lift Hank's body up on the kitchen counter, so it straddled the two big stainless-steel sinks. He was surprised how light Hank actually was. All that gravitas he'd credited to Hank was a result of attitude, not bulk, he guessed.

Keeley slipped the boning knife out of the block and sharpened it on the steel, expertly whipping the edge into shape. The German steel sang on the sharpening stick, so Keeley almost didn't hear the sound of the front door opening.

It had to be the wind, Keeley thought. Or one of those fucking ranch hands, wandering back up the road to complain about something. Whoever or whatever it was, he had to make sure no one entered the dining room . . .

As he flew through the doorway of the dining room, into the living room, he could see the front door hanging open and the rain splashing puddles outside. Keeley reached out to close the door when an arm gripped his throat in a hammerlock.

"You were about to ruin his face" was the last thing Keeley heard.

KEELEY ROLLED OVER on the floor and opened his eyes at four-thirty in the morning. Predawn light, muted by the storm, fused through the door and the front windows.

He was freezing. His cheek where his head had been turned was wet with both rainwater from the open front door and blood from the dining room.

He managed to sit back on his haunches. Everything hurt, including his brains. He stood, and the events of the night before came rushing back.

Hank's body was gone.

Arlen had screwed him over.

The Scarlett family was even sicker than he'd originally thought.

But there was no going back now. No way to undo what he'd done, and what happened afterward.

Keeley formed a plan. It came easily, and the simplicity of it stunned him. There was a way to get back at Arlen and Joe Pickett in one fell swoop.

It was still raining.

26

JOE GOT UP EARLY ENOUGH TO CONSCIOUSLY AVOID running into Missy in her kitchen, made coffee, showered, and was pulling on his uniform shirt when Marybeth said, "Joe . . . should you be wearing that?"

He stopped, puzzled at what she meant for a moment, then remembered he had been fired. He had no right to wear the uniform anymore. But he didn't *feel* that he was fired. He felt normal, or as normal as normal could get while they remained at the Longbrake Ranch and after his encounter with Nate Romanowski the night before.

"This is going to take awhile to get used to," Joe said, stripping the shirt off and replacing it with a baggy University of Wyoming hooded sweatshirt.

He said, "What in the hell am I going to do today? Why in the hell didn't I just sleep in or something?"

Marybeth didn't have an answer to that.

. . .

AFTER RETURNING FROM Nate's house the previous night in the rain, Joe and Marybeth had sat down with Sheridan and Lucy and told them he'd been fired.

Their questions were practical, if somewhat uncomprehending:

Lucy asked if it meant that she would no longer have to go to school.

Sorry, dear, Joe said. *No such luck.*

Sheridan asked if it meant they could get a new vehicle to replace the lousy old Game and Fish truck.

Maybe someday, Joe said. *In the meantime, they'd have to settle for the van and maybe borrowing one of Bud Longbrake's vehicles.*

Lucy asked the toughest question of all: "Does this mean we'll be safer? That we can move back to our old house now?"

Joe and Marybeth exchanged glances. Marybeth said, "We're going to be staying here for a while, Lucy. Our old house doesn't really belong to us. It never did. And as for being safer, I suppose so. Right, Joe?"

Joe said, "Yup." But he had no idea. Whoever had been targeting them might stop now, but then again . . .

"I like our old house," Lucy said, starting to cry and tear Joe's heart out. "I'll miss our old house . . ."

Sheridan studied Joe's face for a long time, saying nothing. Joe wished she would stop. She understood better than he'd expected how devastating it was to him, how doing the thing he loved had been taken away. He doubted she thought much further than that yet. But he was somewhat reassured by the fact that her demeanor reflected concern for his feelings, not what it would mean for the family. Yet.

IN BED, JOE had told Marybeth about finding Nate. He watched her reaction carefully, and she knew he was doing exactly that.

"And how was he?" she asked.

"Naked as a jaybird," Joe said.

"You know what I mean. Was he doing all right? Is he just passing through, or what?"

"We didn't really discuss it. I suggested he put on some clothes and he did. I don't know why he goes around naked all the time. He thanked me for keeping his birds fed. I told him there were a lot of people looking for him, starting with the FBI. Then I left."

Marybeth wanted to ask a million questions, it was obvious, and Joe really didn't want to answer any of them. He was tired, and beaten down. Nate was a subject he didn't have any energy for. Plus, he was unemployed.

"I don't understand men sometimes," she said. "How could you see a friend you haven't seen in half a year—a man you've been through hell with on more than one occasion—and just say hello and go home?"

Joe shrugged. "It was pretty easy."

"Where has he been all of this time?"

"He didn't say."

Marybeth shook her head in disbelief.

"If you're wondering if he asked about you, he didn't," Joe said, turning away from her in bed.

"That was cruel, Joe," she said.

"I know," he said. "I'm sorry I said that."

Someday they would need to talk about what had happened while he was away in Jackson. But for reasons he couldn't really grasp, he didn't want to know. Marybeth seemed to want to explain. Nate had even acted as if he was looking for an opening. But Joe just wanted the entire thing to go away, and thought it had. But that was before Nate came back.

"I CAN'T BELIEVE it," Lucy said at breakfast, lowering the telephone into the cradle. "They haven't canceled school."

Sheridan moaned. Both girls had convinced themselves over breakfast that the rain and flooding would mean that school would be canceled. But Lucy had called her friend Jenny, the daughter of the principal, and received the news.

Joe found himself hoping school would be closed as well. He wanted the girls around the ranch house. He couldn't imagine spending the day not working, rambling around the place, ducking Missy.

"I'll drive the girls out to the bus," Joe said, pushing away from the table.

AS THEY DROVE to the state highway in one of Bud's ranch pickups where the bus would pick them up, Sheridan asked Joe, "Are we going to be okay?"

"Yes, we are. Your mother has a great business going, and I'll find something soon," he said, not having a clue what it would be.

"It's weird thinking we won't be going back to our house. Can we at least go get our stuff?"

"Of course," Joe said, feeling instantly terrible for putting her through this. "Of course we can."

They drove in silence for a few minutes.

"Julie will be on the bus," Sheridan said.

"Isn't that okay?"

"Yeah. I just don't feel the same way about her anymore," she said. "I feel really guilty about that. I used to think she was so cool and now, well, I know she's weird but it isn't her fault."

"Things change," Joe said.

"I wish I could be more girly-girl," Sheridan said. "I wish I could see Julie and squeal and pretend nothing was wrong, but I just can't. Other girls can do that, but I can't."

Joe reached over and patted her on the leg. "You're okay, Sherry," he said, meaning it.

"Look at the ducks," Lucy said, pointing out the window at a body of water that had once been a pasture.

THE BUS ARRIVED at the same time Joe did. Because they were now living so far out of town, there was only one student on board—the first to be picked up. Julie Scarlett pressed her face to the window and waved at Sheridan as the girls climbed out into the mud and skipped through puddles toward the bus.

Joe waved at the driver and the driver waved back.

27

"I NEARLY DIDN'T MAKE IT THIS MORNING," JULIE Scarlett told Sheridan and Lucy. "Uncle Arlen had to drive through a place where the river flooded the road and we nearly didn't make it. Water came inside the truck . . . it was scary."

The school bus had another five miles to go before picking anyone else up on their way to Saddlestring. The three girls were trying to have a conversation but it was hard to hear because huge wiper blades squeaked across the windows and standing water sluiced noisily under the carriage of the bus.

"I still don't know why they're having school," Lucy said. "It's stupid."

"For once I agree with you," the bus driver called back over his shoulder. "They should have given us all a day off."

"Why don't you call them and tell them we're flooded out?" Lucy suggested coyly, and the driver laughed.

"What is *this*?" the driver said, and the bus began to slow down.

Sheridan walked up the aisle and stood behind the driver so she could see.

A yellow pickup truck blocked both lanes of the road, and the bus driver braked to a stop.

"What an idiot," the driver said. "Maybe his motor quit or something. But I'm not sure I can get around him because of all of the water in the ditches."

Sheridan watched as a man opened the door and came out of the truck. The man wore a floppy wet cowboy hat and was carrying a rifle.

Her heart leaped into her mouth.

"I know him," she said, then called to Julie over her shoulder, "Julie, it's Bill Monroe."

Julie screwed up her face in puzzlement. "I wonder what he wants," she said, getting out of her seat and walking up the aisle next to Sheridan.

Monroe was outside the accordion doors of the bus now, and he tapped on the glass with the muzzle of the rifle.

"You girls know him, then?" the driver asked cautiously, his hand resting on the handle to open the doors.

"He works for my dad," Julie said. "But I'm not sure what he's doing out here."

"Well, if you know him . . ." the driver said, and pushed the door handle.

The smell of mud and rain came into the bus as Bill Monroe stepped inside. Sheridan gasped as he raised the rifle and pointed it at the face of the driver.

"This is where you get off," Monroe said.

Beside her, Sheridan heard Julie scream.

A HALF-HOUR LATER, the phone rang at the Longbrake Ranch. Missy was having coffee with Marybeth and reading the Saddlestring *Roundup.* Marybeth was ready to go to work. Joe was in their bedroom, doing who knows what.

Missy answered, said, "Hi, honey," then handed the phone to Marybeth. "It's Sheridan."

Marybeth frowned and took the phone. Sheridan had never called this early because she shouldn't be at school yet. Maybe they had canceled school after all, Marybeth thought. Maybe Sheridan needed someone to meet them on the highway so they could come home.

"Hi, Mom," she said.

Marybeth sensed something was wrong. Sheridan's voice was tight and hard.

"Where are you?"

"I'm on the bus. I need to ask you a question. Is it okay if Lucy and I go out to Julie's house after school tonight?"

Marybeth paused. The scenario didn't work for her. She asked Sheridan to repeat what she had said, and Sheridan did. But there was something wrong in the tone, Marybeth thought. There was something wrong, period. What were Julie and Sheridan cooking up? And why would they want to include Lucy in it?

"You know I don't like it when you spring things like this on me," Marybeth said. "What are you girls scheming?"

"Nothing," Sheridan said. "We just want to hang out. There probably won't be practice."

"You want to hang out with your little sister?"

"Sure, she's cool."

"That's a first," Marybeth said. "Let me talk with her."

"Just a minute."

Marybeth could tell that Sheridan had covered the mouthpiece of the phone so she could discuss something that her mother couldn't overhear. Marybeth sat forward in her chair, straining to hear. She could sense Missy looking at her now, picking up on her alarm.

"She can't talk," Sheridan said, coming back. "She has food in her mouth."

"What?"

"She's eating some of her lunch early," Sheridan said. "You know how she always does that? Then she doesn't have enough to eat at lunch and she has to mooch from either me or the other kids?"

"Sheridan," Marybeth said, dropping her voice to a near-whisper, "Lucy has *never* done that. She brings most of her lunch home with her, and you know it. If only I could get Lucy to eat. Now what is going on? Where are you calling from?"

"The bus," Sheridan said, too breezily. "On my cell phone."

"On your cell phone," Marybeth repeated back. "*Your* cell phone."

"That's why you got it for me," Sheridan said, "for emergencies like this . . ."

Suddenly, the call was disconnected.

Marybeth felt as if she'd been hit with a hammer. Sheridan had been trying to tell her something, all right.

"Oh my God," Marybeth said, standing, dropping the phone on the table and running out of the room while Missy called after her to ask her what was wrong.

"JOE!"

JOE WAS NOT in the bedroom, but in Bud's cramped and cluttered home office. He had recalled his conversation the day before with Tony Portenson's office, how he'd requested a fax be sent to him. But since he wasn't at his house to see what had arrived, he had called again that morning and asked Portenson's secretary to fax the information to Bud's home office instead.

He stood near the fax machine, watching the paper roll out.

. . .

SHERIDAN SAT WITH Lucy on the bus. Julie was in the seat behind them. Bill Monroe had taken the phone and dropped it in his pocket and had returned to the driver's seat, saying, "I hope you didn't just do something there that will fuck us up." His eyes were pulled back into thin slits and his jaw was set. He needed a shave and he needed to clean what looked like blood off his hands and shirt.

The bus shuddered as Monroe worked the gears and did a three-point turn and the bus almost foundered in the ditch. But he got the bus turned around, and it picked up speed, and Monroe clumsily raced through the gears with a grinding sound.

They were headed for the Thunderhead Ranch.

Sheridan held Lucy, who had buried her head into her chest, crying.

MARYBETH FOUND HIM in the office, holding up a sheet of paper.

"Joe," Marybeth said frantically, "I think something has happened to the girls. Sheridan just called me and said she was on the bus, but I don't know where she really is. Or Lucy, either. She said she was calling from her cell phone. Something is horribly wrong."

The look he gave her froze her to her spot. He held up the sheet of paper and turned it to her. It was the mug shot faxed by Portenson's office.

"This is J. W. Keeley," Joe said. "He's an ex-con who supposedly murdered a man in Wyoming and a couple of others down in Mississippi. The FBI is looking for him. But he has another name, Marybeth: Bill Monroe."

Marybeth couldn't get past the name Keeley.

The name of her foster daughter who had died tragically. This man had the same name? And was from the same place?

It all became horribly clear.

28

JOE JAMMED THE MUG SHOT OF J. W. KEELEY INTO HIS back pocket and violently rubbed his face with his hands, trying to think of what to do next. Marybeth stood in the doorway of the office with her arms wrapped around herself, swaying a little, her eyes wide.

"Okay," Joe said, forcing himself to be calm while his mind swirled with anger and fear of the worst kind. "I need to find the bus. A school bus can't be hard to find."

"Should I call the sheriff?" Marybeth asked.

"Yes, call him. Call the school too. Call the FBI in Cheyenne—the number's right here on this sheet," he said, handing her the remaining pages of the fax that outlined the allegations against J. W. Keeley. "My God . . ." he moaned.

"Joe, are you going to be all right? Does this man have our daughters?"

"I don't know," he said. "But he might. I'm going to go find him."

"I can't think of anything worse," she said, tears bursting from her eyes, streaming down her face.

"Stay calm," he said. "We've got to stay calm and think." He paced the room. "If he took the bus into town, it'll be easy to find. The sheriff can find it. Ask for Deputy Reed, he's competent. But if the bus turned around, it would be headed back here or to the Thunderhead Ranch. Or to the mountains. I'd guess he's going that way."

Joe plunged into the closet and grabbed his belt and holster and buckled them on. Then he pulled out his shotgun.

"I've got my cell phone," Joe said, clamping on his hat. "Call me and tell me what's going on since I don't have a radio. If you hear something—anything—call me right away."

Marybeth breathed deeply, hugged herself tighter.

"The sheriff, the FBI, the school. Anybody else?" she asked.

Joe looked up. "Nate. Tell him I'll be on Bighorn Road headed toward the mountains. If he can get there to meet me, I can use the help. If he isn't there in fifteen minutes, I'll leave him. I can't wait for him to do his hair."

Marybeth nodded furiously.

"Tell him to bring his gun," Joe said.

Missy came into the room, said, "What is going on?"

"I'll tell you later," Marybeth said, shouldering past her. "I need to use the phone."

JOE ROARED OUT of the ranch yard with his shotgun on the bench seat, muzzle pointed toward the floor. The sky buckled with a thunder boom that rolled through the meadows, sucking the sound from the world for a moment. He drove fast, nearly overshooting the turn from the ranch onto the highway access road and he fishtailed in the mud, nearly losing control of the truck. He cursed himself, slowed down, and felt the tires bite into the slop. If he got stuck now, he thought, he would never forgive himself.

The ditches had filled even more than when he took the

girls to the bus that morning, and the water was spilling over the road. He drove through it, spraying fantails of brown-yellow water.

The highway was in sight, and he made it and didn't slow down as he turned onto the wet blacktop.

JOE TRIED TO put things together as he drove. He couldn't. He hoped like hell Marybeth had overreacted to the phone call, but he doubted it. Her intuition was always right on, especially when it came to their girls. The thing about the cell phone, that Sheridan was calling from *her* cell phone, tipped it.

If that bastard J. W. Keeley had his girls he would kill him, Joe vowed. Simple as that.

God, how sometimes he hated the distances. Everything out here was just so far from the next. Thirty miles to Saddlestring. Twenty-two miles from his old house. Fifteen miles to Nate's. And thirty miles in the other direction to the first entrance to Thunderhead Ranch. Joe knew enough about Thunderhead and its proximity to the flooding river to realize that there would be only one road still passable, the road to the lower ranch, Arlen's. The other roads would be flooded. Would Keeley take the girls to Arlen's place? And if so, why Arlen?

No, Joe thought. He wouldn't even try to figure out Keeley's motivation and loyalties. That would come later. Now, he just needed to find the bus.

Even if Marybeth was able to get the sheriff on the first call and the department scrambled, it would be a half hour before they could traverse the length of Bighorn Road in search of the bus. The helicopter was grounded because of the weather.

It was up to him.

. . .

NATE STOOD ON the shoulder of the highway wearing a long yellow slicker. His shoulder holster was buckled on over the top, and he stepped out into the road as Joe slowed and stopped.

Nate jumped in and slammed the door. Joe floored it to get back up to speed.

"So we're looking for a bus," Nate said.

"Yup."

"Marybeth said the guy was named Keeley."

"Yup."

"Jesus. One of *those* Keeleys?"

"Yup."

After a beat, Joe said, "Thanks for coming, Nate."

"Anytime, partner," Nate said, sliding his big revolver out of his holster and checking the rounds.

JOE AND NATE passed under the antlered arch with the THUNDERHEAD RANCH sign and plunged down a hill on the slick dirt road.

"There it is," Nate said, pointing.

The school bus was stalled at the bottom of the hill in the middle of the road. Or what had been the road. Now, though, the river had jumped the dike and water foamed around the bus and into the open bus door.

"It looks empty," Nate said, straining to see through the wet windshield. The wipers couldn't work fast enough to keep it clear.

Joe slowed as he approached the bus and stopped short of the water. He jumped out, holding his shotgun. The rear of the bus was twenty feet away, the level of the river halfway up the rear door. The sound of the flooding river was so loud he couldn't hear himself when he shouted, "There's nobody on it. They must have gotten out on the other side before the dike blew open!"

Joe visualized a scene in which J. W. Keeley herded the

girls through the rising water to the other side, marching them toward the ranch buildings two miles away through the cottonwoods. The vision was so vivid it deadened him for a moment.

He wouldn't even consider the possibility that they'd all been swept away by the water.

He looked around at the situation. They were helpless.

They couldn't go around the bus or they'd risk stalling themselves or getting swept away themselves. Joe looked upriver and Nate looked down. There was no place to cross.

"Is there another road in?" Nate asked, shouting at Joe from just a few feet away.

Joe shook his head. All the roads would be flooded, and even worse than this.

He thought about getting to the ranch from the other direction; driving back the way they had come, going through Saddlestring, taking the state highway into the next county and coming back the opposite way. But that highway paralleled the river as well at one point. It would likely be flooded, and it would take hours to get around that way even if it wasn't.

Joe waded into the water, testing the strength of the current to see if there was any way they could cross. Maybe by shinnying along the side of the bus, using the force of the current to hold him upright against the side of the vehicle, he could get to the other side. He was in it to his knees when something struck him under the surface, a submerged branch or length of wood, and knocked his legs out from under him. He plunged into the icy water on his back, his shotgun flying. The current pulled him quickly under, and gritty water filled his nose and mouth. He could feel swift movement as he was carried downstream. When he opened his eyes he could see only foamy brown, and he didn't know if he was facing up or down.

Something solid thumped his arm and he reached out for it and grasped it and it stopped him. He pulled hard, and it held—a root—with his other hand. The surface was slick but knotty, and he crawled up it hand over hand, water still in his mouth, trying not to swallow, until his head broke the surface where he spit it out and coughed.

He turned his head to see Nate upstream, fifty feet away, running along the bank in his direction.

Joe righted himself until he could get his feet underneath him. He shinnied up the root until he was out of the water. He hugged the trunk of the old cottonwood like a lover, and stood there gasping for breath.

"That wasn't a very good idea," Nate said when he got there.

JOE WAS SHIVERING as they backed the ranch truck out and ground back up the hill.

"There is only one way to get to the ranch," Joe said, his teeth chattering.

"The river?" Nate said.

"Yup."

"We'll die."

"We might. You want me to drop you off at your house?"

Nate looked over with a face contorted by pure contempt.

"I'll row," Joe said. "You bail."

JOE BACKED THE ranch truck on the side of the garage of his old house and Nate leaped out. It took less than five minutes to hook up the trailer for the fifteen-foot drift boat with the leaky bottom. The boat was filled with standing rainwater, and the motor of the truck strained to tow it onto the highway. Despite losing minutes, Joe stopped so Nate could run and pull the plug on the rear of the boat. They got back on the highway and drove with a stream of rainwater shooting out of the stern of the vessel. Joe wished he had finished patching up the leaks.

"Have you ever taken a boat like this on a river like *that*?" Nate asked as they backed the trailer up toward the river at the launch site.

"No."

"This is technical whitewater," Nate said, looking out at the foamy white rooster-tails that burst angrily on the surface. Downstream was a series of massive rollers.

"Where are your life vests?"

Joe said, "Back in the garage."

29

IT WAS A ROCKET RIDE.

Nate was in the bow of the boat, holding the sides with both hands to steady himself. His job was to warn Joe, who was manning the oars, of oncoming rocks and debris— full-grown trees, cattle, a horse, an old wooden privy—by shouting and pointing. Joe missed most of them, rowing furiously backwards and turning while pointing the bow at the hazard and pulling away from it. They hit a drowned cow so hard that the impact knocked Nate to the side and Joe lost his grip on the oars.

Without Joe steering, the boat spun tightly to the right. Joe scrambled on his hands and knees on the floor of the boat through twelve inches of icy, sloshing water, trying to get back on the oars, when they hit the privy.

The shock sent both Nate and Joe falling to the side, which tipped the boat and allowed gallons of water to flow in.

They were sinking.

Luckily, the river calmed and Joe was able to man the

oars again. Straining against both the current and hundreds of pounds of water inside the boat, he kept the oar blades stiff and fully in the water and managed to take the boat to shore. They hit a sandy bank and stopped suddenly.

Joe moaned and sat back on his seat. "This isn't going well."

Nate crawled back on his bench and wrung the water out of his ponytail. Joe watched as Nate patted his slicker down, making sure he still had his weapon.

"We need a big rubber raft for this," Nate said.

"We don't have one."

They got out and pushed the side of the boat with as much strength as they had, finally tipping it enough so most of the water flowed back out to the river. With the loss of the weight, the boat bobbed and started to race downstream again. Joe held on to the side, splashing through the water, the boat propelling him downstream, then finally launching himself back in. Nate pulled himself in and fell clumsily to the floor.

Joe pointed the bow downriver, and their speed increased. He could hear a roar ahead, a roar much bigger than what they had just gone through.

"Get ready!" Joe shouted.

Nate reached out for the rope that ran the length of the gunwales and wrapped his wrists through it with two twists.

"Are you sure you want to do that?" Joe asked. "If the boat flips, you may not be able to get out of that rope."

"Then don't flip the boat," Nate called over his shoulder.

Joe could feel their speed pick up. The air filled with spray from the rollers and rapids ahead. They were going so fast now that he doubted he could take the boat to the bank for safety if he wanted to. Which he did.

THE RIVER NARROWED into a foaming chute. What had two days ago been gentle riffles on the surface of the lazy river were now five- and six-foot rollers. On the sides of the river, trees reached out with branches that would skewer them if they got too close.

They had to go straight down the middle.

Joe knew the trick would be to keep the bow pointed straight downriver. If he let the bow get thrown right or left, the current would spin them and they'd hit a wall of water sideways, either swamping the boat or flipping it.

"Here we go!" Nate shouted, then threw back his head and howled like a wolf.

The bow started to drift to the left, and Joe pulled back hard on the right oar. It would be tough to keep the oars in the water as they hit the rollers, but he would have to. If he rowed back and whiffed—the oar blade skimming the surface or catching air—he would lose control.

"Keep it straight!" Nate hollered.

Suddenly, they were pointing up and Joe could see clouds. A second later they crested, the front half of the boat momentarily out of the water, and the boat tipped and plunged straight down. He locked the oar grips with his fists, keeping them parallel to his chin, keeping the blades in the water.

They made it. Only a little splash came into the boat.

But before he could breathe again, they were climbing another roller, dropping again so swiftly he thought he'd left his stomach upriver, then climbing again, aiming straight at the clouds.

Joe kept the boat straight through seven massive rollers.

When the river finally spit them out onto a flat that moved swiftly but was much more calm, Joe closed his eyes for a moment and breathed deeply.

"Damn," Nate said with admiration. "That was perfect."

Joe relaxed his hands and arms and gave in to the terrible pain that now pulsed from exertion in his shoulders, back, and thighs.

. . .

"JOE," NATE SAID, turning around on his bench and facing Joe at the oars, "about Marybeth last year."

"Not now," Joe said sharply.

"Nothing happened," Nate said. "I never should have behaved that way. I let us both down."

"It's okay," Joe said. "I mean it."

"I wish I could find a woman like that," Nate said. He started to say more, then looked at Joe's face, which was set in a mask.

"We've got to get square on everything," Nate said. "It's vital."

"Okay, we're square," Joe said, feeling the shroud that he'd been loath to admit had still been there lift from him. "Now please turn around and look for rocks. Finding my girls is the only thing I care about right now."

THE RIVER ROARED around to the right and Nate pointed at something on the bank. Joe followed Nate's arm and saw the roof of a building through the brush. A moment later, corrals came into view. The corrals were underwater, the railing sticking out of the water. Two panicked horses stood in the corner of the corral, water up to their bellies.

"It's Hank's place," Joe said, pulling hard on the oars to work the boat over to the corrals.

They glided across the surface of the water until the railing was within reach and Nate grabbed it and the boat shuddered to a stop. Joe jumped out with the bow rope and pulled the boat to shore. They tugged until the boat was completely out of the water, so that in case the river continued to rise the boat wouldn't float downriver without them.

AFTER FREEING THE horses, they slogged through the mud toward the lodge. Nate had his .454 Casull drawn and in front of him in a shooter's grip. Joe wished he still had his shotgun because he was such a poor shot with his handgun.

As he followed Nate through the dripping trees toward Hank's lodge, Joe drew his .40 Glock. The gun was wet and gritty. He checked the muzzle to make sure there was no dirt packed into it. He tried to dry it on his clothing as he walked, but his shirt and pants were soaked. He wiped it down the best he could, then racked the slide to seat a round.

Hank's lodge was handsome, a huge log home with a green metal roof. It looked like a structure that would suit an Austrian prince who entertained his hunting friends in the Alps.

Nate began to jog toward it, and Joe followed. The front door was open. Joe could see no signs of life, and no lights on inside. He wondered if the storm had knocked out the electricity.

Nate bounded through the front door and moved swiftly to his left, looking around the room over the sights on his revolver. He had such a practiced way about his movements, Joe noted, that there was no doubt he had entered buildings filled with hostiles before in his other life.

Joe mimicked Nate's movements, except he flared off to the right.

It was dark and quiet in the house. It felt empty.

The floor was wet and covered with leaves from the open door. Dozens of mounted game animals looked down on them from the walls. Elk, moose, caribou, antelope, mule and whitetail deer. A full-mount wolverine, an endangered species, looked poised to charge them. A golden eagle, wings spread as if to land, hovered above them.

"That son-of-a-bitch," Nate said, referring to Hank but looking at the eagle. Nate liked eagles.

Arlen was right, Joe thought. The lodge was filled with illegally taken and poached species. The mounts were expertly done. He knew the work of all the local taxidermists, and whoever had done the mounts was unfamiliar to him. But that was part of his old job, Joe thought. It no longer concerned him.

Nate moved through the living room into a massive dining hall. Joe followed.

Dirty plates covered the table, and a raven that must have flown in from the open front door walked among the plates. The bird stopped and looked at them, head cocked to the side, a piece of meat in its beak. The raven waddled the length of the table until it got to the head of it. Then it turned and cawed, the sound sharp and unpleasant. Nate shot it and the bird exploded in a burst of black feathers.

"I *hate* ravens," Nate said.

Joe's ears rang from the shot in the closed room, and he glowered at Nate.

"Uh-oh," Nate said. "Look."

The chair at the head of the table was knocked over. Nate approached it and picked up a red-stained steak knife from the floor next to it.

Joe began to walk around the table when he felt the soles of his boots stick to the floor. He looked down and recognized blood. There was a lot of it, and it hadn't dried yet.

"I wonder who it was?" Nate asked.

Now Joe could smell it. The whole room smelled of blood.

But there was no body.

They quickly searched all the rooms of the house. It was empty.

As they slogged back to the boat, Joe felt a mounting sense of dread that made it hard to swallow. The river would take them to Arlen's place next.

"Let's go get my girls," Joe said.

30

THE NEXT SET OF RAPIDS WAS NOT AS SEVERE AS THE big rollers they had been through, and although his arms were aching, Joe kept the boat straight and true and they shot through them without incident. The rain receded to a steady drizzle, although there was no break in the clouds. Because the sky was so dark, Joe couldn't tell the time. He glanced quickly at his wristwatch as he rowed but it was filled with water and stuck at 8:34 A.M., the exact time the river had sucked him in.

Joe and Nate didn't talk, each surrounded by his own thoughts. Joe contemplated what they would find at the lower ranch. If he let his mind wander off the oars to the fate of his girls he found it difficult to remain calm. Inside, his heart was racing and something black and cold lodged in his chest. As hard as he tried, though, the faces of Sheridan and Lucy at breakfast kept coming back to him.

He thought: *No matter what, there will be hell to pay.*

. . .

THE RIVER NARROWED through two tall bluffs. Although there were no rapids, it was as if the current doubled in speed. Joe could feel wind in his face as they shot forward. The tiniest dip of an oar would swing the boat about in water this fast, so he steered as if tinkling the keys of a piano, lowering an oar blade an inch into the water to correct course.

As the river swept them along and the bluffs receded behind them, Joe started to recognize the country. To the left, a mile away, was a hill that looked like an elephant's head. Joe had noted it when he brought Sheridan out to Julie's. They were getting close.

The river widened. The tops of willows broke the surface of the water a third of the way to the edge where the river normally flowed. The thick river cottonwoods began to open up a little, allowing more muted light to fall on the surface of the water.

Because his feet and legs were numb, Joe didn't notice at first that the boat was sinking. But when he looked down, he saw the water at his ankles. Somewhere, they had knocked more cracks or holes in the hull and the water was seeping in. He hoped they could get to the ranch before the boat filled again. He didn't want to waste another minute dumping the boat.

Nate started to bail with a gallon bucket. It helped a little, but he was losing the battle.

They rounded a bend and the river calmed for the first time since they'd gotten in the boat. The roar of the water hushed to a whisper. Calves bleated just ahead. The ranch was near.

That's when Joe saw her. She stood on a brushy hillside on the left side of the bank, hands on hips, thrusting her face out at them with an unfamiliar smile on her face. His mouth dropped open and he let the oars loose in an involuntary reaction.

"Joe, who is that?" Nate asked, pausing with the bucket in midbail.

"Opal," Joe said, his voice cracking. "Opal Scarlett."

This was the exact spot described by Tommy Wayman, Joe thought. She was there after all, had been there all along, just as he surmised.

Nate said, "Why in the hell is she standing out in the rain like that?"

"She's watching the end play out," Joe said.

"Jesus," Nate said, screwing up his mouth in distaste.

"Opal!" Joe called out, raising his hand. "Opal!"

She didn't react. As they passed her, she didn't turn her head and follow them, but stared stonily at the river.

"She couldn't hear you," Nate said.

"How could she not?"

"She's old and probably deaf. And definitely crazy," Nate said in awe.

"She's been here all along," Joe said, his mind numb.

THEY BEACHED THE boat on the bank with the water level inside just a foot below the sides of the boat. Another ten minutes in the water and the boat would have gone under.

Joe and Nate leaped out, leaving the boat to settle into the mud.

"Should we go talk to Opal? Find out what she knows?" Nate asked, looking from Joe to the ranch compound ahead and back. He was deferring to Joe, a new thing.

"Later," Joe said. "I don't want to waste time chasing her down. We can find her after we've checked out the buildings. Sheridan and Lucy have to be here."

Nate gave him a look. How could he be so sure?

Joe didn't acknowledge it. He just felt they were near.

The side of a fresh embankment had collapsed into the river from the rain. Something stuck out of the dirt of the wall, something long, horizontal, and metal. Nate approached it and rubbed mud away. It was the bumper of a car. Someone had used a front-end loader to bury it.

"Cadillac," Nate said, rubbing the mud away from the logo.

"Opal's car," Joe said. "She buried it so everyone would think she drove away."

"Why would she do that?"

Joe thought for a moment. "So she could see who won."

AS THEY APPROACHED Arlen's house, Joe's insides were churning and he tried to swallow but couldn't. He glanced down at the gun in his hand and saw it shaking.

"I'll take the front," Nate said. "You come in the back."

"If you see Keeley," Joe said, "shoot first."

"Not a problem," Nate said.

As they parted, Nate reached out and grabbed Joe's arm.

"Are you okay to do this?"

Joe said, "Sure."

"Stay cool."

JOE KEPT A row of blooming lilac bushes between him and the side of the house as he jogged around toward the back. As at Hank's house, he could see no lights on inside or any sign of life. A calf bawled in the distance from a holding pen. Drizzle flowed softly through the leaves of the trees and running water sang through the downspouts of the house.

He stepped over a low fence and into the backyard. There was a porch and a screen door. The door was unlocked and he opened it as quietly as he could and stepped inside a dank mudroom. Heavy coats lined the walls and a dozen pairs of boots were lined up neatly on the floor.

The mudroom led to the huge kitchen where Sheridan had described seeing Arlen and Bill Monroe together. Joe skirted the island counter and stood on the side of the opening that went into the family room.

There was an acrid mix of smells in the home—chemicals Joe couldn't identify, years of cooking residue on the walls, and a sharp metallic smell that took him back to Hank's dining room: blood.

Holding his weapon out in front of him, he wheeled around the opening into the dining room and saw the Legacy Wall facing him. All the pictures were smashed and some had fallen to the floor.

Furniture was overturned. A china cabinet was on its side, spilling coffee cups and plates across the floor. A wild spray of blood climbed the Legacy Wall and onto the ceiling. A pool of blood stained the carpet on the floor. It was a scene of horrendous violence.

"Jesus," Nate said as he entered the living room from the front and looked around.

Joe called, *"Sheridan! Lucy!"*

His shout echoed through the house.

Nate wrinkled his nose. "I recognize that smell."

"What is it?"

"Alum," Nate said, turning to Joe. "It's used for tanning hides."

THEY HEARD A sound below them, under the floor. A moan.

"Is there a basement?" Nate asked.

Joe shrugged, looking around.

They heard the moan again. It was deep and throaty.

Nate turned, strode back through the dining room

toward the front door. "I remember seeing a cellar door on the side of the house," he said.

Joe followed.

OUTSIDE, NATE TURNED and hopped off the front porch toward the side of the house Joe had not seen. They rounded the corner of the front of the house and Joe could see a raised concrete abutment on the side of the house with two doors mounted on top. The mud near the cellar was pocked with footprints leading to it. Someone was down there.

Nate ran to the doors and threw them open, stepping aside in case someone was waiting with a weapon pointing up. But nothing happened.

"Sheridan!" Joe called. "Lucy!"

The moan rolled out, louder because the door was open.

"Come out!" Nate boomed into the opening. "Come out or I'll come in!"

The moan morphed into a high wail. Joe recognized the sound of Wyatt Scarlett when he had cried months before, after his brothers got in the fight.

Joe pushed past Nate and went down the damp concrete stairs. Nate followed. The passageway was dark but there was a yellow glow on the dry dirt floor on the bottom. The chemical smells were overpowering as Joe went down.

He had to duck under a thick wooden beam to enter the cellar. Nate didn't see it and hit his head with a thump and a curse.

What Joe saw next nearly made his heart stop.

It was a taxidermy studio. A bare lightbulb hung from a cord. Half-finished mounts stared out with hollow eye sockets from workbenches. Foam-rubber animal heads filled floor-to-ceiling shelves, as did jars and boxes of chemicals and tools.

Wyatt sat on the floor, his legs sprawled, cradling Arlen

Scarlett's head in his lap. Arlen's eyes were open but he was clearly dead. There was a bullet hole in Arlen's cheek and another in his chest.

Hank was laid out on a workbench, his cowboy boots pointed toward the ceiling, his face serene but white, his hands palms up.

And there was a man's entire arm on the floor near Wyatt's feet, the hand still gripping a pistol. The arm appeared to have been wrenched away from the body it had belonged to. Joe didn't think that was possible, but here it was right in front of him.

Joe didn't even feel Nate run into him accidentally and nearly send him sprawling.

Wyatt looked up at Joe, his eyes red with tears, his mouth agape with a silent sob.

"Wyatt," Joe asked. "What happened here?"

The youngest Scarlett boy closed his eyes, sluicing the tears from them, which ran down his cherubic face.

"Wyatt . . ."

"My brothers are dead," Wyatt said, his voice breaking. "My brothers—"

"Who did it?"

Wyatt's body was wracked with a cry. "Bill Monroe."

Joe thought, *J. W. Keeley.*

"Where is he now?"

"I don't know. He ran away."

"Is that his arm?"

There was a flash in Wyatt's eyes. "I tore it out when I saw him shoot Arlen. Took a few hard twists to get it off, but it wasn't no different than pulling a drumstick off a roast chicken. I thought I killed him last night, after what he did to Hank. But he came back."

Joe thought: the blood on the wall and ceiling upstairs.

"Wyatt," Joe said, trying to keep his voice calm but failing in his effort, so as not to upset the big man and cause him to clam up, "Did Monroe have my girls with him?"

Wyatt nodded sincerely. "And Julie too. But not anymore."

"Where are they?"

"They're safe," Wyatt said. "They're in my shack. Bill told Arlen he was going to hurt them if he didn't give him money. Julie's mom is there too."

Joe felt a surge of blistering relief, although he wondered where Keeley was.

Nate asked, "Why are your brothers down here, Wyatt?"

Wyatt clenched his eyes, shaking his head from side to side. He looked like he was about to explode.

"Nate," Joe cautioned.

Nate pressed, "Why did you bring them down here?"

Wyatt whispered, "To preserve them. So I could preserve my family. We're very important here. And I loved them so much, even though they didn't love each other."

"Like you preserved your mother," Nate said.

Wyatt nodded, then looked up eagerly. "Did you see how I made her smile? Not many people knew how she could smile. They know now."

Joe turned and shouldered past Nate toward the stairs.

"Please stay with him," Joe said. "I'm going to get my girls."

HE RAN ACROSS the ranch yard and down the road on legs that felt as if they could go out on him at any time. The scene in the cellar had scorched his soul, and Wyatt had broken his heart.

J. W. Keeley was still out there, as far as Joe knew. As he ran, he held his gun in front of him with two hands and searched for movement of any kind in the dark trees near the ranch buildings. How far could a man go with a wound like that? he wondered. He'd seen deer and elk travel for miles with legs blown off by careless hunters. But a man?

Then a horrible thought struck him as he ran: Maybe Keeley had found the girls.

SHERIDAN'S EARS WERE numb from the drumming of the heavy rain on top of the tin roof of the shack. So numb, that when she heard a cry outside she doubted herself. Just like earlier, when she thought she had heard gunshots outside and even the unholy scream of a man. In both instances, she couldn't be sure that her mind wasn't playing tricks on her. This time, though, she heard the cry again.

"Is someone coming?" Lucy asked from where she was huddled in the corner of Wyatt's shack.

"Yes," Sheridan said, summoning all her courage to approach the window and brush aside the curtains. The glass outside was still streaked with running rain, and the view undulated with the water. A form appeared in the murk outside, a man running toward the shack, crouching, looking around as if he expected someone to jump out at him. She recognized the form.

She stepped back from the window and turned to Lucy, beaming. Everything was suddenly right with the world.

"Dad's here," she said.

LIGHTS WERE ON in Wyatt's shack. Joe called out again for his girls.

He heard, "Dad!" in response. Sheridan. A squeal from Lucy.

The door was locked. He jerked on it and pushed it but it was solid.

"Just a minute," Doris Scarlett said from inside.

He heard a bolt tumble and the door opened inward. Sheridan, Lucy, and Julie Scarlett were inside, behind Doris. Lucy ran across the floor and bear-hugged Joe around the waist.

Sheridan said, "Boy, are we glad to see you."

Joe closed the door behind him and pulled both of his daughters to him.

Lucy said, "You're really wet, Dad."

Joe sat them down on a couch with Julie. He said, "Tell me what happened."

Sheridan told the story about Bill Monroe taking over the bus, turning it around, and getting it stuck as they tried to cross the river. Monroe made them get out and wade to the shore, and they all walked through the mud to the ranch. When they got to the ranch yard, Wyatt came out of the cellar and yelled at Bill Monroe to go away. When he wouldn't, Wyatt charged him and hit him in the head. Monroe ran, cursing, toward the house where Arlen now stood on the front porch. Monroe went inside and Arlen closed the door. Wyatt told Doris and the girls to go to his shack and lock the door and not let anyone in unless it was he.

That's all they knew, and Joe was relieved. They hadn't seen what happened inside.

"Have you seen Keeley since?" Joe asked, "I mean Bill Monroe," he said, to avoid confusion.

"Keeley?" Sheridan asked. "Like April? The same name?"

"I'm afraid so."

Sheridan and Lucy exchanged glances. "I told you his face was familiar. He has April's eyes," Sheridan said to Lucy, referring to her stepsister.

Joe shook his head, then looked at Julie who sat silent and alone at the end of the couch. She had no idea she'd lost her uncle and her father. Thank God her mother was there.

He stood.

"Keep the door locked, just like Uncle Wyatt told you. I'll be back in a minute."

Doris said, "Please be careful. Don't let Bill Monroe find us."

Her voice trembled as she said it, and Joe could see how terrified she was. "Can't you stay with us?"

Joe considered it, but shook his head. He couldn't assume Keeley had bled to death. And even if he had, Joe needed to see the body. "I need to be sure he can't threaten anyone again," he said.

"Then can we go home?" Lucy asked.

Joe didn't ask which home she meant. "Yes," he said.

ALL HIS THOUGHTS and feelings channeled into one: revenge.

Joe returned to the front porch of the house and studied the concrete. Although rain had washed most of it away, he could still see traces of blood. Nate must have missed it in his haste on the way in. He backed off the porch and looked around on the wet loam. A spot here, a splash there. Headed in the direction of the barn.

It was like following a wounded game animal, Joe thought. He looked not only for blood flecks but for churned up earth, footprints, places where Keeley had fallen as he staggered away.

There was a depression in the grass where Keeley must have collapsed, his shoulder punching a dent into the turf that was now filling with water and a swirl of blood.

Keeley hadn't made it all the way inside the barn. He sat slumped against the outside door, next to a boat that was propped up against the wall. Joe guessed Keeley was going for the boat when he collapsed. Keeley's legs were straight out in front of him. He held the stump of his left arm with his right hand, covering the socket tight with bone-white fingers. Still, blood pumped out between his joints with every weakening heartbeat. Joe couldn't see a weapon on Keeley or near him as he approached. But Keeley watched Joe the whole time, his eyes sharp, his mouth twisted with hate.

"That Wyatt, he is the one I never thought about," Keeley said. "He is one strong son-of-a-bitch."

"Yup," Joe said, remembering when Wyatt snapped the Flex-Cuffs.

Keeley looked up. His eyes were black and dead. "You destroyed my family. My brother, my sister-in-law, my baby girl."

"What do you mean, your baby girl?"

"She was *my* daughter," Keeley said, and his eyes flashed.

"You mean, you and Jeannie . . ."

"Damned right, me and Jeannie. Ote was gone a lot."

"So that's why you did all of this? To get back at me?"

Keeley nodded.

"I did all I could to save April," Joe said, angry. "We loved her like our own."

"Horseshit. Not like a father loves a daughter."

Joe clenched his fists so hard his nails broke the skin on his palms. He wanted to hurl himself at Keeley and start swinging. Instead, he felt his right hand relax enough to undo the safety strap on his service weapon.

"What the hell would you know about being a father?" Joe said. "You were just the sperm donor."

"Fuck you," Keeley spat.

Joe stood over him, looking down, his fingers curling around the pistol grip. "Is there any point in talking to you? Telling you I had nothing to do with the death of your daughter or your brother?"

"I know what I know," Keeley said. "You and Wacey Hedeman were involved in my brother getting killed. You were there when April was assassinated."

Joe shook his head, speaking calmly. "You were the one who poisoned Wacey then too?"

"Yup."

"And the cowboy? The one who got shot on Shirley Rim?"

"That one was the best of all."

Keeley made a cold smile with his mouth but his eyes remained steady on Joe. "I wish I'da taken care of your daughters. I should have. They were right there. I got greedy, though. I got stupid. I wanted to make Arlen live up to his word to pay up."

Joe squatted so he could look at Keeley's face at eye level. What he saw disgusted him, terrified him. He thought of what Keeley had done to his family. What he had done to Wyatt. What he could do to him and others if he recovered, as unlikely as that seemed. J. W. Keeley would always be a threat to him and to everyone around him.

"I need a doc," Keeley said. "Call me a doc. I ain't got long like this."

Joe said, "Six years ago Wacey Hedeman was in a situation just like yours. He was down on the ground bleeding. I let him go. It was the wrong decision."

Keeley studied Joe and sneered, "You got a badge. You can't just do that."

Joe said, "Not anymore," and raised the Glock, pressed it against Keeley's forehead.

Behind him, Nate called out, "Joe! Don't!"

Joe pulled the trigger. Keeley's head kicked back against the barn door and he slumped over to the side, dead. Even Joe couldn't miss from an inch away.

WHEN JOE STOOD and turned, he saw Nate stumbling across the grass toward him. Nate was hurt.

"The son-of-a-bitch Wyatt coldcocked me when I looked away," Nate said unsteadily. There was blood on the side of his head.

"Wyatt did that?" Joe asked, his voice disembodied due to what he had just done. He didn't feel triumphant, or guilty. He didn't know how he felt yet.

Behind Nate, a curl of smoke came out of an upstairs

window of the ranch house. Then another. And the windows lit up with flame inside.

Joe approached Nate, his gun hanging limply at his side. He was numb everywhere. Although he knew what he was watching, it seemed as if it were on a movie screen; it didn't seem real. He could still feel the sharp recoil of the gun in his hand, feel the shock waves shoot up his arm from the shot. Thought about the way Keeley had simply collapsed on himself and pitched to the side, like a side of beef, the evil spark gone that had once lit him up.

Thinking: *Killing is easier than it should be. John Wayne Keeley probably had the same thought.*

Then: *What has happened to me? How could he have dared to threaten my daughters?*

FLAMES WERE LICKING through the windows and front door, the roof was burning. Joe could smell the smoke, hear 120-year-old wooden beams popping inside the structure.

"Where's Wyatt?" Joe asked, his voice seeming hollow, lifeless.

"I think he got out," Nate said, now recovered enough to stand next to Joe.

"Nope," Joe said, pointing. "There he is."

Wyatt appeared on the side of the house through the smoke. He was hard to see clearly because of the pulsing waves of heat. But it was big-shouldered Wyatt, walking straight toward the house with something over his shoulder.

Opal. Stiff as a board.

Wyatt carried the mount of his mother through the front door, straight into the teeth of the fire.

"My God," Nate said. "He's making a funeral pyre."

"I was sure wrong about Opal," Joe said, his voice tinny and distant.

Nate said, "Before he thumped me, Wyatt told me his

mother died of a heart attack that morning after some guide named Wayman threw her in the river. She died peacefully, and Arlen found her. Arlen buried her in secret because he knew about the will giving Hank the ranch, but Wyatt saw him and dug her up. Wyatt made her into what she always wanted to be—immortal. And what *he* always wanted her to be."

"Pleasant," Joe said.

"Hell of a legacy," Nate said.

AS DUSK APPROACHED, Joe sat with his girls in Wyatt's shack. Doris comforted Julie, whispering to her that things would be all right. Julie appeared catatonic. Sheridan reached out to her, held her hand.

The house continued to burn until it collapsed in on itself. The rain stopped and the sky cleared.

Joe was surprised to find out that telephone service was restored to Wyatt's phone, and he called Marybeth.

"I'm with the girls," he said. "They're safe."

He listened with tears in his eyes as Marybeth cried with joy, and handed the phone to Sheridan and Lucy so they could talk with her.

When they finally handed the phone back, Joe gave her an abbreviated version of what had happened. Since the girls were listening, Joe didn't tell her about any of the details, only that J. W. Keeley had brought the girls to the ranch, that they'd been saved by Wyatt, and that Keeley and the Scarlett brothers had had a fight which resulted in the house burning down.

The story shocked her into silence.

"There's a lot more to it, isn't there, Joe?"

It was as if she knew he'd killed J. W. Keeley in cold blood.

"Yes, there is. But it's for later," he said.

She said the sheriff's office had just called and they

were sending the helicopter out. It should be there any minute.

"Is Nate still there?" she asked.

"Yes, but I haven't seen him recently."

"You might want to tell him the sheriff is coming," she said.

Joe agreed and hung up.

JOE COULD HEAR the distant approaching thump of the helicopter as he walked the ranch yard. The smoke from the fire stung his nose and made his eyes tear up.

Nate was gone. So was a drift boat Joe had seen earlier leaning against the barn. And so was J.W. Keeley's body. Joe guessed it was in the fire, where it would be discovered with the others. Neat and clean.

Joe drew his weapon and threw it as far as he could into the river. His holster followed.

It was crashing in on him now: what had happened, what he'd done, how J.W. had forever welded the fates of the Keeley, Scarlett, and Pickett families together by death.

As he saw Sheridan and Lucy walking toward him from Wyatt's shack, he thought: *But we are the ones who are left standing. Unlike Keeley or the Scarletts, Sheridan and Lucy are still here.*

And that was all that mattered.

Sheridan stood close to him and asked, "Are you okay, Dad?"

"I'm fine," he lied.

"What happens now?"

He could have said, "Everything will be different." But he didn't. Instead, he pulled his daughters close to him and waited for the helicopter.

ACKNOWLEDGMENTS

The author, who has read too many overlong acknowledgments in novels lately, would like to thank those who significantly contributed to the research and writing of this book, including Sergeant Nadim Shah of the Wyoming Department of Corrections in Rawlins; D. P. Lyle, M.D.; Jim Hearne of MHP in Cheyenne, who went through hell on earth in an actual ranch dispute much like the one described in the book; Wyoming game warden Mark Nelson and his lovely wife, Mari, who read the book and offered suggestions and corrections, as always; and Mark Weakland, who was my partner in an inadvertent drift-boat rocket ride down the North Fork of the Shoshone River near Cody, much like the one depicted in the novel. Thanks also to Don Hajicek for cjbox.net.

Special thanks to the publishing pros, especially my editor, Martha Bushko, who makes every book better than it ever was imagined; Michael Barson and the Putnam team, who have supported every novel when they didn't have to; and my agent, Ann Rittenberg, who dives deep in the murk of submerged wreckage and surfaces holding up answers.

Turn the page for a preview of

FREE FIRE

The next Joe Pickett novel
by C. J. Box

Available in paperback
from Berkley Prime Crime!

1

Bechler River Ranger Station
Yellowstone National Park
July 21

A HALF HOUR AFTER CLAY McCANN WALKED INTO the backwoods ranger station and turned over his still-warm weapons, after he'd announced to the startled seasonal ranger behind the desk that he'd just slaughtered four campers near Robinson Lake, the nervous ranger said, "Law enforcement will be here any minute. Do you want to call a lawyer?"

McCann looked up from where he was sitting on a rough-hewn bench. The seasonal ranger saw a big man, a soft man with a sunburn already blooming on his freckled cheeks from just that morning, wearing ill-fitting, brand-new outdoor clothes that still bore folds from the packaging, his blood-flecked hands curled in his lap like he wanted nothing to do with them.

McCann said, "You don't understand. I *am* a lawyer."

Then he smiled, as if sharing a joke.

2

Saddlestring, Wyoming
October 5

JOE PICKETT WAS FIXING BARBED-WIRE FENCE ON A
boulder-strewn hillside on the southwest corner of the
Longbrake Ranch when the white jet cleared the mountain-
top and halved the cloudless pale blue sky. He winced as
the roar of the engines washed over him and seemed to
suck out all sound and complexity from the cold midmorn-
ing, leaving a vacuum in the pummeled silence. Maxine,
Joe's old Labrador, looked at the sky from her pool of
shade next to the pickup.

Bud Longbrake, Jr., hated silence and filled it immediately. "Damn! I wonder where that plane is headed? It sure
is flying low." Then he began to sing, poorly, a Bruce Cock-
burn song from the eighties:

> *If I had a rocket launcher . . .*
> *I would not hesitate*

The airport, Joe thought but didn't say, ignoring Bud Jr.,

the plane is headed for the airport. He pulled the strand of wire tight against the post to pound in a staple with the hammer end of his fencing tool.

"Bet he's headed for the airport," Bud Jr. said, abruptly stopping his song in midlyric. "What kind of plane was it, anyway? It wasn't a commercial plane, that's for sure. I didn't see anything painted on the side. Man, it sure came out of nowhere."

Joe set the staple, tightened the wire, pounded it in with three hard blows. He tested the tightness of the wire by strumming it with his gloved fingers.

"It sings better than you," Joe said, and bent down to the middle strand, waiting for Bud Jr. to unhook the tightener and move it down as well. After a few moments of waiting, Joe looked up to see that Bud Jr. was still watching the vapor trail of the jet. Bud Jr. shot out his cuff and looked at his wristwatch. "Isn't it about time for a coffee break?"

"We just got here," Joe said. they'd driven two hours across the Longbrake Ranch on a two-track to resume fixing the fence where they'd left it the evening before, when they knocked off early because Bud Jr. complained of "excruciating back spasms." Bud Jr. had spent dinner lobbying his father for a Jacuzzi.

Joe stood up straight but didn't look at his companion. There was nothing about Bud Jr. he needed to see, nothing he wasn't familiar with after spending three weeks working with him on the ranch. Bud Jr. was thin, tall, stylishly stubble-faced, with sallow blue eyes and a beaded curtain of black hair that fell down over them. Prior to returning to the ranch as a condition of his parole for selling crystal methamphetamine to fellow street performers in Missoula, he'd been a nine-year student at the University of Montana, majoring in just about every one of the liberal arts but finding none of them as satisfying as pantomime on Higgins Street for spare change. When he showed up back at the Longbrake Ranch where he was raised, Bud Sr. had taken Joe aside and asked Joe to "show my son what it means to work hard. That's something he never picked up. And don't call him Shamazz, that's a name he made up. We need to break him of that. His real name is Bud, just like mine."

So instead of looking at Bud Jr., Joe surveyed the expanse of ranchland laid out below the hill. Since he'd been fired from the Wyoming Game and Fish Department four months before and lost their state-owned home and headquarters, Joe Pickett was now the foreman of his father-in-law's ranch—fifteen thousand acres of high grassy desert, wooded Bighorn Mountain foothills, and Twelve Sleep River valley. Although housing and meals were part of his compensation—his family lived in a 110-year-old log home near the ranch house—he would clear no more than $20,000 for the year, which made his old state salary look good in retrospect. His mother-in-law, Missy Vankueren-Longbrake, came with the deal.

It was the first October in sixteen years Joe was not in the field during hunting season, on horseback or in his green Game and Fish pickup, among the hunting camps and hunters within the 1,500-square-mile district he had patrolled. Joe was two weeks away from his fortieth birthday. His oldest daughter, Sheridan, was in her first year of high school and talking about college. His wife's business management firm was thriving, and she outearned him four to one. He had traded his weapons for fencing tools, his red uniform shirt for a Carhartt barn coat, his badge for a shovel, his pickup for a '99 Ford flatbed with LONGBRAKE RANCH painted on the door, his hard-earned authority and reputation for three weeks of overseeing a twenty-seven-year-old meth dealer who wanted to be known as Shamazz.

All because of a man named Randy Pope, the director of the Game and Fish Department, who had schemed for a year looking for a reason to fire him. Which Joe had provided.

When asked by Marybeth two nights ago how he felt, Joe had said he was perfectly happy.

"Which means," she responded, "that you're perfectly miserable."

Joe refused to concede that, wishing she didn't know him better than he knew himself.

But no one could ever say he didn't work hard.

"Unhook that stretcher and move it down a strand," Joe told Bud Jr.

Bud Jr. winced but did it. "My back . . ." he said.

The wire tightened up as Bud cranked on the stretcher, and Joe stapled it tight.

THEY WERE EATING their lunches out of paper sacks beneath a stand of yellow-leaved aspen when they saw the SUV coming. Joe's Ford ranch pickup was parked to the side of the aspens with the doors open so they could hear the radio. Paul Harvey news, the only program they could get clearly so far from town. Bud hated Paul Harvey nearly as much as silence, and had spent days vainly fiddling with the radio to get another station and cursing the fact that static-filled Rush Limbaugh was the only other choice.

"Who is that?" Bud Jr. asked, gesturing with his chin toward the SUV.

Joe didn't recognize the vehicle—it was at least two miles away—and he chewed his sandwich as the SUV crawled up the two-track that coursed through the gray-green patina of sagebrush.

"Think it's the law?" Bud asked, as the truck got close enough so they could see several long antennas bristling from the roof. It was a new-model GMC, a Yukon or a Suburban.

"You have something to be scared of?" Joe asked.

"Of course not," Bud said, but he looked jumpy. Bud

was sitting on a downed log and he turned and looked behind him into the trees, as if planning an escape route. Joe
thought how many times in the past his approach had likely
caused the same kind of mild panic in hunters, fishermen,
campers.

Joe asked, "Okay, what did you do *now*?"

"Nothing," Bud Jr. said, but Joe had enough experience
talking with guilty men to know something was up. The
way they wouldn't hold his gaze, the way they found something to do with their hands that wasn't necessary, like Bud
Jr., who was tearing off pieces of his bread crust and rolling
them into little balls.

"She swore she was eighteen," Bud said, almost as an
aside, "and she sure as hell looked it. Shit, she was in the
Stockman's having cocktails, so I figured they must have
carded her, right?"

Joe snorted and said nothing. It was interesting to him
how an old-line, hard-assed three-generation rancher like
Bud Longbrake could have raised a son so unlike him. Bud
blamed his first wife for coddling Bud Jr., and complained
in private to Joe that Missy, Bud's second wife and Marybeth's mother, was now doing the same thing. "Who the
fuck cares if he's *creative*," Bud had said, spitting out the
word as if it were a bug that had crawled into his mouth.
"He's as worthless as tits on a bull."

In his peripheral vision, Joe watched as Bud Jr. stood up
from his log as the SUV churned up the hill. He was ready
to run.

It was then that Joe noticed the GMC had official State
of Wyoming plates. Two men inside, the driver and another
wearing a tie and a suit coat.

The GMC parked next to Joe's Ford and the passenger
door opened.

"Is one of you Joe Pickett?" asked the man in the tie. He
looked vaguely familiar to Joe, somebody he might have

seen in the newspaper. He was slightly built and had a once-eager face that now said, "I'm harried." The man pulled a heavy jacket over his blazer an zipped it up against the cold breeze.

"He is," Bud Jr. said quickly, pointing to Joe as if naming the defendant in court.

"I'm Chuck Ward, chief of staff for Governor Rulon," the man said, looking Joe over as if he were disappointed with what he saw but trying to hide it. "The governor would like to meet with you as soon as possible."

Joe stood and wiped his palms on his Wranglers so he could shake hands with Ward.

Joe said, "The governor is in town?"

"We came up in the state plane."

"That was the jet we saw, Joe. Cool, the governor," Bud Jr. said, obviously relieved that the GMC hadn't come for *him.* "I've been reading about him in the paper. He's a wild man, crazy as a tick. He challenged some senator to a drinking contest to settle an argument, and he installed a shooting range behind the governor's mansion. That's my kind of governor, man," he said, grinning.

Ward shot Bud Jr. a withering look. Joe thought it was telling that Ward didn't counter the stories but simply turned red.

"You want me to go with you?" Joe asked, nodding toward the GMC.

"Yes, please."

"How about I follow you in," Joe said. "I need to pick my girls up at school this afternoon so I need a vehicle. We'll be done by then, I'd guess."

Ward looked at him. "We have to be."

Joe stuffed his gloves into his back pocket and picked up his tools from the ground and handed them to Bud Jr. "I'll ask your dad to send someone out here to pick you up."

Bud's face fell. "You're just leaving me here?"

"Get some work done," Joe said, gesturing toward the fence that went on for miles. "Come on, Maxine," he called to his dog.

Bud Jr. turned away and folded his arms across his chest in a pout.

"Quite a hand," Ward said sarcastically as Joe walked past him toward the Ford.

"Yup," Joe said.

THE GOVERNOR'S PLANE was the only aircraft on the tarmac at the Saddlestring Regional Airport. Joe followed Chuck Ward to a small parking lot at the side of the General Aviation building.

Joe had heard the stories about the drinking contest and the shooting range. Rulon was an enigma, which seemed to be part of his charm. A one-time high-profile defense lawyer, Rulon became a federal prosecutor who had a 95 percent conviction rate. Since the election, Joe had read stories in the newspaper about Rulon rushing out of his residence in his pajamas and a Russian fur cap to help state troopers on the scene of a twelve-car pileup on I-80. Another recounted how he'd been elected chairman of the Western Governors' Association because of his reputation for taking on Washington bureaucrats and getting his way, which included calling hotel security to have all federal agency personnel escorted from the room of their first meeting. Each new story about Rulon's eccentricities seemed to make him more popular with voters, despite the fact that he was a Democrat in a state that was 70 percent Republican.

Governor Spencer Rulon sat behind a scarred table in the small conference room. Aerial photos of Twelve Sleep County adorned the walls, and a large picture window looked out over the runway. The table was covered with stacks of files from the governor's briefcase, which was open on a chair near him.

He stood up as Ward and Joe entered the room and thrust out his hand.

"Joe Pickett, I'm glad Chuck found you."

"Governor," Joe said, removing his hat.

"Sit down, sit down," Rulon said. "Chuck, you too."

Governor Rulon was a big man in every regard, with a round face and a big gut, an unruly shock of silver-flecked brown hair, a quick sloppy smile, and darting eyes. He was a manic *presence,* exuding energy, his movements quick and impatient. Joe had seen him work a crowd and marveled at the way Rulon could talk with lawyers, politicians, ranchers, or minimum-wage clerks in their own particular language. Or, if he chose, in a language all his own.

Ward looked at his wristwatch. "We've got fifteen minutes before we need to leave for Powell."

"A speech for the Community College Commission," the governor said to Joe before settling back in his chair. "They want more money—now that's a shocker—so they'll be willing to wait."

Joe put his hat crown down on the table. He was suddenly nervous about why he'd been summoned and because there was no way to anticipate what Rulon might do or say. Joe had assumed on the drive into town that it had something to do with the circumstances of his dismissal, but now he wasn't so sure. It was becoming clear to him by Ward's manner that the chief of staff didn't really like the purpose of the meeting, whatever it was.

"Everybody wants more money," Rulon said to Joe. "Everybody has their hand out. Luckily, I'm able to feed the beast."

Joe nodded in recognition of one of the governor's most familiar catchphrases. In budget hearings, on the senate floor, at town meetings, Rulon was known for listening for a while, then standing up and shouting, *"Feed the beast! Feed the beast!"*

The governor turned his whole attention to Joe, and

thrust his face across the table at him. "So you're a cowboy, now, eh?"

Joe swallowed. "I work for my father-in-law, Bud Long-brake."

"Bud's a good man." Rulon nodded.

"I've got my résumé out in five states."

Rulon shook his head. "Ain't going to happen."

Joe was sure the governor was right. Despite his qualifications, any call to his former boss, Randy Pope, asking for a job reference would be met with Pope's distorted tales of Joe's bad attitude, insubordination, and long record of destruction of government property. Only the last chage was true, Joe thought.

"Nothing wrong with being a cowboy," Rulon said.

"Nope."

"Hell, we put one on our license plates. Do you remember when we met?"

"Yes."

"It was at that museum dedication last spring. I took you and your lovely wife for a little drive. How is she, by the way? Marybeth, right?"

"She's doing fine," Joe said, thinking, *He remembered her name.* "She's got a company that's really doing well."

"MBP Management."

Amazing, Joe thought.

"And the kids? Two girls?"

"Sheridan's fifteen, in ninth grade. Lucy's ten, in fourth grade."

"And they say I have a tough job," Rulon said. "Beautiful girls. You should be proud. A couple of real pistols."

Joe shifted in his chair, disarmed.

"When we met," the governor continued, "I gave you a little pop quiz. I asked you if you'd arrest me for fishing without a license like you did my predecessor. Do you remember me asking you that?"

"Yes," Joe said, flushing.

"Do you remember what you said?"

"I said I'd arrest you."

Chuck Ward shot a disapproving glance at Joe when he heard that.

The governor laughed, sat back. "That impressed me."

Joe didn't know it had. He and Marybeth had debated it at the time.

Rulon said, "So when we were in the air on the way to Powell, I was reading through a file that is keeping me up nights and I saw the Bighorns and I thought of Joe Pickett. I ordered my pilot to land and told Chuck to go find you. How would you like to work for the state again?"

Joe didn't see it coming.

Chuck Ward squirmed in his chair and looked out the window at the plane as if he wished he were on it.

Joe said, "Doing what?"

Rulon reached and took a thick manila file off one of the stacks and slid it across the table. Joe picked it up and read the tab. "Yellowstone Zone of Death."

Joe looked up, his mouth dry.

"That's what they're calling it," Rulon said. "You've heard about the situation, no doubt."

"Everybody has."

The case had been all over the state, regional, and national news the past summer—a multiple homicide in Yellowstone National Park. The murderer confessed but a technicality in the law had set him free.

"It's making me crazy and pissing me off," Rulon said. "Not just the murders or that gasbag Clay McCann. But this."

Rulon reached across the table and threw open the file. On top was a copy of a short, handwritten letter addressed to the governor.

"Read it," Rulon said.

Dear Gov. Spence:
   I live and work in Yellowstone, or, as we in the

*Gopher State Five call it, "the 'Stone." I've come to
really like the 'Stone, and Wyoming. I may even
become a resident so I can vote for you.*

*In my work I get around the park a lot. I see
things, and my friends do too. There are some things
going on here that could be of great significance to
you, and they bother us a lot. And there is something going on here with the resources that may
deeply impact the State of Wyoming, especially your
cash-flow situation. Please contact me so I can tell
you what is happening.*

*I want to tell you and show you in person, not by
letter. This correspondence must be held in complete
confidence. There are people up here who don't
want this story to be told. My e-mail address is
yellowdick@yahoo.com. I'll be waiting to hear
from you.*

It was signed "Yellowstone Dick."

Joe frowned. He noted the date stamp: July 15.

"I don't understand," Joe said.

"I didn't either," Rulon said, raising his eyebrows and
leaning forward again. "I try to answer all of my mail, but I
put that one aside when I got it. I wasn't sure what to do,
since it seems like a crank letter. I get 'em all the time, believe me. Finally, I sent a copy over to DCI and asked them
to check up on it. It took 'em a month, damn them, but they
traced it with the Internet people and got back to me and said
'Yellowstone Dick' was the nickname of an employee in Yellowstone named Rick Hoening. That name ring a bell?"

"No."

"He was one of the victims murdered by Clay McCann.
The e-mail was sent to me a week before Hoening met his
untimely demise."

Joe let that sink in.

"Ever hear of the Gopher State Five?"

Joe shook his head.

"Me neither. And I'll never know what he was talking about, especially that bit about deeply impacting my cash flow. You know how serious that could be, don't you?"

Joe nodded. The State of Wyoming was booming. Mineral severance taxes from coal, gas, and petroleum extraction were making state coffers flush. So much money was coming in that legislators couldn't spend it fast enough and were squirreling it away into massive trust funds and only spending the interest. The excess billions allowed the governor to feed the beast like it had never been fed before.

Joe felt overwhelmed. "What are you asking me?"

Rulon beamed and swung his head toward Chuck Ward. Ward stared coolly back.

"I want you to go up there and see if you can figure out what the hell Yellowstone Dick was writing to me about."

Joe started to object but Rulon waved him off. "I know what you're about to say. I've got DCI, and troopers, and lawyers up the wazoo. But the problem is I don't have jurisdiction. It's National Park Service, and I can't just send all my guys up there to kick ass and take names. We have to make requests, and the responses take months to get back. We have to be *invited* in," he said, screwing up his face on the word *invited* as if he'd bitten into a lemon. "It's in my state, look at the map. But I can't go in unless they *invite* me. The Feds don't care about what Yellowstone Dick said about my cash flow, they're so angry about McCann getting off. Not that I blame them, of course. But I want you to go up there and see what you can find out. Clay McCann got away with these murders and created a free-fire zone in the northern part of my state, and I won't stand for it."

Joe's mind swirled.

"You're unofficial," Rulon said, his eyes gleaming. "Without portfolio. You're not my official representative, although you are. You'll be put back into the state system, you'll get back pay, you'll get your pension and benefits back, you'll get a state paycheck with a nice raise. But you're on your own. You're nobody, just a dumb-ass game warden poking around by yourself."

Joe almost said, *That I can do with no problem,* but held his tongue. Instead, he looked to Ward for clarification. "We'll tell Randy Pope to reinstate you as a game warden," Ward said wearily, wanting no part of this. "But the administration will *borrow* you."

"Borrow me?" Joe said. "Pope won't do it."

"The hell he won't," Rulon said, smacking his palm against the tabletop. "I'm the governor. He will do what I tell him, or he'll have *his* résumé out in five states."

Joe knew how state government worked. This wasn't how.

"Without portfolio," Joe said, repeating the phrases. "*Not* your official representative. But I am."

"Now you're getting it," the governor said, encouraging Joe. "And that means if you screw up and get yourself in trouble, as you are fully capable of doing based on your history, I'll deny to my grave this meeting took place."

Chuck Ward broke in. "Governor, I feel it's my responsibility, once again, to advise against this."

"Your opinion, Chuck, would be noted in the minutes if we had any, but we don't," Rulon said in a tone that suggested to Joe that the two of them had similar disagreements as a matter of routine.

The governor turned back to Joe. "You're going to ask me why, and why you, when I have a whole government full of bodies to choose from."

"I was going to ask you that."

"All I can say is that it's a hunch. But I'm known for my good hunches. I've followed your career, Joe, even before I got elected. You seem to have a natural inclination to get yourself square into the middle of situations a normal thinking person would avoid. I'd say it's a gift if it wasn't so damned dangerous at times. Your wife would probably concur."

Joe nodded in silent agreement.

"I think you've got integrity. You showed me that when you said you'd arrest me. You seem to be able to think for yourself—a rare trait, and one that I share—no matter what the policy is or conventional wisdom dictates. As I know, that's either a good quality or a fatal flaw. It got me elected governor of this great state, and it got you fired.

"But you have a way of getting to the bottom of things, is what I see. Just ask the Scarlett brothers." He raised his eyebrows and said, "No, don't. *They're all dead.*"

Joe felt like he'd been slapped. He'd been there when the brothers turned against each other and went to war. And he'd performed an act that was the source of such black shame in him he still couldn't think about it. In his mind, the months of feeding cattle, fixing fence, and overseeing Bud Jr. weren't even close to penance for what he'd done. And it had nothing to do with why he'd been fired.

"When I think of crime committed out of doors, I think of Joe Pickett," Rulon said. "Simple as that."

Joe's face felt hot. Everything the governor said seemed to have dual meanings. He couldn't be sure if he was being praised or accused, or both.

"I don't know what to say."

Rulon smiled knowingly. "Yes you do. You want to say YES! You want to shout it out!" He leaned back in his chair and dropped his voice an octave. "But you need to talk to Marybeth. And Bud Longbrake needs to hire a new ranch foreman."

"I do need to talk to Marybeth," Joe said lamely.

"Of course. But let me know by tonight so we can notify Mr. Pope and get this show on the road. Take the file, read it. Then call with your acceptance."

Ward tapped his wrist. "Governor . . ."

"I know," Rulon said, standing and shoving papers into his briefcase. "I know."

Joe used the arms of his chair to push himself to his feet. His legs were shaky.

"Tell the pilot we're ready," Rulon said to Ward. "We need to get going."

Ward hustled out of the room, followed by Governor Rulon.

"Governor," Joe called after him. Rulon hesitated at the doorway.

"I may need some help in the park," Joe said, thinking of Nate Romanowski.

"Do what you need to do," Rulon said sharply. "Don't ask me for permission. You're not working for me. I can't even remember who you are. You're fading from my mind even as we speak. How can I possibly keep track of every state employee?"

Outside, the engines of the plane began to wind up.

"Call me," the governor said.

Joe Pickett thought he was saddling up for his last patrol. If only he'd known how true that might turn out to be...

NEW YORK TIMES BESTSELLING AUTHOR

C. J. BOX

NOWHERE TO RUN

A JOE PICKETT NOVEL

It's Joe's last week as a temporary game warden in the mountain town of Baggs, Wyoming, but his conscience won't let him leave without checking out the strange reports coming from the wilderness: camps looted, tents slashed, elk butchered. Not to mention the Olympic hopeful who'd been training in the region and then just...vanished. What awaits him is like something out of an old campfire tale, except this story is all too real—and all too deadly.

www.penguin.com
www.cjbox.net
facebook.com/AuthorCJBox

C. J. BOX

BLOOD TRAIL

Game wardens have found a man dead at a mountain camp—strung up, gutted, and flayed as if he were the elk he'd been pursuing. Is the murder the work of a deranged anti-hunting activist or of a lone psychopath with a personal vendetta? Wyoming game warden Joe Pickett is the man to track the murderer and stop him before someone declares open season on humans.

penguin.com

New York Times bestselling author

C. J. Box

The mystery series about Joe Pickett,
a Wyoming game warden trying to keep the wilderness—
and the family he loves—safe from danger.

OPEN SEASON
SAVAGE RUN
WINTERKILL
TROPHY HUNT
OUT OF RANGE
IN PLAIN SIGHT
FREE FIRE
BLOOD TRAIL
BELOW ZERO
NOWHERE TO RUN
COLD WIND
FORCE OF NATURE

THE JOE PICKETT NOVELS ARE:

"Muscular." —*The New York Times*

"Heartfelt." — *The Washington Post*

"Fascinating." —*USA Today*

"Suspenseful." —*New York Daily News*

www.cjbox.net
www.penguin.com

M25AS1112